D0933698

WOLFNIGHT

Books by

N I C O L A S F R E E L I N G

Fiction

LOVE IN AMSTERDAM

BECAUSE OF THE CATS

GUN BEFORE BUTTER

VALPARAISO

DOUBLE BARREL

CRIMINAL CONVERSATION

THE KING OF THE RAINY COUNTRY

THE DRESDEN GREEN

STRIKE OUT WHERE NOT APPLICABLE

THIS IS THE CASTLE

TSING-BOUM

OVER THE HIGH SIDE

A LONG SILENCE

DRESSING OF DIAMOND

WHAT ARE THE BUGLES BLOWING FOR?

LAKE ISLE

GADGET

THE NIGHT LORDS

THE WIDOW

CASTANG'S CITY

ONE DAMN THING AFTER ANOTHER

WOLFNIGHT

Non-Fiction

KITCHEN BOOK

COOK BOOK

WOLFNIGHT

A NOVEL OF SUSPENSE

NICOLAS FREELING

Pantheon Books, New York

Library of Congress Cataloging in Publication Data
Freeling, Nicolas.
  Wolfnight.

  I. Title.
PR6056.R4W6 1982   823'.914   81–48220
ISBN 0–394–52266–4   AACR2

Manufactured in the United States of America

First American Edition

A dogday was ending.

Sometimes, just before twilight, the sky will go a washed pale blue. After a still, beautiful day at the very end of autumn. The sun has gone, but scattered feathers of cloud are glowing and sparking from the bushfire that has just passed. Castang stared out of his window in the PJ offices.

Some clock-watching computer had switched the car-park lights on; a pinkish orange like anaemic gladioli on their long curving stems, hanging insipidly in the sky. They had the effect upon Castang of instant impotence; the self-pity known to the poets as Look On My Works, Ye Mighty, And Despair. You piddling little man.

It was still a dogday, and still not time to go home. It is always Time for something, if not Christmas then Elections, if not chocolate then apple-blossom-shampoo. All those executives are still out there Marketing, and I'm sitting here doing nowt.

Now he was a family man, it was due to his position to be a Commissaire, and so he was; recently enough to feel uneasy about it, wondering what it meant. He was the same, wasn't he? Only a Commissaire-Adjunct, the lowest kind. But the Step: money, standing, position. He was exactly where he had been, doing exactly the same work. In nominal charge of the Serious Crimes Brigade, in a provincial city in France, of something under half a million souls.

Commissaire Richard, too, was exactly where he had been. A divisional commissaire, the highest kind, but that was the end. Richard was pushing sixty, and would no longer be called to Paris for the choice desk, after which you become Comptroller, Sub-Director and Director of the Police Judiciaire. Those are political jobs, and Monsieur Richard had said, once too often, "You know, it's possible to be a cunt. I'm one myself. But when it comes to being an Abject cunt . . ." Richard would not get sent to the Basses-Alpes, or even the Basses-Pyrenees. He would just stay the way he was. Finish.

1

You got promoted – it's Buggins' turn next – and between forty and sixty you too would go tranquilly on until you too – in Pau perhaps, or Valenciennes.

Lasserre was gone. There had been malfeasance if not malpractice: the less said the better. It had not splashed over on to Richard. A tightlipped person from the Inspectorate had spent hours closeted. Prosecution had been avoided. Lasserre, a Principal Commissaire, was replaced by a person who really had come from Pau; had in his office a banner to prove it; green and white, colours of the Section Paloise rugby club. A nicer person than Lasserre. But what's all this Nice and Nasty? They're all just cops.

And Cantoni was gone, promoted like Castang and replaced at the head of the violence brigade by yet another close-knit, loose-moving tricky runner with a mongol moustache. But Castang hadn't been sent to Pau or even Valenciennes. Perhaps it was meaningless: most things in Administration are. Some professed to read subtle shades of influence and manoeuvre into every smile or frown, much like political journalists examining the entrails of a presidential speech.

He would have been happy in Pau: he liked the Navarrese, spoke a bit of Spanish. Vera would have knitted him a green and white scarf and he'd have worn it, too. Happier still in Valenciennes: he loved the North. He'd learn Flamand, and Polish too: and drink gin, and what were the colours of the Valenciennes Football Club? – he didn't care how hideous they were. They are always underdogs, and he was one too. What would have been depressing would be a town last heard of getting besieged by Sir John Falstaff during the Hundred Years War. He liked this town – a noble and an ancient city. A dump too, of course. Maybe he loved it – it didn't do to love things. He had grown to love the flat, with its view of a disused canal and poplar trees.

He had an office to himself now, and whenever Serious Crimes had no great urgency about them he found himself alone. Being senior, he had a window on the courtyard side. A view not inspiring, being mostly parked cars, but there were plane trees too of a design slightly less unimaginative.

When he looked again the twilight was coming down fast, and somebody was moving behind a plane tree. The somebody had a crouching, furtive manner and Castang frowned. It would not do if somebody put a bomb in a PJ car: no. It would not even do for

2

somebody to glue subversive manifestoes to windscreens. Or execute graffiti in aerosol dye. Then the somebody straightened up and showed the unmistakable bullet head of Orthez: a PJ inspector who was skilful with cars and liked to play with them.

Castang sat upon the desk in the darkening office and lit a cigarette, enjoying his discomfiture. Twilight made things sinister. Why else is the moment before darkness falls called 'entre chien et loup'? Between dog and wolf; when even Orthez could have snarling fangs and mad blazing eyes. And when, conceivably, the werewolf could still present a blameless air of domesticity.

Wolves: an animal for which he felt esteem. Respect. Liking. Now dogs were a very different matter. These thoughts were abruptly broken by the typist from the Secretary's office; coming bursting in: a fat girl.

"There's someone asking for the boss."

"Richard's out."

"Yes, I know."

"Well tell Domenech."

"He's out too."

"Tell him to come back then."

"We thought" – meaning the Secretary – "you had better see him."

"Why?"

"You'll see," with irritating coyness. He had barely time to put the bureau lamp on, sit hastily behind the desk, and look official.

"Miss."

"What?"

"Put the overhead light on," in a voice sharp enough.

"Yes, sir." Light was shed upon a personage who had entered majestically, a man recognisable: a face familiar.

This familiarity was that given by television sets. The phenomenon is known to all, but have we come to terms with it? Most of us have not had the opportunity. Castang hadn't, up to this moment. A man whose face, and voice, had been in his livingroom a score and probably more of times. One knew the facial and vocal mannerisms very well; the rapid, practised way of taking the spectacles off and putting them on again. But one did not know the man. His political opinions, yes. The fact that he is a skilful public debater and appearer, yes. What more? – nothing. It is such a long time since Richard Nixon's five-o'clock-shadow and sweaty, over-eager,

3

ingratiating manner. Marketing techniques have grown so much more subtle and sophisticated. What do you know now of the fellow in your livingroom? Precious little. Wolves look increasingly like dogs, and dogs can be trained to perform.

"Please sit down. Monsieur Vibert, right? Monsieur Marc Vibert – correct?" Good name for a politician. Vibrates. Easy to pronounce and remember. A solid, people's name. Sure. Trust me. All of Castang's invisible antennae were clustering and waving about, mobilised to catch the unsaid.

"I am listening." In the offices of the PJ means being in public and at that moment you have to make a speech. He just can't help it: he is conditioned.

A speech. The existing generation of French politicians, between fifty and sixty years of age, was formally educated, brought up upon 'a solid grounding in the humanities'. Bossuet, Cicero, Demosthenes: logic, rhetoric, the turn of a phrase. Paragraphs beginning with 'Now Therefore'. Winston Churchill, an embodiment of all that the French detest, was forgiven everything because he too had been brought up upon Gibbon and Antithesis.

One or two of the youngest do not orate. But perhaps the chief characteristic of French life, be it public or private, is their unwillingness to change any of their habits.

Castang became aware of the rise and fall of practised, polished, rehearsed paragraphs, foaming, breaking. Upon the granite cliffs of Finistère, or the broad sandy beaches of the Gironde; Atlantic rollers, ample and majestic. He had to stop it.

"A cigar?"

"I never smoke. Now therefore –"

"Then I will. Monsieur Vibert. Won't you please listen a moment? You come to me. I am a senior police officer. Competent to take charge. That does not mean only that I know my job. I am invested with the authority of the Republic. Reduced to words of one syllable, a life has been lost, so you tell me. I must now tell you; in the absence of Divisional Commissaire Richard, Principal Commissaire Domenech, I'm the one who carries the can. Who empties the pot? That's what the Procureur de la République will ask, what the Instructing Magistrate will ask. Okay? You accept that? Then we're stuck with one another. All right? So your style of things, my style of things . . .

"You understand? I take a piece of paper, I write. I write slowly,

4

in longhand. I make it very brief, very curt. To keep up, you understand, with my pen. All right? I put the brief, factual question. You agree?"

The silence was for once not rehearsed: one beat: two beats.

"Yes."

"This took place where?"

"The uh, commune, the locality . . . is called Saint-Julien-sur-Eze."

"Good. This took place when?"

"In the early hours of this morning."

"As far as you are able, be more precise."

"Uh – one-thirty. Perhaps two."

"The time is now – eighteen hundred. Minus ten minutes. Seven, but we won't be pedantic. You agree, as to the time?"

"Commissaire, I have explained to you –"

"Leaving the time factor aside. Saint-Julien-sur-Eze is a country district. Outside the jurisdiction of the urban police. Within, thus, the sphere of authority of the gendarmerie. You have, if I understand aright, made no approach to the gendarmerie . . .? They haven't been notified at all . . .? They know nothing . . .? Is that correct?"

"Commissaire; I have explained."

"No need to explain afresh."

We've got to get it reduced to basic bedrock. Outside the urban limits of whatever municipality, the urban police has no authority. In whatever country district, authority over all things – be they criminal, or just technically infractions – is held by the gendarmerie. A para-military body, organised upon military lines. Answerable to the Ministry of Defence.

Now the Police Judiciaire, a specialised and elitist body, has authority over a district, a department, even a province. It overlaps thus – putting the heart of the matter in euphemisms – both the municipal police and the gendarmerie, and is by the most natural consequence in the world heartily detested by both.

That's putting it factually, right?

Now from the point of view of a politician, a well-known public figure. The law states that in the event of unexplained loss of life, to put it laconically, there shall be enquiry. By whom? The law could not state it more precisely. The legal authority is the Procureur, who will delegate enquiry (and any legal sequels) to a Judge of Instruction, an examining magistrate. Who confides the technical

5

and administrative aspects to – the PJ? The Gendarmerie? Brief answer; whoever gets there first.

Since, my dear boy, after a time-lapse of sixteen to seventeen hours this well-known politician has chosen to confide in the PJ, it is to be concluded that he is on better terms with the Ministry of the Interior than with the Ministry of Defence. Full stop. Paragraph.

Castang, boy, you're saddled with this. No use looking around for Richard, for Domenech. The shadow on the sundial is pointing at you.

"I think it advisable, Monsieur Vibert, that in view of the very large lapse of time –"

"Commissaire, I have tried to explain . . ."

"Lapse of time, that we proceed together to an examination of the ground."

"Commissaire, I –"

"Monsieur Vibert, these scruples do you honour." But this was no mere frightened bourgeois, no smalltime notable out of his depth. He was determined to take charge, not to allow the control of affairs to get out of his hands. What after all is a little police officer in a provincial city? He'd better keep quiet, if he knows what's good for him.

Come, that is somewhat crude. A PJ officer, of enough rank and experience to know his way about, has learned not to break any china. Vibert wanted this made clear.

"Monsieur Castang. Let's be quite sure we understand each other. An accident took place, a very dreadful accident from which I escaped with my skin more or less whole. In great distress – I can use the word distraught – I sought the help of a deeply trusted friend who happens also to be a medical man of acknowledged eminence. I wished of course to bring this dreadful occurrence to the notice of the proper authorities without delay. You will, I feel sure, distinguish readily between the problems of being a nationally known figure – and the responsibilities accruing – and those of an ordinary private citizen. It is of course impossible – the press . . ."

"We're discussing this quite quietly, like two sensible prudent men," said Castang. "So we need not cover up our words too much. It wouldn't do – quite so – to go tottering into some country gendarmerie post, all deranged and distraught – covered in blood and dust – no, no."

"I'm so glad you understand."

6

"So that the moment you feel sufficiently collected and coher –
ent –"

"Against medical advice, in fact."

We're getting on beautifully. He'll be calling me Castang next –
we've been friends for years.

"So that another half-hour can't make any difference." It was a
very intelligent face there across the desk.

"I'm not altogether sure that I'm following you."

"There's an unpleasant fact, and I see no possibility of its
remaining unknown."

"My dear Castang, there's no question of anything being
withheld or disguised."

"No. If nothing has been found, which appears to me most
unlikely, the woman has been down there for seventeen hours."

The pause was a short one.

"Yes. That's a very dreadful thought. You realise of course that
this has only been brought home to me – I mean that my recall has
been total – for, well, perhaps an hour." There was a longer pause.

"I see," said Castang. "Without entering upon technical medical
jargon – mm, we're looking for a blanket word. Blanket's not quite
the right expression. Amnesiac, perhaps?"

"Something of the sort, perhaps. My medical adviser very kindly
drove me here. I insisted on coming in here alone. He was unwilling
to take the responsibility."

"You think perhaps we should have him in?"

"As a witness you mean? If you think it advisable."

"I was just wondering whether you felt up to answering a few
questions."

"I'll do my best," said Monsieur Vibert gallantly. "I must warn
you, I'm still a bit on the giddy side. Had a bit of a knock on the head,
you know. And full up rather of various assorted medications. Not
quite sure how these might affect my realisation or recollections.
But go ahead, my dear chap. This isn't formal, is it? If I understand
aright, you are seeking the essential information on which to base
the action you see fit to take."

"That's roughly it," perhaps a little too drily.

"Have I left anything out?" with cooperative warmth.

"We'd do better perhaps to leave the questions for now. Till
you've had a good night's sleep. Or perhaps just the one. How did
you know she was dead?"

"How did I know... ? I'm at a loss."

"The car skidded. Hit something, there was an impact, you think that sprung the door open, there was a violent lurch, conceivably an overturn – you were flung clear?"

"Those were my impressions. They may be inaccurate. Piecing it together after . . . you see, otherwise, I'd hardly be here to tell the tale. Would I?"

"No safety belt?"

"Perhaps not. I don't recall. If not, then just as well, I should think."

"And you were driving? Or was she?"

"You know, Commissaire, this is very strange... I simply had not asked myself that question, hitherto . . . Quite honestly, I don't know."

"What would have been normal?"

"Normally she. I dislike driving at night especially, when tired or preoccupied . . . the weirdest things happen to one, under stress. Only now does it begin to come back to me... of course, this sort of precise, professional questioning . . ."

"Yes? You were going to say?"

"I came to, after a moment. And then when my eyes got accustomed to the night I could see this frightful ravine, and thought Good God, the car's gone down that. And by some fantastic miracle I hadn't. And that was all that occurred to me. I must have thought at that moment that I was alone in the car. Or I suppose – but naturally; I would have made efforts to get down there. Or if that proved impossible – nearly a sheer drop as I see it now – I would have tried of course to get help. But I seem to have had the conviction that I was alone.

"This morning or this afternoon – coming to, at all events – then I remembered that she was in the car with me. But it was all disjointed somehow: still is, very largely . . . Commissaire, do you really judge it indispensable that I should accompany you back there now? The medical man, I think, would advise against that."

"On second thoughts, no: I think you should get to bed and have some sleep. I'll come and see, in the morning, how you're getting on. Will you give me the address?"

"I can't call it to mind. But his name is Joinel. It'll be in the book."

"You recalled it this morning?"

"I looked in the book then. There was a public phonebox, in the village. In the country, everyone's asleep early."

"Didn't you bang on anyone's door?"

"No . . . no. I just waited by the phonebox, for Doctor Joinel to come and get me. I was in a daze, of course."

"Didn't you get cold?"

"I suppose I did. I have a notion of walking about, to keep warm."

"I don't want to prolong your ordeal any longer, Monsieur Vibert."

"Thank you so much, Commissaire. I knew I could count on you."

"Yes."

There are episodes which catch the public imagination, and because of their political consequences remain tenaciously in the memory. Watergate is one such. Chappaquiddick is another.

"Orthez? Ring up hither and thither, in a colourless fashion saying nothing: find out if a car accident was reported in the mountains round Saint Julien in the early hours. Specifically, hairpins climbing the col, above the village."

"Okay. We interested in this car?"

"We are if there's a dead woman in it. You see who went out?"

"No."

"Monsieur Marc Vibert."

"That the one I keep seeing on television? Z'a fascist bastard, no?"

"Probably, presumably, and is that going to worry us?"

"No. None of um ever give straight answer twennything, right?"

"So better not plan things for the evening just yet."

The great advantage of Orthez was his looking immeasurably thick. Left to himself, Castang practised for a moment looking very very bright, taking imaginary glasses off and putting them on again, before reaching for his telephone. It rang at the other end: he waited patiently: Vera was not and never would be very quick on her feet. But especially since having a child – biological shake-up or something – she'd got both quicker in the mind and sharper in the tongue.

"Oy. Things all right? I might be late. I say might, because it's the sort of tale that could technically be true, might be total claptrap all the way, and either way is political."

"How boring that does sound. Anything else?"

9

"No, that's all."

Castang opened the window. The parking lot was emptying as people scurried off home. Above was the orange glow of the city at night. Above that was a calm sky, black, overcast, not very cold, little or no wind: no feel of rain in the air. Nonetheless he got boots out of his cupboard, a raincoat with a fleecy lining. In the hills it was always five degrees colder, and if he was going to plooter about in ravines . . . Orthez returned, with a Make-what-you-like-out-of-that expression.

"Gendarmerie have got it."

"Never expected they hadn't. Been there all day."

"Down in streambed, thirty, forty metres. Got it out wither helicopter."

"She must have been pretty smashed up."

"Who? Wasn't anybody in the car."

"Ho," said Castang.

His first reaction had been Good Luck to the gendarmerie; let them disentangle Monsieur Marc Vibert and we hope they enjoy it.

Whereas now . . . A clash of interests between two police forces is to be avoided if possible. And an empty car is just a wreck, and of little interest to anyone.

"So?" Orthez had what there was written on a message pad.

"Peugeot, the big one, six-o-four. Paris plates. Registered to a – uh – Madame Viviane Kranitz. Presumed stolen."

Making matters simpler. Stolen car would be on the computer and signalled: PJ interest would not arouse gendarmerie curiosity.

And not-simpler: if the car was empty, what had Monsieur Vibert been gassing on about? And where was Madame Viviane Kranitz?

A jockey coming up to the first fence on the Aintree course isn't worrying about Becher's Brook. He takes them one at a time.

"All right," lacing his boots, "let's go out and see."

They had a nearly new Renault with a turbo motor, the sort of thing Orthez took pleasure in, in his hands hopping up the difficult hill road like a hare. Whereas the big heavy limousine – if one were sleepy, or going a bit too fast . . . The hairpin was built over a narrow stone bridge. High up here, some nine hundred metres. Could have been a bit of fog, or enough moisture to make the surface slippery: too early for black ice. On the other hand, going up or down you were prepared by several other dangerous bends, and all clearly signalled.

There was little enough to see by torchlight. Cars had parked up here; a lot of scuffling and trampling had effaced any traces on the soft shoulder beyond the bridge. And several people had been down in the ravine, scrambling and holding on to bushes. There were a lot of broken bushes. There were stones, and boulders. If anybody had gone down there in a car it was inconceivable that they should escape injury and climb back up again.

If one person got flung clear, so might another – as a rough rule, either both driver and passenger have fastened the belts, or neither have. Gendarmes had thought of this, of course. There was no thick cover on the steep stony slope, and they had combed the terrain carefully.

It was five kilometres down – through two hairpins – to the village of Saint-Julien-sur-Eze. As one left the village there was a large clear notice saying 'Dangerous bends over 9 km'. On the street was a phonebox, and in the phonebox a directory. The houses on the street had been shuttered since nightfall. Nobody showed curiosity at their stopping: there was small likelihood of a witness to anyone on foot, stopping to phone in the small hours. They asked, though. There was also a small village café, and plenty of voluble tongues.

Of course it was well-known to be dangerous. In ten years five or six cars had gone over. Even without black ice, ground moisture and oil on the roadway made it a naughty one. Tail end of last winter a big truck went over. Loaded too with dangerous chemicals. Just showed you. Not a road at all for them big things, but the way round through the valley is thirty kilometres longer, see?

The gendarmerie barracks was in the next, bigger village in the valley. Never tell lies when you can tell at least some of the truth. This axiom kept Castang as a rule on quite friendly terms with bristly officers of other police forces, even those dug out at suppertime in their shirtsleeves.

"We got a jolly-up on top of the signal – seems the wagon is the property of some politician's secretary, so they pressed the panic button. Stuff inside it?"

"Sure, lot of clothes and papers, haven't looked at that. Wagon's in the garage – total write-off, of course. Something funny about it?"

"If there is I haven't been told."

"Well, what are we to do? Been a lot of work, and that's enough."

"Only the one query, I suppose. If it was stolen, did it go over by accident or did they tip it over just for fun?"

11

"Nobody in it, so odds are they tipped it a'purpose. Who knows what games these clowns will play, or why? Your guess is as good as mine."

"Just wondering why this female doesn't turn up and say, 'Hey, my car, my clothes, and so on."

"If she's a politician's secretary, maybe she's being kept busy," grinning evilly.

"And we can do the work," said Orthez.

"One thing occurs to me," said Castang. "The local people would know that was a good place to tip a car over. But suppose you wanted to fake an accident?"

"Still be well-known," said the gendarmerie officer. "A truck went over last winter, and there was a fuss about that. We went up. Chemicals it said. Turned out to be nuclear material – had to get a special team: decontamination and everything. There was an enquiry, and it leaked into the public eye a bit. Kept out of the press, naturally, but word gets around."

"It's possible somebody would remember that," said Castang yawning.

"All right; been a long day. Home, Orthez."

It was seventy kilometres. Orthez had made it in an hour coming out, and not much more going back. Doctor Joinel would have taken longer, being a prudent gentleman, and elderly. Monsieur Vibert had spent that much time walking up and down outside a phonebox?

The clothes and papers, in the back of the car – hers? His too? He would have quite liked to have taken a look.

In gendarmerie eyes, the car was of no interest and would be left in the local garage – untouched – waiting for a visit from some insurance company. For as long, at least, as nobody tumbled to the notion that Madame Viviane Kranitz was supposed to have been in it. He was getting quite curious about Madame Kranitz. And almost as much about Monsieur Vibert.

What had he said, at the start? My secretary? No. An adviser, helper, friend? No. A collaborator; that had been the expression used. How close a collaborator?

Car registered to her. A 604 is a big car. Not the thing a woman, even a businesswoman, chooses as a general rule. Unhandy in the town and to park. Heavy on gas. Not what you run to the supermarket with, to do the shopping or drop a parcel off at the cleaners. On top of an odd story, this all made quite a few oddities.

12

What sort of official handle could be given to an enquiry? If you have no body you have no death – so far. Have you even a missing person? What evidence, in fact, have you that she was in the car at all? Monsieur Vibert said she was, but his tale is vague and confused. Maybe he's a bit off his rocker. And even if he isn't, Doctor Joinel could say he was a bit unhinged by the shock, you know. And who was going to contradict that?

If you send the Identité Judiciaire specialists to look the car over without an order from a magistrate, are you overstepping your powers a wee bit? – not that you were, but suppose the gendarmerie took it into their heads that you were being unduly inquisitive – they can be very touchy about their prerogatives. In any case they've got the clothes and papers – and anything else there may be. You can't get that without a magistrate's order. Monsieur Vibert can: he's only to walk in and ask.

It was nearly ten when he got home. He warmed up soup and said little. Vera's cooking was not macrobiotic. She made soup every night on the grounds that this was easy should he be late. And that one needed a fresh vegetable every day.

Eating alone in the tiny kitchen, able to put his elbows on the table and pig it, he was reminded for the nth time that there was not really room for two adults and a child now at high-chair stage (a real old-fashioned high chair, of solid turned hardwood, with an abacus: found in the fleamarket, sandpapered and revarnished by his lily hands). A splendid thing, but there wasn't room. There wasn't room for anything, anywhere, any more. The livingroom, full of books, pictures and drawing materials, was now full of child's objects: no room for living. The bedroom, which had contained a cradle as well as the big bed, did not allow for a cot. The bathroom . . . It was a problem of long standing already, growing steadily more acute, and he still didn't know what to do about it. Like several more of his problems.

A little wearily, for the day had prolonged itself in tedious fashion, he undressed. Pyjamas were far too expensive and he hated them anyhow. When his expensive cotton shirts wore out, Vera cut the sleeves off and turned the collars, and they became Nightshirts. Her – extremely expensive – cotton nightdresses were a Burden upon the Economy, but were part of the irreducible minimum. The domestic budgets of the Commissaire of Police were wearisome. But made a change from politicians; and on this note he fell asleep.

13

Breakfast was important: oat, wheat and barley flakes came mixed together out of a tin which had contained Uncle Ben's Rice (kept because of nice colours and pretty Art Déco lettering). There was a slight friction, because instead of Corinth raisins, preserved with a small quantity of oil, he had bought Santa Clara sultanas, preserved with sulphur dioxide.

A problem to go to work on: if some gangster imports disgusting Californian raisins instead of honest Greek ones, is this an affair for the Police Judiciaire?

Divisional Commissaire Richard was in his office, trim of clothing, silvery neat of hair; stropped like an antique razor upon a broad good-smelling leather strap. What had he had for breakfast? – nobody knew. He was conducting his early-morning review of currant – sorry, current – affairs. Castang, infected by politicians and Santa Clara sultanas, rambled; was pulled up. Be concise, and answer the question.

"Is there any criminal offence? Anything to charge anybody with?"

"No."

"Then do nothing. If the man has any complaint to make, let him make it. You've investigated the matter he saw fit to report to you. It makes no sense at all. Very well, that's his worry, not ours."

"There's obviously more to it."

"Castang, if your training has not yet taught you elementary truths about politics in police procedure you aren't even fit to empty wastepaperbaskets. This is going to be one office that isn't infiltrated by any neo-nazis; we had enough of that with Lasserre."

Nobody had ever got an answer to the question (unspoken and it had better not be spoken) how actively Richard had conspired towards Lasserre's downfall.

Neo-nazi is a bit strong. Monsieur Vibert is sort of right wing. So was Lasserre, and not just sort-of. But Monsieur Vibert is a great deal more intelligent, and less crude. And in politics, you talk a great deal about clarity, while taking great pains never to say anything clearly.

Current affairs were no more urgent than they had been last night. He read the local paper, a thing he rarely did. It called itself conservative: so did the municipal government. Vibert was a big shot around here, and well thought of by the electorate. There was lots of stuff about the speeches he would be making, and the

14

expected announcement that he would be a candidate in forthcoming presidential elections. And there was a late-insertion notice, what used to be called a stop-press:

Monsieur Vibert escapes from
a potentially dangerous car accident

Yesterday on his way to the city the car in which Marc Vibert was travelling left the road at a notoriously dangerous bend in the mountains. By good fortune he was thrown clear and escaped serious injury. He continued on his way suffering from slight bruises and shock. It is understood that this minor incident would not delay the announced programme (see p 1) and that a day's rest would be sufficient for his recovery. Last night he was not available for comment, but a spokesman confirmed that his injuries were trivial.

See our political pages and Domestic Affairs section, p 4.

No word about the 'collaborator'; no word whether he was alone in the car.

The telephone rang: Richard's voice, extremely mild.

"Castang, give me a moment would you, if you're not too busy?" Sarcastic, since Richard knew perfectly he wasn't busy? Or just conciliatory?

Smoking the small black Brazilian cigars to which he was addicted; things nobody else would touch: was this why? Like most things about Richard it was unexplained.

"Sit down. I've had a call. Not through official channels – not, in other words, the Chief. Obliquely, by inference, the more official. Cabinet of the Minister. Through this mouthpiece, the Minister is talking about his Colleague."

"Is Vibert a minister?"

"No; has been; several times; sharpen your wits. Erstwhile colleague, but buddybuddy, definitely. The minister is exercised at rumours that have reached him – I'm sparing you the roundabouts. You are to follow this affair carefully and with discretion. Confidential report is to be made by me."

You mean you're to follow carefully: careful that I should do it instead. Richard though was a loyal person, and would protect him. Whatever had been done to Lasserre. Because there's no politics here, but on the very rare occasions Richard's had a drink too many, he's not 'conservative'.

"There's no legal action envisaged," said Richard, staring at the ceiling.

Since the Police Judiciaire is the machine for execution for decisions by judicial authority, as its name implies, Castang asked the obvious question; however naive it might sound.

"Then why not RG?" The political police goes under the shrinking-violet name of Renseignement Genéral, which means simply Information. The art of politics is to be both pompous and meaningless.

Richard drew on his cigar.

"I feel quite certain that RG has been given the same message. To be open, I should think that this was just the Minister taking out a little insurance. And of course to keep me in line. Being a little bit more open than is needed, the colleague at RG is perhaps rather right wing."

"I understand," said Castang. "Instructions?"

"It's the sort of thing," colourlessly, "that is a key to further promotion being rapid. Or retarded . . . Monsieur Thing made you an approach, as a bit of cover and as invitation tc the same.

"So you reply in kind. You are friendly and voluble, showing that your instruction is to be cooperative. He'll expect no less from the servants of his buddy the Minister. Once he feels secure . . . Discretion is something that has to be paid for."

Not an attractive job. But most police work is in the nature of pathology.

Now if I were a German policeman I would just push the button. The Bundeskriminalamt possesses an extremely powerful computer. All that there is to be known about thingummy would come tumbling out. In fact a great deal more than one wished to know; a print-out fifty metres long before you could stop it. Information, says the good Herr Herold, is the key to police work.

Jawohl, but the expression is a bit rotund. It's the quality of the *entrecoupages*, the cross-references, that counts. We are much poorer, much more old-fashioned, much less sophisticated. We are still almost entirely in the days of the fifty-year-old joke: if France's coalmines run short she can always keep warm by burning her dossiers. Innumerable minor civil servants have to be kept in jobs and grey dustcoats, all of them the last word in sloth, apathy, and incompetence – and don't think for a moment that they're just rude to strangers.

16

We're buying computers as fast as we can go. But we've still a library, and a librarian, and policemen spend a great deal of time there, burrowing away, eager little doggies.

There isn't a criminal file on Doctor Joinel: one hadn't expected there would be. A glance at the medical 'Bottin' shows him to be an eminent scientific personage with honorary degrees from . . . Rather younger than you expected. First name Hippolyte (which tells you quite a lot about his family). Fascinating but do you progress? You can go to the local paper, which has voluminous files on local notabilities, mostly cuttings from their own back numbers, and will that advance you? Mate, the way to gather information is to go out and gather it. There are facts, but what do they relate to?

Whereas concerning Madame Viviane Kranitz . . . few facts. Quite a lot of rumour. He had no wish to add to the rumour by disclosing that the PJ was taking an interest in the lady.

There were interesting features about Doctor Joinel's house, which was a large, ugly villa standing in a large, ugly garden; the whole bespeaking more wealth than taste, but appearances may be misleading. On the street outside a cop was loitering, the sort you find outside Arab consulates, armed apparently with nothing more aggressive than a raincoat and a radio, who looked at him and said nothing. Inside the iron grille was a choice of gravel paths, leading to a professional entrance (Appointment only: the Doctor was in private practice, very, and didn't have queues outside consulting rooms) and a private entrance saying Private. Looking at the house Castang could guess that it housed oriental carpets or Chinese pottery. That it was one of the few enjoying the privilege of burglar alarms linked to the central police commissariat he knew already. That the gentleman in the parked car taking a sidelong interest from behind *Paris-Turf* was wearing a gun he didn't need telling. That was Box. Box was the one who opened the door. Weighty people with sharp corners: pushable, but so is the kitchen dresser.

"Castang: commissaire: PJ." He then said, "Good morning."

"That's right. The boss is expecting you. Good morning," not sure whether it was or not but trained to be polite, to cop officers anyhow.

"I'd like to see Doctor Joinel."

"Doctor Joinel?" as though he'd got on the wrong bus. "But the boss is expec −"

17

"I'm sure he is very busy."

"Well of course . . . I'll see." At the back of the very clean, very polished hall an elderly female appeared and waited, staring at him till everyone had had time to take up position. Cox said a word to the female who said, "This way," and led him down a passage to a study next to the consulting room. There was not much light: outside the window was a verandah with a lot of plants: what light there was bounced off mahogany bookcases, was absorbed by dim brown bindings. There was a large bureau with a lot of papers. Doctor Joinel walked in, portly but not conspicuously overweight, sat at the bureau and then said, "Good morning, Commissaire. Sit down then, do. And how may I be of service to you?" Polite but not much more. "Cigar?" The gambit is universal. Take it and you're servile: refuse it, you're hostile. Castang's gambit was to take it, light it, put it on an ashtray and disregard it.

"I know that my friend Marc Vibert went to see you. I don't know what he had to say to you. I don't want to know. I can't see anything I could usefully add to that."

"I don't have a mission. If there was one it would be confidential."

"On my side, what I hear in this room stays in it." Small, sharp, grey eyes, gold-rimmed glasses also small.

"Likewise."

"What does that mean?"

"I understand myself." It is a formula phrase, *je me comprends,* whose meaning goes by intonation.

"If you're not going to smoke that cigar, put it out."

"I am not asking for confirmation of Monsieur Vibert's account of his adventures. His word is enough for me."

"So it should be."

"On the other hand there are things it would be indiscreet to ask him. Whereas a doctor is professionally discreet."

"Quite so."

"As is a PJ officer of a certain rank."

"If you have a question, put it."

"Madame Viviane Kranitz?"

"She's a highly skilled political analyst who serves in a confidential advisory capacity. As plenty of people could tell you."

"And did. Anything more personal than that I could always ask her. If she was around, which at present she doesn't seem to be. I have in fact only one question, but I'd hesitate to put it to her.

18

Whereas nothing embarrasses a doctor."

"You have just the one question?"

"At present. If I were to have others, why, I could always make the fact known to you."

"Depending upon circumstances?"

"Exactly. Like the present ones."

"I see. In any circumstance, my reply to your present question would always be silence; which, naturally, you would be free to interpret as you pleased."

"It's very good of you, to give me your time," getting up.

"I'm not calling any press conferences," said Doctor Joinel, "so I'll confine myself to saying that Monsieur Vibert's health, which is robust, will permit of his carrying out rather too heavy a programme. He drives himself too hard of course – always does. He's staying here as my guest while in this town. That is quieter than any hotel, allows of some much-needed rest. And I can keep a discreet eye on his health."

"Yes," said Castang. He had a hand on the doorhandle when some small echo in the air made him pause. The intonation – or something in the phrasing? "A little shock, and some bruises. He's quite recovered?"

"Speaking as a medical man, without breach of confidence, some residual shock. And there's always a considerable nervous strain, and a tendency to overwork. He really shouldn't be worried or bothered – any further. I know, Commissaire, I can rely upon you and that what I say – already too much – will go no further than this room. Remember," smiling, "that I'm an old friend as well as a doctor. He's a national figure. Irresponsible rumour can be very damaging, if maliciously fomented by political opponents." Rather a long speech for Doctor Joinel. Sounding rather a prepared speech. Perhaps Castang's getting up precipitately like that had taken him aback.

"Yes," he said. "The residual shock you mention – that would be the loss of a valued – close – collaborator."

"Naturally."

"You think she's dead, do you?" Doctor Joinel was still sitting placidly behind his desk. He raised his eyebrows.

"My concern was with the living, I grant. An accident of that nature holds out, I fear, no hope at all of survival."

"On your way back – passing the gendarmerie post – it didn't

19

occur to you at all to stop and report that accident?" Joinel frowned.

"Are you reading me a lesson? I would not expect discretion from a country constable. From yourself, however . . ."

"Within these four walls, and those your own. If I were to repay your confidence of a minute ago with one of mine."

"I fail to understand."

"She isn't dead."

Joinel did not move but the change on his face was considerable.

"What makes you say that?"

"In speaking of her a moment ago you used the present tense. She is: she serves."

"A slip of the tongue." He admired the man's self-control.

"That's what I would be thinking, if there'd been any body in that wrecked car."

There was a longish, nasty pause. Doctor Joinel got up slowly.

"I think, Commissaire, that you forget yourself, and exceed your instructions."

Castang opened the door and took a step outside.

"I do admit," he said pleasantly, "that it's a bit of a puzzle to me, being told of a death, and finding no body. Doubtless there's some simple explanation."

"In the absence of all knowledge of the matter," said Joinel politely, "I must arrive at the same conclusion."

"Sorry again to have troubled you."

In the hallway the gorilla, seeing him, held up a hand in a gesture of wait-a-moment, opened a door and said, "Here's the Commissaire now."

"But my dear man, ask him to give me a second of his time," boomed the hearty, jovial voice of a public speaker. In the doorway of what looked a pleasantly furnished library appeared Marc Vibert, radiating bonhomie and vitality.

"My dear Castang. I was asking myself where could you have got to? They told me you were here. Ah, you've been having a chat with my host. And he'll have told you that Richard's himself again. Now I'm altogether at your service: is there anything at all I can do for you?" with so much charm that one scarcely perceived patronage.

"It was only a routine enquiry," said Castang smiling, "to ask about your health."

"As you can see, never better. Poor Joinel's the man that suffers – drowned in business papers – the comings and goings."

20

"And bodyguards," smiling.

"Yes, aren't they a pest! They won't mind my saying so," grinning and clapping the gorilla on the shoulder; he beamed self-consciously, like a schoolchild given a prize. "The fact is that as we see, I'm sometimes tempted to slip away from them, because alas a public man too seldom calls his life his own – and then; isn't that," with ironic amusement, "exactly when we need them most?! A lesson to me. I was punished for my own irresponsibility."

"Then let's hope there'll be no more evil consequences," with hearty goodfellowship: everybody laughing gaily but Doctor Joinel.

"Quite, quite. You need nothing from me – no little technical hitches, signatures on bits of paper?"

"Just the one," hunting in his pockets. "You got your luggage back all right?"

"Yes, a man went out yesterday to pick it up. The gendarmerie were most courteous and helpful. I apologised, for giving them so much work and trouble."

"This concerns the car – oh, here it is. Just the usual release form – we propose to give it the usual technical lookover for signs of possible mechanical failure. The insurance company will like that: their claims adjuster will be the happier."

"I see, I see," reading. "Empowering release from sequestration at Provenchères pending eventual judicial enquiry – yes?"

"Since there'll be no judicial enquiry," humbly, "it's just a bit of bumf."

"I understand: certainly," with a practised autograph for the housewife; 'my son's collection, you understand', "I can safely leave all that in your hands, Castang?"

"You won't be staying long, and there might not be another opportunity."

"Right, alas. Love to stay longer, but meeting tonight, back to Paris tomorrow, my friend Joinel will be delighted to see the back of us."

"I'm like the Commissaire," said Joinel in his dry, quiet way, "my chief concern is for your health, quiet, and peace of mind."

"Which thanks to you both is quite restored. Well, Castang," offering a hand as a reward, "to our next and happy meeting." The phrase was well-used.

"I will have much to congratulate you upon."

"Now now, that's a secret. We're not actually convinced right

21

now that the moment is ripe for an announcement."

"You're speaking of your candidacy?" politely.

"Correct. 'Overshadowed at this moment by a sense of loss' – I'm just drafting a personal statement. To give to the press, you see."

"Of course. I must leave you to it."

"You feel, do you, Castang, that I am safely discharged of legal and judicial obligations?" like a prudent man.

"You did your duty as a citizen in reporting the incident to authority," blandly. "Authority will not be unduly officious."

Monsieur Vibert extracted a card from a little morocco folder in his pocket.

"Personal address, in Paris – unlisted phone number. Just in case. Always welcome. But don't leave it lying around," with a laugh.

"Confidential," agreed Castang solemnly.

He had used his own car for the errand and brought it back to the police parking lot. On the next street in this wealthy residential district there was a small car in step behind him. Nothing to notice, and was only noticed because it was an Alpine, unlike his or other trundle-wagons. Still there on the boulevard. It could pass him easily; why didn't it? A quickened interest disclosed two gentlemen in Arab head-dresses. Beards and dark glasses; the street where he had picked it up was full of Arab consulates. Wealthy gentlemen like expensive toys. He had enigmas enough: instead of solving them he went round collecting more. Don't go searching for gratuitous puzzles in the street.

Back in the office, with a comforting sense that here at least the stairs went upward and the corridor stayed straight, he found a piece of paper and after a small struggle a pen that wrote, and wrote 'Looking-Glass-Land'.

No, realities first. He searched for his piece of paper with the autograph while telephoning to Identité Judiciaire to say tow-truck; Provenchères; big Peugeot what-fell-in-the-ravine; gendarmerie; soothing noises.

Mm, they would not be foxed by the soothing noises, but they would pretend to be. The gendarmerie in France is notoriously courteous, intelligent and efficient; all that other police forces aren't. An object of envy. Why not be a gendarme? Rhetorical question: one wouldn't want to be a soldier, wear a uniform, and be for ever saluting tourists. If there was a body, you'd get that car the

22

way you won the lottery. There being no body, they wouldn't want to know anything about Monsieur Vibert's nocturnal divagations: any more than Richard had.

He got back into looking-glass-land. All he knew about that was that you had to run very fast indeed just to stay in the same place. In order to get anywhere you would have to run a great deal faster than that. If, thus, such a thing as a brown study still exists and it is possible to fall into it, Castang had fallen in.

With a bang, Lucciani entered and tossed an envelope on the desk.

"What's that?"

"Heart-throb assignation. They gave it me downstairs. *Courrier du coeur.* Dear Abigail, my boyfriend is unscrupulous about personal hygiene – look, how should I know?" The envelope said simply 'Mons. Castang. Serv. Reg. Pol. Jud.' and was not stamped or franked. Inside was a sheet, rough-torn from an ordinary exercise book, containing quite a neatly hand printed message of two lines unsigned:

'Castaing let's hope that after marrying that Czech pig you haven't forgotten you're a Frenchman' He tore downstairs. Who left this? Nobody knew. It had been found dropped in the passage. What the hell, there are ghosts round here? Things that go bump in the night? Sorry but you know how it is, people walk in and out of here like it was the Gare Saint Lazare.

He took it up to the lab knowing what they would say. Even perfunctory tests – no need for anything sophisticated – showed up Science at a loss. No prints, stains or dust. Standard material sold by every stationer. Written left-handed by right-handed person, the oldest trick in the book: no graphologist will ever make anything of that. So he was left with the text and a nasty one it was, because of Vera. If it told him more than he knew before, it was because then he had known nothing.

Written by a Frenchman, because Castaing is a common name and this the common spelling: someone who had heard his name but did not know him personally. Anybody snuffling round his home would find his wife was Czech: it was no secret. Neatly written and no other spelling mistakes. That all got him nowhere. A name spelt right on the envelope and wrong inside, the familiar '*tu*' form – it was contemptuous, thinking him of no importance. Then why bother at all? Why send him threats? He hadn't even known what he was going to do, and whatever it was it wouldn't be much. Not anybody in the *entourage* of Monsieur Vibert or the good Doctor Joinel. They had understood perfectly that his instructions were to be unaggressive, and this was aggressive.

But before he had had no dossier: now he had one, because this was the first piece. Anonymous letters are two-a-penny, but this did not relate to any 'current affair'.

Somebody who knew that Vibert had come to see him with a tangled tale – a thing perhaps not too difficult to find out. And who did not want him to show zeal. What zeal had he shown? He had gone out to Saint-Julien, he had looked at the road, he had retraced steps, he had questioned a few villagers, he'd gone on down to the gendarmerie. Observable by anyone hanging about. A hanger-about, so many hours after whatever had happened, meant someone concerned in same.

Whatever Vibert said or left unsaid, forgot or pretended to, he was blurring a situation potentially very embarrassing. She had been in the car: that was certain.

You are with your mistress in a car: it's her car. That she is your mistress is known to quite a few people. The situation does not seem all that explosive. You're on your way to Doctor Joinel's house: it's late at night; you've got rid of secretaries and bodyguards; you're planning a discreet and peaceful night with your mistress. So far so good. What happened then was most unclear.

They'd been stopped, or held up. The 'disappearance' of Viviane Kranitz meant she'd been kidnapped. For fun, or the pleasure of being nasty, or to confuse matters, or impress Vibert further (take your choice), the car got tipped down the ravine: that's what'll happen to Viviane unless you are good, but the chief effect, by design or not, is to embarrass Vibert. Is he to report the accident and what is he to say? After consultation with a few close friends (including the Minister) he comes in with a ridiculous bullshit tale about amnesia. No Chappaquiddick – he didn't tip anybody down the ravine.

Technically it might be possible that he did, or someone did it for him, and that the scenario went wrong, but now, Castang, you are hypothesising far ahead of your data. There isn't any body. To put any effective pressure on Vibert they'd keep Viviane alive.

Now who would put pressure on Vibert, and why?

24

Politician; the purpose is political.

Unless somebody wants to make it look political. And since hypotheses are now arriving in volleys don't just sit here turning brown at the edges. The telephone is a mighty instrument: use it.

"Vera? I wanted to say, if you haven't already been out, it would be as well if you didn't. Trivial, but like most trivial things needing long, complicated explanations."

"I've already been out. How else would you have any dinner?"

"Oh. Well, I would have got something."

"There was nothing in the house. Anyway, what's this nonsense about not going out?"

If it were nonsense she was already inside his guard. If it were not she'd start arguing; was very argumentative these days. The female was in revolt against pretty well everything. If he said simply 'don't go out' she'd go out straight away just to be anti-authoritarian.

"Go out or not; just as you please," ringing off rather crossly. That way, you call two bluffs together.

Unless it isn't a bluff. But of course it is: he'd done nothing yet. Except, of course, sending the I.J. to collect the car. He would, though. Castang was a person mild in manner: these people have often an unreasonable dislike of being bullied: a truism, but so are most things.

Well, to work. For a start he needed a collaborator: jargon word and one he disliked – a partner. For criminal brigade work he would have picked a woman. He liked working with women, and was proud of having brought more women into his group than anybody else; in the country as far as he knew. But not this time. There was a smell of violence about these hints and rumours.

Orthez: he'd started with him, he'd stay with him. It had been Orthez, he recalled suddenly, who'd been there on the parking lot at the moment when you couldn't tell dog from wolf; when a dogday became imperceptibly a wolfnight. Orthez was a good dog: better, a good man. Not just a good-man-in-a-fight, a man you could turn your back on. A man.

Castang, like many more, had been foxed for a longish time by the air of impenetrable stupidity. Nobody was better than Orthez at letting his jaw hang and looking dense. He liked things Castang had no patience for; judo, and childish mechanical toys like autos. How on earth had he become an inspector? How had he ever got into the PJ at all, a body employing numerous barbarians, but they're

25

supposed to be able to add, subtract, and spell otorhinolaryngologist?

Well yes, childish; if by that you meant kindness, candour, and total simplicity; the things you looked for in Vera, not in a PJ man. There were unexpectedly deep waters: Castang had found by accident that Orthez belonged to a confraternity for which secrecy has a noble meaning; that bury the dead, care for the poor, work for the old, the sick and the smelly. Orthez lived in a one-room studio flat and was not married. What did he do there? What kind of girls did he have? A southerner from the Pyrénées, the Cathare country, who liked to drop into the langue d'oc when he met a compatriot. They are a strange and secretive people.

Castang went and got him, sat him in the office and explained this and that.

"Maybe terrorists," Orthez mumbled in his dense way. Richard had forbidden the use of this cliché."Mean extremists. Mean p'raps a job for Intervention," meaning Salviac's brigade of toughs, all guns, grenades and paralysing gases.

"No – instruction is total discretion. If Vibert were to say openly here, this woman of mine has been pinched for ransom or blackmail purpose – but he hasn't, he won't: for obvious political purposes. No cops, no press. There might be a snide remark or two in *Monde* say, or a weekly, whatever happened to Marc Vibert's confidential adviser, but no more."

"He was screwing her, I s'pose."

"Since nobody's saying, of course he was. Saying so, that's a personal smear and political. Each way you turn you've a hand and a foot tied, where it's not both. Richard's got to report to the Minister. I only tell you that to show that the bottom line of this calculation is my job. There's a move made already to block us off. Here, what d'you make of this?" showing him the 'message'. Orthez got it quicker than he had.

"Someone knows where we were last night, and why. That's pretty close. Vibert himself? Or this doctor-pal?"

"What I thought first. But Vibert's old friends with the Minister, must know we're in check-reins and a martingale: why bother? Why stir the shit up further? It's a decoy, to see whether we'll come out into the open at all, whether they're safe from us."

"Who are They?"

"Exactly, and start from zero."

" 'Hoping you're a real Frenchman' – who makes shit talk like

26

that?" Orthez had always sound common sense.

"That's it, that's where we start. We go to lunch first. We thin
about it separately; come up with whatever we can construct as a
staircase to action; synthesise that."

"You going home? You want I should set a couple of boys in the
street by your house: dissuasion, or *qué*?"

Castang laughed.

"That's just a bluff."

There was no sense in trying to be secretive with Vera. "Threat
made to Czech pig. Am I a Frrrench man? No, I'm just me. No more
is Orthez."

"What's he?"

"Oh him," said Castang comfortably, "he's a disgusting savage
from Bagnères-de-Bigorre, so about as French as I am. Shepherd.
Good shepherd too, likes wolves as well. What are they up there? – a
bit Spanish, a bit Catalan, a bit Basque, a bit Navarrese, and highly
anticlerical."

"He going to wheel Lydia in the pram?"

"Will if you ask him," roaming towards the window. He was
always looking out of the window: it was an occupational disease.
Well, for him.

The child was in a nest made of two chairs wedged so that it would
not fall out. He made a huge jump and seized it, fell down clutching it
to his stomach, rolling and curling up, bellowing at her, "Down, get
down." Even while wide-eyed at these antics she flopped.

Glass fractured and disintegrated all around: bullets whined and
screamed, the room seemed shaken as though by an earthquake,
walls reverberated under loud hammerblows, the noise outside
seemed nothing to the noise inside. Afterwards it all seemed
strangely trivial. Was that all? A small amount of dust, mostly from
the plaster of the walls and ceiling. Glass everywhere, yes, and glass
is very dangerous stuff; the flying splinters are as mortal as bullets,
and bloodier. But the high-velocity small-calibre stuff of a modern
assault rifle does not project great shards of hurtling glass: it's not
like a bomb. Probably, being machine-gunned in the good old
tommy-gun days was a lot more impressive: monstrous forty-five
calibre things and a lot more of them.

Castang did not leap up and crouch at the balcony with his gun
out. A lot of good that would do, when his ear had told him that the

accelerating was off around the corner. He got up slowly and ꞓsted his trousers. Child was all right, finding indeed the whole ꞓhing vastly entertaining, staged expressly for its benefit, and wishing it would do it again. Wife all right, lying on her back with eyes wide open, mouth slightly open and a 'dear me' look. Needed helping up, but quite undamaged. Chief casualties were the thick plaster of an old house, a fake-Tiffany lampshade, and one of the potted plants.

"Be back," said Castang-the-cop. "Got to see if there were any witnesses." The empty, peaceful, lunch-time street, the quieter for being a quay really, bordering a disused canal, was full of respectable bourgeois behaving like disturbed wasps; a great deal of buzz and a tendency to attack the innocent, which meant him.

Very good shooting from a moving car. Nobody else's windows were bust, and there was no more than a chip or two off the façade. None of the witnesses had seen anything in the least useful, though all were as always very voluble. Complaint and altercation flew like glass, like bullets. People when frightened are nasty. Every one of the ejected cartridge-cases from an automatic weapon had been pocketed as souvenirs . . . It didn't matter much. By the mere good fortune of being by the window he had seen more than anyone, and that was very little. He couldn't even say what kind of car it was. After all, he'd been thinking of his family. It had had a sliding roof. People in gangster movies poke guns out of car windows, but a sliding roof, frankly, makes the job simpler.

Their flat was on the second floor. Bullets from street level would mostly go into the ceiling. Neither Vera nor the child would have been hit in any case. Almost certainly, not even him. There would never be any dramatic tale about his being saved by the quickness of his reactions, or how something-warned-him to look out the window just-at-the-crucial etcetera. He could have been standing sleeping on his feet and it would have been no different. Just a theatrical effect, meant to frighten him. Teach him a lesson: well it would; several.

Much annoying delay was caused by helpful neighbours calling Police Secours, and the Fire Brigade. Neither of whom ever clear up the mess. Never a dull moment! Just like Paris! Remember Whats-isname, the television announcer? Was he gunned, or bombed? Jumping about there in the street in his underpants – simply killing! I saw the photos in *Paris-Match* – uproarious. It's a disgrace, though.

28

Red Brigade again. Fat lot of good the police are.

When Castang finally managed to get home Vera was stolidly cleaning up and the landlady, elderly and acrid widow who lived in the second floor back, had got over being sympathetic-to-the-poor-baby and was conducting a tirade.

"I've put up with a lot, Monsieur Castang, and I don't say you aren't quiet, and I've always liked Madame's nice plants on the balcony, but I've thought often and I've said as much to you, and the other tenants never have liked it and I don't see why I should be forever putting up with their grumbling, a lease is a lease but there are provisions for breaking it and it's no good talking about acts-of-God, because that's just like the insurance company who always finds excuses for not paying and look at all this, who's going to pay for this damage? It's not that I'm hard or unfeeling, but a person has to protect themself and if gangsters are going to come shooting at you how am I to stop people saying that the police make undesirable tenants and —" Castang picked up the phone and got Commissaire Richard.

Richard knew the house: he had been there two or three times.

"Pretty professional job," he said, digging with a penknife for a mangled bullet, "lovely all this old thick plaster, absorb anything, good soundproofing too. Assault rifle of some sort, how many does the magazine hold, twenty odd? We'll have to have you out of here, it's much too vulnerable. Damage in the line of duty, we'll have it made good out of public funds. I'll tell the Comptroller to smooth your old biddy's feathers out."

Practically the whole criminal brigade was soon engaged in the enjoyable task of house-moving. My private life, thought Castang desolately. Given we had to move, all right. But I could think of ways I'd like better.

The Intervention Brigade was likewise much in evidence. More to please the press than anything else, said Richard. They don't know what they're looking for and neither do we. Yet. Nobody connects it with your Mrs Thing, Vibert's girlfriend.

"What are they after?" lighting a cigar in his own office.

"Why overreact in this way? Good, you get an intimidating letter, and then straight off you're bombed; that's all very amateurish. While the gunning was professional. Every fact here is self-contradictory. Good, let's not lose our heads."

At least the Comptroller served a purpose, at last. A bedrock individual – probably with right wing sympathies. Stuffed with iron filings, steel shavings, and the like: certainly not human. Invariably disagreeable about restaurant bills, taxifares and damage done to clothing in the line-of-duty. But, it had to be admitted, just the right person to deal with banks and insurance companies and the faceless folk who own large buildings, and see to it that they are Fruitful Investments. Castang found his family installed on a fourteenth floor, in small boxes of hollow brick and prestressed concrete. Very expensive. Very nasty. A view, though. You got something for all that buzzing up and down in elevators. And Security, said the Comptroller very dryly indeed, was Adequate. Hardly anything we need add.

But whatever we do need to add, said Richard just as dryly, we'll see to it is added. "Go home then, Castang," he added. "In the official car while this lasts. Orthez driving, and young Thing in the back. And Think."

"Oh my poor girl." As controlled about crying as everything else (too controlled?) Vera did not gulp or snuffle. Tears oozed silently; the hanky was very tight-clutched; horrid little white marks came and went at odd corners of her face. "It's a beastly flat, and all I can promise is that we'll get out, and soon." Never mind the how.

"It's not that bad at all and there are two bedrooms. It was Liliane." The tough, busty chief-inspector on his crime-squad, so called because she was from Lille; nobody could now remember her real name. "She was so kind, and worked like stink to help me and then she offered to cook supper and I was horrid and I hurt her."

Oh yes, Monsieur Castang. Highly intelligent, extremely sensitive and good people, and that's the way people are. They are being very balanced and rational, and trip in some idiotically crude emotion of pride and hidden vulnerability. Liliane, excellent psychologist and thoroughly nice woman, would have understood even while slamming the door and storming out. The machinegun had not hurt Vera. It had invaded her privacy, which is much worse.

"The misery," said Castang, "is that I still have work to do. You're very tired; leave everything as it is and go to bed and I'll –"

"You go out and leave me to it. When I'm insufferable that's the technique anyhow."

"I bought some onion tart so you needn't bother cooking." He

30

had a slightly peculiar supper of onion tart and cocoa, and went to Marc Vibert's meeting.

He'd never been to a political meeting. In his trainee days, and as a young sub-inspector given shit-chores, he'd done plenty of crowd work. But the police on principle avoid political meetings – bar those shady types from RG with their little hidden cameras. They hover about in the neighbourhood. There may be Over-excitable Elements, but it's nothing to Europa-Cup football; in crowd-control terms that's a really shitty chore.

So that his experience was limited to television: young girls with enormous breasts wrapped in the Stars and Stripes, who then leapt up and down: flags got put to peculiar uses.

As to trooping in as one of the faithful, the idea would never have entered his mind; there wasn't a politician on earth for whom he would have crossed the street.

The faithful were being very carefully filtered indeed. The crowd marshals' clothing did not bulge with guns or blackjacks, but with muscles, very: clean-living boys these, and karate adepts to a man. Message clear. Cause any disturbance whatsoever, even a breath of a heckle, and you'll be put out and it will hurt; written on those great barrel-chested T-shirts in large print. Castang, being a cop, had no confusion in his mind between democracy and demagoguery, and quite admired their professionalism.

The people on the platform were making the lead-up speeches. They were the usual municipal politicians, in or out of office; a deputy or so, a senator, Councillors, one or two ex-Ministers who'd found soft spots to fall on; Secretary-Generalship of something or other. Languid distaste gave way to boredom. A dreadful-looking crew, masking squalid self-interest and piddling self-importance with the dregs of cliché and rhetorical hyperbole. A row of tin kettles with holes in, that no tinker could save. You see, Missus, the metal was too thin from the start. He would have fallen asleep but for Vibert.

The faithful had come for Vibert too. A few imbeciles, and more than a few, can always be found to lean forward with shining eyes through Elmer Gantry saying that with God's help we shall yet make of these United States a Moral Nation, or even Doctor Pickerbaugh explaining that venereal disease is due to Immigrant Labourers. But most were leaning back with their eyes shut; they'd

31

come for the star. No warm-up needed by cheerleaders, no Hail to the Chief for Tricky Dick. Vibert sat in the middle like a hawk among drowned rats, effortless.

Very nervous, playing with his glasses, his pencil, his glass of water, his microphone, but the nervousness of a crack horse going into the starting-gate, the gently patting hand of a crack jockey. The man was completely relaxed; all his attention on the crowd. There was Doctor Joinel in the front row, stonefaced and immobile, sharp little eyes missing nothing. Vibert's quick flickering eye suddenly caught Castang's and a brilliant smile flashed, a long finger, white and supple, flicked a joyous little greeting. Good, the man has the professional skill of total concentration, and whatever private worries there are have been cleanly sliced off and set aside. But that much command is damned impressive, or . . .

Doesn't drink or smoke, doesn't suck toffees, chew peanuts or munch jellybeans. Drugs, now what are drugs? They ain't just opium derivatives. Anything manufactured by the pharmaceutical industry is a drug, and words like addiction or dependence are polarised political words used to condition a reflex. The pro is addicted to his profession – cops as well as politicians. The man takes a lot of pills, crafty things like beta-suppressors. And the moment he got up, Castang knew that the man was addicted to women.

Magnificent speaker: Castang even found himself listening. Got everything; extreme intelligence, rapier repartee, delightful humour, an immense charm worn very lightly. Good and perfectly pitched speaking voice, homework excellently done, every statistic at fingers' end, snap crackle pop. The timing a delight, the pacing exquisite. You round the curve into the straight lying just right, and when you take the whip and really start riding it's there, you have it under you. A theatrical performance, the little look to left and right as you pull out fifty metres from the post, but what a damned nice finished job, what a pleasure to see that insolent mastery.

Rhetoric, sure. A Mussolini job. Hell, man, you're in France; stop nit-picking.

The vanity is to be expected. He's young, remarkably so for a man so far advanced upon his career, he's tall and handsome, he's even quite good-looking. Very few horses win the Prix de l'Arc de Triomphe two years running: admire the silky negligence with which the jockey dismounts.

What Castang didn't like was the theme; all that Nation stuff, so incredibly old-fashioned. Of all European countries, it's really only in England and France (is that why they hate each other so?) that you'll hear quite so antique a peroration.

It was what the audience came to hear: they were joining hands starrily to sing about Hope and Glory. Glory, good grief, and Grandeur, thought Castang racing for the emergency exit. A muscular young man held a hand up: Castang smiled with immense warmth, and instead of his police medal exhibited Marc Vibert's autographed calling-card. The karate king bowed and lowered his great bulging forearm.

The fellow is a hell of a nice fellow, but he's still a frigging fascist. And the extremist group who pinched Madame Kranitz would like to force him to go further still. But had she been pinched? Or had the whole thing been stageplay, like the machinegun this afternoon?

Castang stopped, on the way to his own office, to make himself agreeable to Liliane, whom he met in the passage.

"But of course," she said, "I'd have done just the same in her shoes. There could be nothing a woman hates more than a pestiferous stranger sniffing in her linen cupboard, laying violent hands on the kitchen pots." Castang made deprecating noises.

"In the South it's different maybe, but I'm a northern woman myself. Our house is our fortress."

"Men somehow " recalling that no one had ever been known to set foot in Liliane's flat: the consumption therein of furniture polish was said to be staggering . . .

"Men have no sense of privacy. They ramble in and out of each other's houses, borrow pullovers, use people's toothbrushes without a qualm – what have you been doing then, to get yourself gunned – rounding up Basque autonomists?" Curiosity had been piqued, in the PJ. Statistically, it is no more dangerous a trade than many others. On average, eighteen policemen a year get killed on duty.

"Eeny-meeny-miny," said Castang shrugging.

Monsieur Richard was in a metaphorical sort of lotus position, contemplating.

"You recall after the synagogue in Paris got bombed, how very difficult it was to lay hands on any solid information about right wing dotties? We didn't have any trouble here." Both recalled with secret glee the spectacle of the Minister of the Interior, abjectly ingratiating, explaining that perhaps there were just a very few nasties in the police force. All the fault of that dreadful general in Libya, seeking to Embarrass the Fatherland. "Not a Local affair," went on Richard with much sarcastic emphasis. "Masterminded elsewhere. Parachuted from Paris."

"Teleguided," suggested Castang.

"You took the words from my mouth. I hear that Marc Vibert had a highly successful meeting last night."

"Delirious popular enthusiasm," agreed Castang, taking the paper Richard handed him. There was a great deal about Marc Vibert: reported *in extenso*. There was also a nice little block about the Outrage, with a photo of the balcony. Spectacular, but no real bottom to it. A possible change in the management of the football team (which had lost three times on the trot) got much more space. The public has got accustomed to assassination attempts upon the Guardia Civil, the Carabinieri, tra-la. There are far too many extremist groups, most invented the previous night. Nobody can be bothered learning all their new names. Whenever there is an Outrage they all ring up to claim responsibility, hoping for a bit of free publicity. The public is left with a vague notion that if the police gets shot at, that's more or less what it's paid for. Information is as devalued a currency as any South American coinage. By this evening nobody would remember Castang's name.

"There was a photo of you," murmured Richard, "but I had it suppressed.

"We'll go very carefully indeed, Castang," after more meditation. "He that believeth shall not make haste. I'm in no hurry to have Madame Viviane Kranitz liberated from confinement in a damp cellar. I've a feeling we've not come to the end of spectacular Interventions."

Castang had not been in his office thirty seconds, had indeed just opened the window to air the stuffiness (not without a look at whether any terrorists were lurking in the parking-lot) when a girl announced that there was a lady to see him. Not a woman; a Lady. Him by name.

"Three minutes to get the stink out of here." Shall we light a stick of Harekrishna incense? They've all sorts, suitable for everything between contemplating-the-infinite through tired souls to sex. He lit a cigarette instead and stood up politely.

The Lady was small, thin, forty-fivish. Very good legs displayed by stockings much too pale. Anonymously dressed, but crocodile handbag and silk-scarf-with-horses, very eponymous, screaming Rue Saint Honoré a kilometre off. The face and figure both pretty, but oddly faded, as though left too long in strong sunlight, or perhaps she'd been slimming too strenuously.

"I'm Murielle Vibert," she said abruptly. "I'm his wife." She was stuck: Castang nodded kindly and said, "Is there anything I can offer you?"

"No thanks. This is very personal, very painful, intensely humiliating."

"My flat got machinegunned yesterday, which is the same, but still all in a day's work for me. My wife though felt the invasion of privacy acutely."

"Yes," she said nodding. "I'm glad you understand."

"So don't hesitate. But one brief question, if I may – you asked for me by name?"

"Yes, my husband told me. Oh, we're on speaking terms. I realise it's all confidential. I didn't give my name to the young woman."

"I did not recognise you, but," cautiously, "someone else might have?"

"I'm not in the public eye, you know. I play no role in public affairs. I don't get photographed much."

"But a reporter, if alert, would recognise you, isn't that so?"

"I just have to take a chance on that. In fact, I'm not sure I care." The tone of desperation made Castang knit the brow.

"Let's get this clear, Madame," lighting another cigarette, "I've been instructed to follow up an incident which might or might not be criminal, but which could embarrass your husband, uh, in his capacity as a nationally-known figure."

"I don't know that I care about that, either."

"But I do, here's why. Nobody even in this building, bar my superior, knows of the instruction I received. But if anyone recognises you – not a very hard task – the link with your husband is at once manifest."

"I don't care about that either," impatiently. "I think that now, the less cover-up the better. I'm considering a statement, to the press." Oh merde, thought Castang, we're back in Chappaquiddick country. "And if I don't give this to the press," she added, "there

35

may be others who will." Castang, who had suppressed the thought that people seemed unaccountably interested in his own doings these days, agreed without saying so.

"If there's any milk spilt it's too late now," smiling. Come in her own car very likely – Paris plates – parked carelessly on the street outside . . . This discretion thing is going to go up with a bang. What the hell is Vibert playing at?

"I forced his hand," she said, guessing his thoughts. "My husband got back early this morning. I won't conceal that I made an immense scene. I've been up all night. I left early. He's gone to bed." An oddly irrelevant observation. "I've made my mind up – it's her or me."

How had she known? Is this the Minister again, playing a sneaky game, ringing up with reassurances – no, no, he's not hurt, set your mind at rest! I've seen a lot of things, thought Castang wearily, but this – can't move a step without falling down a secret trapdoor cunningly set under the carpet, and woosh – the oubliette. And the Seine, sewn in a sack.

"Good, you want to say what's on your mind. I have to hear it. That is at the present my job. We won't be interrupted," lifting the internal phone, not switching on any tape-recorders.

"When the cat got in among the pigeons," said Castang crossly, "there was a lot of loud flapping, feathers around the place, probably blinding the goddam cat. In any case a moment later the pigeons are strutting about as though nothing had ever happened. Perfectly self-satisfied – it's the cat that's feeling frustrated, right?"

Richard let all this pass. Castang being rhetorical; a familiar phenomenon.

"But when the fox got into the henhouse there were a lot of dead hens. The one at the top with my name on. If this woman gives it all to the press . . . She's a woman of strong character; she's not going to be easily deflected from her purposes."

"Cool off," advised Richard pleasantly. "What have you done to deflect her purposes?"

"Told her the truth – or what may be the truth, for all we know. That Viviane Kranitz has disappeared and we don't know any more about how or why than about what happened to the *Marie Celeste*."

"Stop raving," said Richard irritably. "No, no, I understand," he added kindly. Commissaire Richard concealed the fact, with

36

success, but the truth was that he was a kind man. There was no question of replacing Castang. He had nobody better: he had nobody even as good. Castang did get into flaps; a personality needing a strong back-up, which did not detract from his intelligence and courage. Having a woman like Murielle Vibert stamping around the room, on top of being shot up, had put him momentarily under too much strain.

He knew the type well. Woman from an old-fashioned strain of high bourgeoisie, with high if very narrow ideals, extremely rigid morals and unbendable precepts. Catholic to the core, early Mass and regular Communion. Devotion, fidelity: both to your charitable works and the precepts of your sophisticated Jesuit confessor. And to your husband! They were trained to total submission and to closing the eye resolutely to every male villainy. Men were frightful creatures! But this one was given you by God, and men shall not put you asunder.

Just don't push a woman like that too far! Once the barrier of her self-control has snapped, there's no stopping her. She will kill, and walk with perfect calm and dignity into the police station immediately after.

"If we could even –"

"Shut up: I'm thinking."

It was not that Vibert had flaunted this Kranitz as his mistress openly, provocatively: common political prudence had forbidden that. But from all Richard could gather, and he had been busy gathering, the woman had acquired an extraordinary influence over a popular, dynamic personality widely viewed as having a very considerable political future. If he played his cards skilfully, it was in most places thought, there was almost nothing Marc Vibert might not rise to. Even the Presidency of the Republic. Not this time . . . but next . . . And this woman Kranitz was not just good in bed. As a confidential adviser she'd got very close indeed. Her whisperings in his ear were not just pillow talk. And the man was insatiably ambitious.

Because of all this Richard was himself worried. Vibert was at the moment out of office after a well-publicised brawl with the present First Minister: a fact giving him plenty of freedom for political manoeuvre. But the man had held ministerial positions of much importance – this was no ex-State Secretary for Transport, whose misadventures would never much disturb the government.

37

The Broglie scandal, at no great distance in the past and vivid in Richard's mind, had, by threatening to involve an ex-minister of importance, close in the councils of the mighty, crucified half a dozen policemen and forced the resignation, a year ahead of his pension, of the Director of the Police Judiciaire in person. And Divisional Commissaire Richard, while only the chief of a provincial brigade no more important than eight others, had no intention of going the same way. Officially let off the hook, but a disgraced and ruined man.

"Has she gone back to Paris?" he asked sharply.

"I hope so: I begged her to," said Castang soberly. "I told her that until we could form an opinion whether the woman was dead or alive, whether she had been really kidnapped and by whom, and above all for what purpose, conceivably implying blackmail or at the least strong pressure upon her husband, she would be impeding justice by making any public statement, causing great and perhaps irreparable damage. I hope I convinced her."

"I'll go to Paris myself this afternoon. But understand this, Castang, if there exists any file on Madame Kranitz, we won't get to see it. Now synthesise. No extremist group known to us, be it left or right wing, and I may fairly say that in my district I've pretty extensive knowledge of both, has laid claim to kidnapping Madame Kranitz.

"Now you, on your side. It's known, not widely but sufficiently, that you, acting upon information received, made a brief, formal enquiry into Marc Vibert's traffic accident. He wants it kept dark, the Ministry wants it kept dark, we see no good reason for not keeping it dark – all right? We don't even know that she was in the bloody car – officially."

"IJ's report upon the car," said Castang baldly, "doesn't advance us a step one way or the other. Property of hers, prints all over, presumably hers. Both he and she had driven the damn car, with nothing much except his are superimposed, so he was driving then. No mechanical sabotage, no sign of the car being stopped by a tripwire or whatever. At that point it wasn't doing over thirty: anybody jumping out on the roadway could stop it. The doors were both sprung open – at what point of the crash into the ravine is not clear. No sign of any third person either in the car or on it. But of course she was in the car. Why should he say that she was killed in a crash? Because he didn't know what happened to her, save that something did, and that something violent."

"The same day," went on Richard imperturbable, "as you smear syrup over all this and Vibert is patted on the back, you get a warning note with a right wing patriotism smell to it – meaning what? You've done nothing, and only an hour or so later, your flat is shot up in a noisy, flamboyant way. Another sort of warning, but seemingly unconnected to the first. The same evening, Monsieur Vibert has a large much-publicised – very successful – political meeting, but does not, as was apparently intended, announce his candidacy for the President's job. In a brief press statement he announces that Madame Kranitz, hitherto a trusted associate and adviser, no longer figures in his entourage: asked whether this is for personal or political reasons, declines to comment: asked whether there was a difference of opinion – declines comment: asked what this has to do with a traffic accident says No Connection. That there was an accident, in her car – a teacupful of gossip. There was an accident, reported to the police, who see no need for further enquiry: that'll be all, gentlemen, thank you. Now add up all this together and what have you?"

"Quite a lot, or anyway too much – but what it is I've no idea."

"Madame Murielle Vibert obviously does have ideas, and storms in to make them forcibly known."

"That the woman Kranitz had him under a spell. *Envoûté* was the expression used. That she was trying to force him into a far more extreme, and outspoken, right wing attitude in public, and a candidacy based on a tubthumping law'n'order grandeur-of-France act."

A train ride to Paris took a bit under three hours: roughly the time – were you imprudent enough to take the car – that you would risk sitting blocked on the Boulevard Periphérique.

Richard had changed his mind about going. "You can kill both birds with one métro carnet," was all he said: about long and tiresome conversations on the telephone with the Ministry he had nothing to say beyond, "They're knitting their brows a good deal." Having the Direction of the PJ knitting its brows on the Quai des Orfèvres is tedious enough. Faces being made on the Place Beauvau is even more of a trial.

Orthez had been left with a small instruction: are there any Arabs with a dark blue Renault Alpine, and if so who are they? Tape-record and cherish any messages for Castang, filter any callers, and if Mrs Castang goes shopping, tag along, would you?

A car, on or off the autoroute, admits of small mental effort beyond choosing between Europe No. 1 and the Citizens' Band (illegal but practically everything in this legalistic country is. You can eat, and fornicate, but think twice about breathing).

A train however admits of thought: Castang had been told to Think: he Thought: Descartes' principles are still paid lip-service.

Has Madame Kranitz, for reasons known to herself, arranged a kidnapping for eventual publicity and to force Vibert's hand? That's what Murielle says: is it as silly as it sounds?

What are these 'warnings'? The letter could mean anything. Roughly don't be anti-Vibert: don't discover or disclose anything prejudicial to the Cause. Possible source, Joinel; for what that's good for.

The gunning: almost certainly unconnected; work of people believing in flamboyantly violent action (like hijacking cars and kidnapping people?). Message saying Watch your Step, which is what everybody's telling me. Source thus, absolutely anybody: could even be RG's way of saying Piss Off. Meaning, as far as there is any, do nothing, especially about Kranitz.

Well we *haven't* done anything. There had been no calling out of gendarmerie, mustering of CRS brigades, helicopters, searches, roadblocks and all the paraphernalia of a Strong Reaction to Extremist Threat.

We wait, until this – call it a group for lack of a definition – comes out and runs up its colours.

Vibert had been fairly clever, given no great space to be clever in. Dissociated self from Kranitz; controlled hysteria about attacks: he'd pinched out the fuse of the drama.

His wife – Marc would be very cross with Murielle if he knew – had done her best to light it again. She'd been damped a bit, but she was an uncontrollable element.

If nothing happened, the group, be Kranitz an accomplice or not, would now try something more spectacular. If logic meant anything, which it seldom does.

Mumblings on the tin loudspeaker, and everyone struggling into overcoats, announced Paris. He tumbled with the others from

40

overheated air into chilly draughts full of bangs and smells, and dived into the bowels of the earth. He didn't think anybody was taking an interest in his movements, but performed the act anyhow of bewildered-provincial taking the wrong metro line.

At Party Headquarters the way was not barred by gorillas, but by numerous young women of impenetrable imbecility, dressed in funny raiment. No bowler hats and ponchos this year: a tendency to work-overalls of bum-boy design, coloured pink or lilac. Once Vibert's voice had bidden it admit him, a luxuriant bottom served as guide. Telescripters, computer-terminals and all manner of music counterpointed these Hungarian rhapsodies. He would have been impressed, but the last time he'd been in Paris had been an errand at Communist Headquarters, where Colonel Fabien presides over an even fancier get-up. A relief to find Vibert in a pleasant room, a place where actual work could get done. He sprang up; broad beams and athletic bounds.

Castang had made his mind up: no mincing, no beating around bushes.

"I am grotesquely handicapped, not so much by enforced discretion, since we're used to that, but by all the accounts given us which are of staggering silliness."

"Yes," murmured Vibert. "It's a pity there's so little I can do about that."

"Everybody's silly from time to time. At present, me, I had my flat machinegunned. I look silly. I am silly."

"I heard about that. Believe me, I was most sincerely sorry. There's help I could perhaps offer. But you might not like to be thought under obligation."

"Oh, we're quite comfortable. Puzzled, a bit."

"So'm I," said Vibert.

A girl of rare beauty came in carrying a porcelain cup of coffee.

"Freshly made," she said smiling. "Do you like cigars?"

"Tiny ones," said Castang smiling. He watched the play of her legs across the carpet, banishing lechery.

"It's said," he offered, stirring the cup, "that intimate relations with the girls in the office is not a brilliant or original idea." Vibert smiled.

"Very well-organised girl, that."

"Our girls are of a plain sort. Homely. Not a temptation. My

41

God, we never get any privacy even in the lavatory." Smile broadening, in sympathy. "Now Madame Kranitz – would she be described as homely?"

"You mean you don't know?" surprised.

"We haven't even a photograph: I'd rather like some."

"I've none, I fear."

"A description would be illuminating."

"I wouldn't exactly say homely. I might describe her as striking-looking. In the sense of maturity rather than youth. She's . . ."

"I notice you no longer say was." This time Vibert broke into an outright silent laugh. Castang could see why people liked him.

"Suit yourself. As to a photo, there might be one in her flat."

"I haven't the right to go breaking into people's flats," said Castang scandalised. "But you'll have a key, I feel sure."

"Have you been talking to my wife?"

"Your wife?" shocked. "Good God, no."

"Just that I'd be glad to know how you come by the supposition."

"Ministries . . . dreadful gossipshops!"

"Yes," murmured Vibert, "we've gone too far now . . . Suppose, Castang, I were to entrust you with this key."

"Nobody would even know I'd come and gone."

"I'd like a little more than that. I'd like it that you didn't make my wife, whom I value above everything," seriously, "a party to any of the gossip you get exposed to, in your profession."

"Readily. But I can't answer for her thinking, you know, and I've no restriction to place upon anybody's movements."

"Yes. That's understood." He opened a drawer, tossed Castang a key-ring. "May as well remain in your possession," pleasantly.

"If I meet the owner I'll give them back. No concierge?"

"A porter – the sort one only sees on a television screen."

"There is a gentleman," agreed Castang, "who has no wish to be noticed by the other gentlemen."

"And you won't be worrying me any further; is that fair?"

"Unless something forces me," shaking hands on it.

He felt both like a burglar and a voyeur: he had been both, upon occasion. A crime-detail cop has learned that there is a dreary similarity about the ways people hide their valuables (burglars become skilful at the rapid recognition of patterns) while there is a multiplicity and variety to what goes on behind the bedroom door

42

which will stretch even the older cop's eyes. In general perhaps the patterns are not very complicated: dull people have dull houses. Conventional people – which most people are – live in strange discomfort forced upon them by the rigidity of their notion of what an interior ought to look like. The rich are no exception: it is pathetic to see how little their money has been able to do for them.

Never before had Castang been left alone like this in a house, with no fear of interruption, and least of all by the owner. He had thought he would learn a great deal about Madame Viviane Kranitz, and found himself strangely baffled; a baffling sensation.

The flat was small and awkward, albeit quite large and even luxurious, by Paris standards. The chief impression was that the owner was quite uninterested in it. Money there was in plenty, but the feeling persisted that she had pointed at things in expensive shops and said 'I want that', without ever thinking of the relation pieces of furniture have to one another and the room. There was no articulation, nothing organic. Both livingroom and diningroom reflected dead flat boredom. He could not imagine her ever coming in here in her slippers and curling up contented. Few books and those technical, on political science and economics: office-reading that she had forgotten to take back to the office. Some pictures, aggressive in form and acrid in colour. He didn't mind finding them hideous – they weren't his – but how did anybody live with them? Were they there as talking-points for the guests? Because these were rooms for entertaining people in, not for living in. The television set was for looking at the news, the big lacquer table, too large and too square, for standing drinks on, a – nice – antique dresser only for containing drinks . . . it was as though she never came here except for the purpose of having people in'. There was presumably a cleaning-woman: it was all tidy, the film of dust was thin. Windows all sealed against pollution; if you wanted air you pressed the button and got it conditioned. No plants, flowers, animals or music were there: none would have survived.

The kitchen was elaborate, lavishly equipped. She would cook cunning dinners for select little parties, using flashy recipes from restaurants. There were two bathrooms. Hers was obviously the most personal room in the place. A cocoon; here she would be comfortable, but in a completely selfish way: nobody else was allowed in. The pharmacy cupboard was huge, and brimming with sophisticated medicaments meaning nothing to him. For any tiny

43

thing a phonecall, a prescription, a battery of nostrums. The 'guest' bathroom had an electric razor, a lot of expensive men's perfumery. and a lot of anti-allergy stuff. Yes, Vibert would be a sufferer from skin troubles and hay fever: so many of these hard-ridden men were. In the passage were bookcases – novels taken to read in bed – half left unfinished and none reread. Looked like a bookshop's remainder counter: the dead bestsellers of the last four years. The guest bedroom was so conventional it looked to have been lifted complete from a shop window; mahogany veneer in imitation-English; after a Sheraton patternbook, but a long way after. Vibert never slept here . . .

Remained what should have been the plum; her own bedroom, but another disappointment. Things feminine, even frilly, even at a pinch sexy, but perfunctorily so. She could organise herself no doubt to be an accomplished mistress, including being-good-in-bed. The way she was good-in-the-kitchen: it was expected of her. A sharp mind, a disciplined intelligence. But the woman herself was elsewhere. The flat was a shelter, a place to change clothes in, to sleep the whole day when tired, to take pills in, have breakfast in, lose surplus weight in – for the rest, a place to telephone from. Her 'office' might tell one more: she must have had an office, back there at Headquarters. He hadn't thought to ask. Too late now. Badly organised policeman.

There was a spareroom at the end, but used only as a dressingroom and dumping-ground for stuff out of season: skis and ski clothes. Chucked about and not taken care of. She had plenty of money: if she wanted things, she would flip into a good quality shop wherever she happened to be, choose an armful rapidly, decisively, take a taxi home. He looked at labels: Avenue Montaigne, Avenue Victor-Hugo, Rue de Sevres: well-cut, good taste, and that was all. Plenty of things still in the bags in which they'd come back from the cleaners. Underclothes the same – sensible, comfortable, plain. No cleavage bras or black lace knickers. She'd packed a bag before leaving – all-purpose clothes: trousers, blouses, a suit had been considered and discarded. The departure had not been hurried, or unplanned. She'd left of her free will, under her own steam. There were no clues to anything at all: neither bedroom nor bathroom showed any sign of a break in the usual patterns.

The bedroom telephone had a telephone diary beside it, but the names were no help. Paris numbers, and the first names of both men and women.

Remained the writing-desk, put in the diningroom because there was no space for it anywhere else. Gloomily Castang shuffled through paper, cards and envelopes; neatly arranged financial papers. Owned the flat, owned two more – a healthy rent went into a healthy bank balance. Just an ordinary bureau – no fancy locks. He glanced about. Probably there was a safe – but he wasn't equipped for opening one, and had no need or desire to. The telephone diary here was longer and fuller. Doctor, dentist, bank, tax accountant. Flowershop and theatre agency, restaurants – he was wasting his time.

These weren't all local numbers. Some discreet initials, and a few enigmatic codenames (anybody can pick up a telephone book). Code prefixes for foreign towns too – names scribbled in: Hamburg, Düsseldorf, Zürich – and French provincial towns. Including his own. Castang shrugged, and slid the whole thing into his inside jacket pocket. At that moment there was a loud click and the outside door opened. He hadn't shot any bolts.

He had no particular wish to meet any of Madame Kranitz' friends. It might be interesting to know which of them had keys to her flat – or who had borrowed her keys . . . It wasn't the lady herself. A man's steps paused in the lobby. Not furtively or cautiously; more like a man looking casually around; rather as Castang had himself. If the man went towards the bedroom one might slip quietly out. If the man came into the livingroom – well. The diningroom curtains were not long or deep enough to hide behind at all efficiently. Castang wasn't a very good hider-behind-curtains anyhow. A cop prefers to see, and in general too to have his hands and feet free. If need be. The man came into the livingroom, saw nothing of interest there, came on, and Castang stepped out into the doorway.

A big man, heavily built – and startled. He jumped back, and his hand went to the V of his overcoat in a gesture familiar to any television-watcher.

"Don't," said Castang pleasantly.

"Don't what?" in a loud nervous voice, gripping his lapels and sticking his chest out.

"I can shoot quicker than you," still pleasantly; brushing his jacket back and resting his hands on his belt: the wooden butt of a big gun sat there above the holster. He was smallish for a cop and – odious word – dapper, but, in the eye of the beholder, at times a plain-looking fellow wearing a plain-looking piece: nine-millimetre S. & W. revolver.

"Cop?" said the man in some doubt. The accent was a bit funny – an American intonation?

True, Castang didn't look very like a cop, being given to whipcord breeches, and the pride-and-joy, a Harris hacking-jacket. With a check shirt this ridiculous get-up emitted a strong racecourse aroma, as of straw and horsepiss. Completed at present with one of his numerous idiotic hats, green velours with a cord round it, so that he might have been about to break out in a yodel.

"Now let's hear who you are," putting his warrant-card back and still pleasantly. The big man, in quite good shape too – only about three kilos overweight – looked through narrowed eyes and thought about it calmly.

"You're on private property here, seems to me."

"So're you," propping his backside against the table and crossing his ankles: he was on delicate ground and better be unaggressive.

"I've some right. I'm Stanley Kranitz." Castang held his hand out palm up in a peaceable gesture.

"Give. Let's see the piece. Illegal you know, even if you've a permit."

"You going to make a fuss about it?" in a tight voice.

"One thing at a time. Give . . . Better. Tends to make a cop nervous."

An under-shoulder gun, a seven sixty-five: Walther, a good make. Heavy in the butt.

"Loaded," said Castang, springing the magazine out, laying both gun and magazine beside him on the table. "About the fuss, I'll make up my own mind." The man brought out a pack of cigarettes, offered it, lit one.

"Hundred-dollar bill any use to you?" which was exactly what Castang needed.

"Mr Kranitz, you're on enclosed premises wearing a gun and offering a bribe to a police officer: the judge would simply love you. So you tell me very convincingly all about yourself, if you like."

"The woman who lives here is my wife."

"You wear a gun to visit your wife? That what they do, back in Oklahoma?" The man spoke perfectly good French, but there was still something funny about the accent and not just American.

"Look, let's not horse around. I'm divorced from her but we're on perfectly friendly terms. I live in the States, she lives here: we get on all right. French woman, you know; they don't export easily." True.

46

Bretons, Auvergnats, people from poor places, yes. But the French bourgeoisie does not function properly outside its lovely Hexagon.

"Stanley – would that have been Stanislas in earlier times?" running the accent home at last.

"That's right: Polish. Businessman. Honourable credentials. Can show you. Now my wife – I don't know what your business is, but she's pretty well fixed, sort of government employ and from the business angle she knows a few people that are sometimes handy to know, contract-wise, if you take my meaning." Castang did. "So we aren't hostile to one another because the friends she has, they like too to have amicable relations with the American business community. I'm making sense?" The heating of the flat was turned down: he let his overcoat and scarf dangle, moved like a man who knows where the drinks are kept, poured himself out a whisky and one for Castang, took a cigar as an afterthought. Very relaxed, but a person to keep an eye upon.

"Explains most things perhaps, except the gun."

Kranitz drank some whisky, thoughtful. Pale skin, flat fair hair going silvery. Fifty odd.

"I get off the plane in Charlie Airport, go to a little pad I keep here. I'm in Europe maybe eight times a year; don't like hotels much. Keep some stuff there, the gun among other objects. Doesn't mean anything. Ring my wife; she's not here. Ring here and there, she's nowhere. I ask around, naturally it seems to me, and begin to hear funny stories, don't know much what to make of them, but start getting a funny feeling in my bones which I'm not too happy with. I don't come here ordinarily. My wife's personal affairs concern her. Maybe though there's some indication here about where she might be and maybe who with. I've got a key I always had, never bothered giving back, all right?"

"The gun," said Castang gently. Kranitz finished his whisky and began on another.

"You come here," he said at last, "and you're wearing a gun. Maybe you wear it all the time, I wouldn't know. You're a cop. I might have an interest in what you were looking for, hereabouts.

"I go to a meeting in somebody's office, I might take a diary. In a bar, I might take some money. In some hotel room I might take along a pocket recorder. Well now, when you don't quite know who you might be meeting and where, there're moments you might find it prudent to pack a gun along. Yourself now, you do the same."

47

It was an argument Castang had heard too often and with which he had small sympathy, but he was a cop, he wasn't going to give a sermon on non-violence to Polish-American businessmen from Cleveland. The women too carried guns. He didn't know either the firearms regulations in the State of Ohio, and it was a piece of information he could do without. They'd all watched too many television serials. A great many of which were showing in France six months later: time to dub the soundtrack. In France John Wayne talks French. In France are plenty of people who think the deceased gentleman's view on morals excellent, and approve wholeheartedly. We could do with that over here: let's be methodical. In France are quite an incredible number of people with even bigger guns than Castang's under their jackets.

He reached out, put the gun together, handed it politely butt first to Kranitz.

"Put it away. As a favour to yourself, and to me, don't carry it around here." Kranitz looked at him silently, stowed it away; a laborious process under an overcoat and the jacket of a suit. Very suddenly Castang drew his own gun and pointed it. Kranitz' mouth opened and he dropped his cigar on the carpet.

"Mister, there are cops here who would have put a hole in you, seeing you come in that door and make a move like that. You'd be picked up with the hole, and they've got a perfect self-defence plea." The cigar had not made much of a burn in the wool carpet.

"You going to forget it?" asked Kranitz.

"For three hundred dollars. Or if you prefer a lot more information – a lot more, and detailed. I've got my little notebook with me too," cheerfully. "We'll start with all your papers, just in case you're really Zbig – spying for the National Security Agency."

"Fair deal," said Stanislas.

"Your wife, Mr Kranitz, has disappeared, and this fact is interesting some few people including me. Castang, Police Judiciaire, crime detail. Now please, all you know, about her friends, acquaintances, and business relations, specially the ones who make contracts."

Wolfnight, thought Castang ruefully: the shadows along the road through the forest are sinister. It is very silent. The hoofbeats of a tired horse are muffled and stumbling. People hear their own heart, and keep their hand on the gunbutt.

48

Tired. Cops get tired too. Gare de Lyon ten at night. No time to eat. There is a nice restaurant in splendid Art Déco style called the Blue Train, but he wanted above all to be at home and in bed. Hours after midnight count double, and not in pay.

Private person, going home from Paris, with private thoughts. Vera was frightened when he was in Paris: she didn't know why; she just was. In Castang's city there were night-people, plenty, but the province goes to bed early. There is still a feeling that the honest are not afoot after midnight; that those who are must be whores and thieves.

Which doesn't prevent there being a great many whores, and thieves too, innocently and peacefully abed.

A good day's work? Perhaps. This was a complicated business, and a silly one. Stan Kranitz was another complication, and a silly one. Ol' Stan from good ol' Akron.

It wasn't like going home to the old flat: even at midnight a creature-comfort wife waiting up with cosy plasters to take the sting out of fatigue and anxiety; pain too sometimes, and fear often. Vera herself was become a rawer, harsher person. The times they are a-changing, Castang, and are you a bit belated, finding out? That fellow with the assault rifle who emptied a magazine into your balcony window (assault is a good word) – maybe only now are you waking up (waking up is a good word) to some realisations that were overdue? He ripped the plaster off: a thing it's no use trying to do gently. You had it easy, Castang, you didn't want to move. You were getting lazy and self-satisfied. He had grumbled a good deal about the new flat – jerrybuilt rabbit-hutch – would have grumbled more if he'd been given the time. 'Shut up', Vera had said.

What is it you want? – a nice little house in the country, hey, with green shutters and roses round the door? Oh yeah. He dozed.

Getting out of an overheated train into the raw air did him good: digging the car out of a wet-concrete-smelling underground dungeon (overtones of piss) did him good. While he was waiting for the lift to take him rabbithutchwards, a cop walked slowly out into the lobby and took a good stare, and that did him good too. Cop was on duty and so was he, and they only nodded at one another. As the lift came down he found a cigar Kranitz had given him, still in his breast pocket, and held it out as a peace-offering. The cop showed his teeth in a tight grin.

Vera was asleep. She wasn't asleep, of course, but when he came

49

in she fell asleep. He was ravenous, and made a hearty meal. There was a dishwasher in this flat. A stupid thing, wasting energy. Well, he had wasted energy enough, washing dishes. If he was stuck, enslaved momentarily to these imbecile gadgets, it was enough for the moment that he knew it: he stacked things carefully, and got into bed.

"Good," said Vera, "you've understood. We were getting into a tight little pattern – too turned in upon ourselves. No, don't fuss; when I say I'm going out I won't be putting Monsieur Orthez – he's very kind – to trouble. When it all blows over . . . I've plenty of work. One no longer hammers nails in walls," said Vera, who had just found this out, "one takes the electric drill and one makes a hole, with a great deal of work and mess, and then one puts a little plastic thing in the hole which costs a great deal of money, and that might hold a screw, conceivably. And that's modern. Wood is now a great, great luxury, which is as it should be when you think of it."

"Where did this drill come from?" asked Castang. Where was his? Lent to young Maryvonne at the office: why didn't people give things back?

"Orthez lent it me,' said Vera happily.

The car didn't blow up when he started it either: really life was getting quite peaceful.

Richard he found in sarcastic frame of mind. The Adjunct Director of the Police Judiciaire, who Coordinates – whatever that may mean – the sixteen regional services of PJ in France, had been making his life a misery.

"I told him I had two master plans, one for left wing terrorists and one for right. Their code names are Naiad and Dryad," proudly. "Gauche, you see, Castang, and Droite."

"Should be Gaiad then, no?"

"I haven't been able to get round that yet, but both Master Plans are in full schwing. They're both you, so get on with it."

" I'm not quite sure which is which."

'A wood-nymph and a water-nymph, but I don't know either. That's exactly the point," said Richard tartly, "they have to be readily interchangeable. Right, let's have it."

"Working theory: what this country needs is a solid, reactionary, ultra-right-wing government, okay, and get shot of this wishywash liberalism. Can't have an army putsch. Must have an acceptable civilian candidate. Vibert likeliest man. Mind on the right track, but nowhere near extreme enough. However, it's noticed, a confidential adviser, likewise mistress, thus well-placed on two counts, is there to shove him into more extreme positions.

"He's very strong around here, lots of popular support, and he's here to announce his candidacy: he's running for President, but his platform is too vague to please this blackshirt pack. Somebody plans thus an outrage. It seems to have gone wrong at one or two points, but we'll probably never find out just how and why. Suppose the notion is for Viviane Kranitz to be kidnapped, and I'm postulating at present her complicity. A fake attack by left wing extremists, menacing our Fatherland with doubtless-commie-inspired Destabilisation: a great witch-word that."

"Go on," said Richard nodding. "This last twenty-four hours the town's been plastered by Red Front anti-Vibert Slogans, incidentally."

"Bears it out – anyhow Vibert smelt rats and was prudent enough to cut loose. Joinel may be the nigger in that woodpile. Vibert looks foolish, but by being consistent avoids getting bogged down the way he was supposed to. He's not getting his arm twisted for a woman he may have decided was more of a liability than an asset.

"In short, the firework got a bit damp. No major scandal, no great press coverage. The general idea is that there was an emotional scene between them, they had a fight in the car and tipped off the road: nobody's making much of that.

"So this group – call them that – has been hesitating, not quite knowing what to do next. There were a few things planned – like bombing my house; destabilise the police, huh – but my guess is they were called off in a hurry while Mastermind decides what to do next. First squib is damp: they've got to play harder. But what . . ?"

"Castang," said Richard, "I'm not quite taking all this with as much merry laughter as it seems to merit, because the Ministry's being very guarded, but is quite undoubtedly much embarrassed. And then? Have you run out of bright ideas for Act Two?"

"I'm not quite sure – who do I run across yesterday in Paris but Mister Viviane Kranitz. Acting very innocent; I was able to twist his arm a bit by catching him wearing a gun. What does he want a gun for up there in Neuilly, haven of bourgeois respectability?

"Good, he fed me a lot of bullshit. What I didn't tell him was that in Madame Kranitz' flat – no, okay, I made Vibert gave me his key in return for a vague blanket guarantee of immunity – I picked up her phone list. One of the numbers caught my attention, Kranitz had mumbled a great deal, but one name kept cropping up."

"I'm all agog," said Richard, who was looking very much the contrary.

"You ever hear of a woman called Alberthe de Rubempré?"

"Yes; she was one of Stendhal's girlfriends."

"Can't be that one; she'd be too old."

"So it's a fake name."

"I thought it sounded a bit too good to be true. I've had the number checked. It's a house up in the hills, and what might not be altogether a coincidence it's about twenty kilometres from the Col de la Charité, which is where that nice big Peugeot car got tipped in the bushes."

"And Alberthe de Rubempré?"

"Is a real person. Owns a lot of land out there. It's a château. Oh, and there's one more thing. I was followed or might have been by something so obvious that I thought maybe I was supposed to notice – blue Alpine Renault; two Arabs in dishcloths like Mr Muttonfat. Avenue Reine Astrid, where all those consulates are – Joinel's house is round the corner. I had Orthez check them out – no such car registered. So what are we supposed to think – that those Colonels in Libya are supplying the Red Brigade with funds and weapons? – it's just that the bullshit is laid on too thick."

"Go on following it up," said Richard placidly, "and I'll find out whatever I can about this lady for you – but without telling Paris. Is it a naiad – or a dryad?"

"I'll see if she'll invite me to lunch," offered Castang.

The first thing Castang noticed, next to the fact that the police car had a sardine-can economically replacing its gearbox, was that it was a beautiful day. In the city, in the early morning of a day in late autumn, it had just been brumous: immense wreaths of watery vapours half of which was smog, with a watery sun struggling to pierce the nimbus. Once out into the forest country the sky became blue, with at the summits of the taller trees vaporous scarves of gauze, such as pictorially – see, passim, the works of French classical painters, Le Brun, Le Sueur, boring old Poussin – conceal elegantly the pubis of the Naiads and the Dryads.

But once into the hills . . . the sky, ever more open, grew steadily deeper and bluer with the luminosity of a classical Mediterranean landscape. The more beautiful since this was a temperate forest, a thick cover of beech, oak and chestnut; on the poorer soil birch and pine: a dark green and gold that flung into yet higher relief the purple and scarlet of the broad-leaf trees. Captivated by happiness, Castang stopped the car. The world had no right to be so beautiful.

It was windless, and not the remotest feather of cirrus even to hint at wind to come. For the last stage of his journey he had just branched into a narrow rural road. The main road ran on up the valley, clinging to the skirts of the hill, zigzagging upward to the col on the northern side of which Marc Vibert had had his little adventure . . . A large truck he had passed ten minutes before went thudding up this road, with a stink at its passage and a whining, complaining noise that faded into the distance, and in its wake a cloud of small golden leaves left a tree and flew soundless and exquisite across the road. Castang thought at first they were birds. The flight was like that of citified starlings rising when disturbed to settle again three trees further. Goldfinches or yellowhammers. Something Chinese. Certainly the Chinese would have great quantities of bright yellow sparrows in their landscapes. If they didn't, well, they would invent some. The Zen Master says all art is bullshit and should be thrown away, but we'll hit him over the head with a stick, the way he does his disciples. Serve him right. With this refreshing thought Castang started the car again, and the synchroniser made a horrible jarring noise. Orthez again – all those rally-drivers who can't be bothered with a clutch. Castang wished he had a faded blue overall; and a straw hat; and perhaps a pointed stick, with which to prod the donkey.

He had entered upon a feudal landscape. In the dales of the massif are villages still as they were in the thirteenth century. In winter snowbound for four months at a time. He had just passed through one; something out of Breughel: old women with faggots on their heads.

Immediately past the village was a pair of tall wrought-iron gates, modern but good work: the massive stone piers were not modern, lichened and patined by seven centuries of weather. He got out and pushed them: they opened. He drove through and got out to push them shut.

Beyond was a park. The top of the dale flattened into a rolling false level three kilometres long, watered by the rills of the mountain beyond. Large trees grew in the park: there was something about

53

these trees, at once striking and puzzling – in the end he stopped, to have a good stare and satisfy himself. Yes, not just trees – an arboretum. One had to turn around, facing the way he had come, to understand, because the perspectives opened out like the blades of a fan. He knew nothing about trees, but Vera, much under the influence of Japanese artists, had taught herself something. In the time when she had been paralysed and he had had to push her in a chair they had spent much time in the town gardens. The Jesuit Garden, laid out in the romantic style of the early eighteen hundreds, had many varieties: the Botanic Garden had more. He had learned to look. A policeman found much to learn, in trees.

The nearest were the natives, the oldest: hundreds of years, some of those. Plenty of space cleared around them: they were there to be studied, thought about for their character, majesty, port. Half a lifetime spent in weighing the decision to take out a branch: you were working for unseen, unknown great-grandchildren. Further, as far as the eye could fathom, were the foreigners, and some of these as best as he could judge had been there a hundred and fifty years, planted by a Restoration magnate, anglophile, at the time when English explorers, prowling around the confines of their marvellous new Empire, were sending stuff back to Kew so fast it would be another sixty years and the Diamond Jubilee before the eye could begin to take it all in, and the great botanical names would be muttered like incantations. Sir-Joseph-Banks, said Castang to himself (Vera had a monstrous tree book), Veitch-of-Exeter. Some need shelter, the company of their kind and others friendly towards them, and clustered in the dales. Others, precisely like human beings detesting People, went and stood by themselves in high places, wanting all the sun and space they could get, in no mood for a lot of society.

He realised he had come at exactly the right moment for the American oaks and the maples. This was what Vermont looked like in the fall, and today – even if it only lasted a day – was the Indian Summer. Epitaph for the Mohawks and the Susquehannas and all the others whose forgotten gravestones are only marked by polluted rivers and industrial slums.

And over there to the left, stretching away along a spur of rocky outcrop, the conifers culminating in that fierce stiff old boy exactly like the Duke of Wellington surveying the enemy dispositions; though presumably that wasn't why the English called it by his

54

name. Sequoiadendron, muttered Castang in another incantation, relishing it. Giganteum. It was all much too much for him, and it took him five more minutes to get back into the smelly tin auto, shaking his head and mumbling. What had he come here for? To Botanise, my boy, he told himself, intelligence coming belatedly to the rescue. To classify.

Over the last kilometre the roadway bent around to the left with the slope of the hill. Somebody very grand indeed in Renaissance times had made the final approach to the house a formal perspective with an avenue of trees down each side of a Tapis Vert. He did not see it until the minute when the roadway curved in over a cattle-grid and his tyres were crunching on gravel. When he did see the house the impression – for the second time – of a massive clonk over the nut with a large rubber hammer gave him the galloping vertigo and he sat there like a fool.

It wasn't largeness: the house wasn't large. Or well, bits of it were, but it was so well-proportioned, so harmonious in its setting that there was no feeling of size. Simply of beauty.

Orthez hadn't done his homework because there wasn't any to do that the poor boy knew of. Every imaginable kind of house and most of them perfectly hideous is in France called a Château. Some of these places have been in private occupancy for nine hundred years and aren't in any bloody Guidebook, neither.

Try to avoid guidebook lyricism and antiquarian rambling, Castang: a Plantagenet castle, circular towers of ashlar masonry. Of this nothing remained but the two massive round gate-towers – about two-thirds of their original height? – the rest had been smashed by the Black Prince or Brave Talbot. In the Renaissance Monsieur le Marquis, tacking about after King Francis the First and his extravagances along the Loire, had rushed home, got some Italian artists of his own, knocked out the old barbican (frowning portcullis etc.), put in a beautiful gateway instead, a splendid airy, lofty gallery back into the courtyard, and was doubtless planning a magnificent pile when most opportunely he ran out of money. What was accomplished had been so superb that no succeeding generations, however bad their taste, had ever been able to spoil it. An enlightened modern age had indeed peeled away the accumulation of hideous excrescences added at times of bourgeois ostentation (Louis-Philippe certainly, the Third Republic probably) and over the last few years had finally cleared up all the rubbish, landscaped it and made it into a water-garden at the back.

He got out of the car: a Great Dane came and looked at him. He did not feel happy about this: wolves he would have known better how to deal with. Cautious approaches and polite remarks were made. He was permitted to examine the architecture, observe heraldic devices, and get to a bellpull: a bell tolled in a quiet grave dignity. No Childe Roland at any Dark Tower. The stone, of all colours between beige and ochre, was soaked in a light luminous sunshine like the palest, driest sherry.

A very old man opened the door: dry; head on one side. Looking and behaving much like Mr Flintwinch, dressed as a French countrified version, dating from around then too.

"Good morning," said Castang. "I should like it, if Madame de Rubempre would receive me." The old man studied him, taking his time, quite dispassionate, perfectly polite.

"To whom does Madame la Comtesse owe the honour?" This marvellous antique formula just about finished Castang off. He mumbled a bit, and found a card – not even engraved! He might just as well have sold vacuum cleaners and be done with it. but was treated with a courtesy as old-fashioned as the phrasing.

"I shall go and enquire of Madame la Comtesse." Nor was he 'stood'. He was shown into one of the ground floor rooms of the round towers. Library: very good library.

Here he was left for a longish time. Time to overcome the rubber-hammer effect, time to get-a-good-grip-on-himself, for all this to ebb away again. Time to observe dispiritedly a lot of art, like it all and never mind about understanding any of it. Time to feel again an utter fool. Saved by Mr Flintwinch coming in and saying drily, "Madame la Comtesse will be with you within a little time," and going out again: replunged into gloom by this woman taking her time, damn it – theatrical effects? – resaved by Flintwinch with a silver tray, a decanter, a glass, sherry made of the sunshine outside. Sun was not allowed in here: might spoil the fine bindings. The window embrasures in the old masonry were anyhow two metres deep.

Well! He'd have another glass of sherry! And the hell with Mr Flintwinch . . . and stuff his countess while at it: he'd been heel-cooling here for exactly twenty-five minutes. He was pouring it, nervous of spilling any, when a voice said behind him, "I am confused, Mr Castang." He couldn't even turn quickly because of the glass in his hand.

56

He put the glass and the decanter down with care. There are people with a talent for making one feel an oafish slob. One gets out of it as best one can. He smiled at her and said, "Rather full."

A stupid woman would have said 'I startled you' with a malicious amusement. Instead she said, "But you are absolutely right. It is disgusting to have kept you waiting, but I had some serious work and I could not send you away. Now I shall feel better. Do give me some too."

He looked for a second glass.

"Ring a bell," she suggested. Wasn't he supposed to be a detective? Act like one, then.

She was tall, taller than him and built like a deer. Her hands and feet were large and well-shaped. Her face was an undistorted oval, the features remarkably classical. She wore a grey dress matching her eyes and her fair hair. Too well-bred to wear jewellery at home in the daytime.

Never would he forget that first moment: never had he had such an instant impression of quality, which seemed to lend him a rare lucidity.

"Remarkable," said Castang.

"Unusual," corrected Richard, perhaps thinking his subordinate had had too much sherry.

"The unusual is remarkable." Perhaps he had.

"She doesn't if I understand admit it openly?"

"Maybe she would, for two pins. She certainly doesn't trouble to deny it. Everything in fact but spell it out. I don't know what to call it."

"Call it vanity," said Richard. "Because that's what they all of them have in common. Think of her as a perfectly normal commonplace crook, and that, you'll find, will cut her down to size. She's thrown you. I don't blame you. I've been thrown myself, more than once. Lunch . . . Your main trouble," said Richard getting up like a man with a good appetite, "is an empty stomach." It was experience talking. "Start thinking of her as though she were Madame Laure Dissard."

"You know Laure Dissard?" asked Castang amused. The lady was a classic in the annals of the Police Judiciaire. Now well into her seventies and still going strong, like Johnnie Walker, she was a confidence-trick artist of legendary impudence, and undaunted by

57

little official discouragements like prison where she had spent some twenty years: no sooner out than installed in a suite at the Ritz, more fetching than ever and no time lost in finding a Dutch businessman ready to buy the Eiffel Tower for scrap.

"I arrested her once," said Richard with reminiscent affection, "but she threw me first. Heavily."

Vera had imposed her style upon the new flat. Castang was in general an obsessive-meticulous type, forever polishing things and rearranging them into the right positions, and Vera said he ought to have been a barman: all those lovely clean glasses. She lived in a happy encrustation of innumerable jamjars full of pencils, paintbrushes and noxious liquids, but this was incidental to her Attic simplicity. A wooden board scrubbed to show the grain: a cup and saucer whose one ornament was its shape. In form, line or person – purity. There had been something in Alberthe de Rubempré – a directness, a singlemindedness of vision. Perfectionism?

She'd thrown him all right! Richard's experience; a scepticism, to those who knew him at all, by no means all sterile; surprisingly far from the gross cynicism of most senior police officials, had seen that accurately. Vanity? – right there too; the common denominator of all criminal behaviour and impulse. Pride. And upper-class arrogance carried to the extreme of an indifference that the shrink would call psychopathic to all but her own interests, the fulfilment of her desire.

Vera, who hobnobbed in byways of romantic literature, read English, and in secondhand bookshops hunted out all Tauchnitz editions, threaded a needle (his strenuous existence was hard upon buttons), sniggered, and said, " 'She-who-must-be-obeyed.' " Having had this explained he said primly that romantic stereotypes were misleading.

"Made a conquest of you by the sound of it."

All right, he'd shut up and say no more. It was partly jealousy. He would have had to admit that Madame la Comtesse was sexually very attractive and highly desirable: he wouldn't agree that she was cheap. There hadn't been a breath of come-hither.

'You interest me' she had said. An entrapment for his own vanity, to be sure. There were very few people around whom he could be said to interest . . . But what she meant was that he was an adversary, and even a petty one will repay study. And entrapped or not he was

58

there to study her. What were the little shabbinesses, the slight shoddiness that would show if one looked hard, and with a Vera-trained eye as well as a cop eye?

'You have a remarkable house' he had said. 'I've never seen anything like that outside the Very Rich Hours of the duke of whoever it was,' and he'd found himself telling her about the golden Chinese sparrows, which struck her.

'Did you ever want to be a painter, Monsieur Castang?'

'As a boy, yes – I was brought up by an auntie, who dealt in art materials.'

'And don't you regret it? – one must always pursue the best, the noblest. There is so little of it.'

'My wife is a painter,' he had said simply. He wasn't going to discuss Vera! She'd known, of course. There wasn't much about him she did not know, and she let him see it in a negligent, throwaway fashion.

'You had the removers in as I hear.'

'You hear right,' he'd said, smiling.

'However skilled, or well-meaning they may be it is intensely painful. They lay hands upon one's privacy, and it is as though they tore one's clothes off.' He'd kept silent. She couldn't surely have known how Vera had snapped at poor Liliane – it must be a spontaneous remark, and the more interesting.

'You are vulnerable, you see.'

'It was designed to make me feel so, yes.' She left that alone, but pursued her own thought.

'I would not wish to discourage you from your career. The police are necessary, and it is necessary to have good ones. But aren't you tempted to resign, from the pettiness and vulgarity of this existence?'

'I have been, very often. There's a lot of humbug about state service. Then I decided not to.'

'You have your reasons, no doubt. Now that you're a family man, and find yourself – at your age – in temporary lodgings, doesn't it strike you that you're worth something better?'

'Most people think that.'

'I could arrange it,' she said simply. 'I can do most things, if I set my mind to it. It would not be difficult to find you a house, and work both valuable and interesting. And leisure to paint.'

'But there's always an employer,' said Castang 'and one has to please that employer.'

'True,' she nodded. 'Think about it.'

'Where?'

'Wherever you please. I have interests all over France. And also elsewhere.'

'You are very rich.'

'I am wealthy naturally, since one can do nothing without wealth. That gives it a certain importance. And wealth brings responsibilities; a truism which nonetheless has also its importance. So that one needs auxiliaries, and these must be of high calibre. Now I notice – is it another truism? – you might give me some more sherry if you would – it's to your liking? – good – that most persons of any calibre are not employed anywhere near the limit of their abilities. We hear a great deal about waste, and this is one of the most pernicious kinds.'

'You're making me an offer – this is flattering.'

'You are thinking basely, and you shouldn't: it is a vile habit of mind. Flattery is base. You will know me better.'

'The state isn't that bad an employer. We know where we stand. The means are devious, and mostly detestable. But the end is public service.'

'The service of the people,' she said pensively, too clever to let contempt creep into her voice. 'Well, we shall see. Recall that I have made you the offer, and shall not hesitate now that I have met you to repeat it.'

'I don't want to lose sight of my immediate aim, which is to find out what has happened to Madame Viviane Kranitz.'

'I can give you good advice. I know her well. She's a hard-headed and determined woman of much force of character, sometimes degenerating into obstinacy. If she makes a mistake she's slow to admit it. I think it likely that when she has come to terms with the consequences of a mistake – I think it must be undeniable that she made one – she will reappear among her friends. I think that if I were you I'd leave it at that. There's no law against a person dropping out of sight to do a little thinking or just have a holiday from busybodies. By which I don't mean you – you are simply doing your job. But politicians – would you give me one of those cigarettes? – try one, they're Cuban – are wearisome. As you will have noticed their occupational disease is that they cannot stop themselves talking. Viviane is also a great talker. Silence in her is unexpected, I agree, but I can't help thinking will do her good.'

'As long as her dropping out of sight is voluntary.'

'It isn't?' enquired Madame with polite surprise.

'The circumstances were a bit obscure.'

'Yes. I understand your curiosity. For my part I am rarely curious. I find in a general manner of speaking that usually I know enough. If I don't then it's probably a matter that doesn't merit curiosity. Leave them alone and they'll come home. Wagging their behind them. Like Marc Vibert.'

She'd had a parting shot.

'My regards to Commissaire Richard. An able man – perhaps a little old.'

Vera who had been busy with her own thoughts – much of the meal had been eaten in silence – said suddenly, "What colouring does she have?"

"Pale," answered Castang. "I've never seen anyone with that sort of pallor. Not bleached or washed out. Pale like marble. The pallor is healthy and powerful." He thought for a moment. "Like light was behind it. Lit from inside – from within." Vera looked at him queerly, but said nothing.

Richard was sitting where Castang had left him: had he even been out to lunch? Quite often he used the interval for a quiet think, and his secretary, Fausta, made him a 'frugal meal', the crumbs from which got tidied carefully into the wastepaperbasket. He lost no time.

'Paris now takes the view, Castang, that no criminal action was intended: even if there were, there is no evidence to support it."

"Meaning you release me from further interest in Mrs Kranitz. I'm glad to hear it."

"I'm not altogether sure that I can conquer my dislike for having people on my brigade shot at. Incidentally, I've been having a nice time looking up your great new friend Madame de Rubempré. Counts and countesses are five a penny, mm? They have however a tendency to alliances. The interminable ramifications of their own cousins and those of their marriages – this one has more relations than anyone since Robert de Montesquiou.

"We all know about the bourgeois clans, don't we? Polytechnique, and Ena: once you're in you're set for life or so they say, because the old-boy network will see to it that you never lack a good job and a candle to light you round the passages in the basement, hey?

61

"This crowd didn't seem to matter, did it, in the technocratic world? Not part of the mandarinate; nomenklatura as it's now fashionable to call it. We think of them as hunting the fox or the slipper over their still surprisingly extensive estates, and too bone-headed for anything else.

"Mistake, as I somewhat belatedly discover. They're in director-ships in everything from nuclear power stations to banking. And they're especially thick with the Elysee.

"They're adept at playing the sedulous village mayor, walking around the cornfield in leather gaiters chatting about partridges and making play with their roots – and I don't mean sugarbeet – until you discover that what gets them really excited is off-shore oil in Sarawak and a nuclear power station to add to the tourist attractions in Peru."

"I've got the message," said Castang resignedly, who had been puzzling over this lengthy exposition. "Rubempre means really one of the Establishment and a big shot in chemical engineering. So totally protected; inviolate to the likes of us."

"Maybe you can guess too that I don't much like it. I daresay she's right. Too old," said Richard. "Hanging on for his pension."

"She offered me a job," said Castang.

"Did she really?" amused.

"Wasted in the PJ. I have enough aesthetic sense to mow her lawn until she sees what I could be entrusted with."

"I'd encourage you to take it," said Richard seriously, "if it weren't that I'd find you troublesome to replace. I'm old, and I've got selfish. You're an awkward object, and frequently an embarrass-ment, but I've got accustomed to you I suppose. Rather like a zoo-keeper with a particularly tedious camel."

"Suppose we did it the other way round," said Castang. "I stay where I am. Might she rather like having me in her pocket? In all humility, I'm nothing much, but a PJ commissaire, it's a catch. She wouldn't have insulted you unless she felt you a thorn in her flesh. If she had a highly-placed spy hereabouts . . ."

Richard lit a cigar, smiling a little sadly.

"Has merit, my boy, but you exaggerate, I fear, my importance. As I have come to realise over lunch – the Minister is satisfied that a regional service of the PJ dances to his tune. You don't have to be in her pocket, and neither do I. You see, the Minister is, already."

"What can we do?"

62

"I've been wondering," said Richard knocking the ash off carefully, "whether Vera wouldn't fit the bill."

This was a surprise. Richard hardly knew Vera, had hardly laid eyes on her. Didn't let 'personal relationships' get in the way of professional duties; when Vera after much labour, and pardon the pun, had produced a baby, Richard to everyone's surprise had come floating in with flowers, and chockies, and encouragement. The PJ's private grapevine (centring around Fausta) agreed that this was largely the doing of Richard's mysterious (seldom seen, never heard) Spanish wife Judith. Judith was the greatest enigma around: the most obscure economic fraud was as crystal in comparison. Was she a Jewess? (all intelligent Spaniards have Jewish blood, through Moors . . .) Judith never uttered: was popularly supposed to speak no French.

Vera was obscurely, secretively thick pals with Judith: had made a drawing of her. Commissaire Richard, to whom Judith was a professional embarrassment, had never said that he liked this drawing very much.

Fausta (as was well known the real power behind the entire SRPJ) said that Commissaire Richard, officially ashamed of a wife who had spent childhood years in Spanish-Republican concentration camps at Perpignan (secretly not at all ashamed), had a soft spot for Vera.

Vera you see is a blot, thick and dark, upon Castang's record. It is Not-Done to have a wife who is a Transfuge from the East. Vera, a Czechoslovak girl who happened to be a substitute on the Czech gymnastic team, had Chosen Freedom in fashion embarrassing to the queasy-stomached French government. Castang had bull-headedly gone and married her, doing himself and his career no good at all.

Nonetheless Castang's career hasn't gone too badly. Protected by Richard. Why? Well – so argued Fausta and her females (both Richard and Castang showed a peculiar liking for females and the Ministry would be rather disturbed by this) – there isn't any difference really. Judith crossed the curtain (going north) from a fascist dictatorship. Vera crossed the curtain going south, from a Stalinist dictatorship. Now, said Fausta triumphantly, you find me one single difference between the fascists and the communists.

There isn't any?

Right!

Castang's quite fairly bright, and although this is a handicap quite a fair PJ officer. But you don't imagine he'd ever have got anywhere if it wasn't for the protection of the Commissaire Divisionnaire – do you?

In this silence made up of 'THINKS' with a balloon around it the telephone rang; a discreet purr sounding like a pneumatic road-drill. Richard made a long arm, fairly languidly.

"Yes? . . . Put him on . . . Richard here . . . Ah . . . Very well. Thank you." He put the phone down expressionlessly. "All these . . . speculations. Day-to-day sordid business, I fear. Oh well, makes a change. With a corpse at least one knows where one stands. The Proc has been notified, Castang," reaching for the internal telephone.

"Don't tell me we've got a homicide."

"Get yourself over as quick as may be to the underground parking beneath the Place d'Armes," said Richard syllable by syllable. "There's a dead woman there in a parked car. I'll have the medicine-man and the IJ there within five minutes and I want you there before them." Castang was already in the passage bawling, "Orthez!" The way we're fixed at present, thought Richard, the boy will welcome a homicide with open arms, even his own.

The Law: in case of an unexplained death the Procureur de la Republique shall be called. That's a very important legal dignitary and it takes more than a mere homicide to get him out of bed. But he has active young assistants, known as the substitutes. If the conclusions tend toward the existence of a crime the affair is confided to a judge of instruction, and under the authority of this gentleman – or, frequently, lady – the police enquiry will be placed. Some homicides – most, mercifully – are sad and squalid domestic disputes and the criminal, generally, is alcohol. These will go to the Criminal Brigade of the Sûreté Urbaine, inside a city's limits. The odd one, smelling of entanglements, goes to the PJ: they are more Sophisticated.

The Place d'Armes, a large and draughty formal square, is more or less the centre of the city. The parking lot beneath it is very large, excessively ill-lit, and the air-conditioning is not strong enough to extract exhaust fumes at all speedily. They say you won't die of carbon-monoxide poisoning, but one is by no means convinced of this.

Nobody is thus much surprised at finding a dead woman down there. The only thing is, this one had been shot.

"Stand back," said Castang.

"Allez," said cops, "circulez." Like the cars, like the air: go on, circulate, and get a move on.

Once the eyes are accustomed to the dimness one does a little better. The woman was slumped down in the passenger seat, and had not been noticed for some time. When noticed, thought asleep. Peculiar place to sleep, but it happens: not just drunks, either. It had taken a real Hawkeye to notice she was dead: the head had fallen forward. Hawkeye was telling his story with relish to everyone: Orthez went and shut him up. In these warm conditions rigor would be slow setting in: Castang pushed tentatively: the head came up. The Identité Judiciaire photographer would be here any minute, but . . .

A head wound, even in the back of the head, even with a small-calibre bullet, will render the face unrecognisable: the very facial bones . . . but this was not strictly a head wound. The nape of the neck is a very vulnerable target.

The police medicine-man had arrived. Castang had been looking for the gun, knowing he would not find it. People shoot themselves in the eye, the ear, the mouth, or the big toe, but not the neck.

"Not a suicide," said the doctor unnecessarily. "Small calibre: still there – here."

"No gun?" asked the Substitute.

"No." Castang, no gun.

"Very well then. Monsieur le Commissaire – Monsieur le Juge – all yours."

"Let me hear these witnesses," said the judge. "Monsieur l'Inspecteur," collaring Orthez.

A horrible feeling had been gathering at the place there at the top of Castang's stomach. Solar plexus, yes. He took another, longer look at the woman's face: it wasn't that much distorted. Draggingly he sought in his pocket, fumbling amid a lot of rubbish. No, it had been a big photo and he'd left it on his desk. So he wasn't sure. Not quite sure anyhow. And anyhow this wasn't the time or the place for that sort of announcement.

"I'll be in my office, Castang, up to six anyhow, so let me have the basic by then." Yes Monsieur le Juge.

Pretty well certain. In any case the lab expert from IJ, the moment he had these photos – and that other – in his hand for comparison . . . a quarter of an hour from now.

No mistake. Viviane.

Madame Kranitz, missing a couple of days now, had reappeared. In a not very favourable light, but was that her fault? Not, in any case, her idea.

"I'd like your preliminary conclusions as soon as may be," said Castang to the doctor "– this evening?"

He shrugged: cops – always in a hurry.

"The outside – not the inside."

"Any signs of physical maltreatment – or restraint."

"She didn't put up a struggle, you know."

"I'm talking about had she been tied up?"

Some divisional commissaires, like the directors of some schools, think that being distant and inaccessible lends weight to their authority. Richard practised neither the freezing manner nor the little frown, and Fausta provided barrier enough. She only said "What, again?" when Castang appeared both war-worn and travel-stained.

"He wants it verbal, and he'll want it fast," and she put on her face of 'Rely upon my discretion'.

Monsieur Richard was seeking intellectual refreshment in the pages of *Le Journal*, that remarkable newspaper into which one can sink, and vanish without trace; which actually believes in conveying information: causing thereby much ill-feeling in the ranks of the French government. It is however of manageable format; quite easily folded, quite easily put down; and Richard did.

"Madame Viviane Kranitz has been assassinated. Pistol, small, in the cervical vertebrae: no fuss, no noise. Car almost certainly stolen; Orthez is looking into it."

Richard simply said, "I see. Is that all?"

"Superficial medical this evening: for anything better we'll have to wait for Deutz. Light was foul, but as far as I could see not tied, gagged or blindfolded."

"Who's the judge?"

"Rombout."

"We'll go and see him. You, and I. As of now, Castang, you have a rogatory commission."

"True. Now at last we've some legal footing."

66

"Now what about your friend the Baroness? This being a little too much coincidence, or isn't it?"

"Use your phone?" hunting for his little notebook. Dialling. "Commissaire Castang, and I'd like to speak with Madame." Richard was listening to the extension earphone. The rusty file voice of Flintwinch.

"I much regret, Monsieur. Madame la Comtesse left this afternoon."

"I see," said Castang, hastily buttering some dry bread, "and when was that?"

"Immediately after lunch, M'sieur."

"And when will she be back?"

"I fear that I have no information about that."

"What a pity; I was hoping to catch her – you've no idea where she went?"

"I am uninformed, Monsieur. The instruction I was given for the driver was the airport."

"Oh. He might know her destination?" But Flintwinch decided he was being pumped.

"I regret that Monsieur should have been troubled."

"Get the airport," said Richard, turning it around and doing it himself. "A passenger that conspicuous . . ." Provincial airports in France do a roaring trade with Paris, but being in general monopolies of Air Inter, with nowhere else much. For international destinations there are no more than half a dozen flights a day. Freddie Laker hasn't quite caught up yet: on that day Air France will be pulling long faces.

"Police post, please. Richard here, PJ. I'm interested in the movement of a lady named Rubempré: you'll look up if need be the passenger lists." Castang's turn to listen.

"No need for that, Monsieur le Divisionnaire," obsequious, not to say soapy. "We know the lady well: she often flies."

"I'm only interested in where to," unimpressed by this dog's range of acquaintance.

"That I couldn't say – she has this private jet, little Dassault job you see Mo –"

"Then ring the tower; they'll have given her a flight plan, and get a move on, mate." Richard never bellowed at underlings but they generally managed to get the drift.

"Tower says cleared for Düsseldorf."

"What time was that?"

"Let's see, three-oh-four was just in: fourteen hundred give or take."

"Accompanied?"

"Well the passports to tell the truth Mo –"

"You hardly gave them a glance. I'm aware. Just that whatever you say, make sure you get that much right. If you don't know, say so."

"Two were French. One German, one American. One sec., that would be Madame, her secretary – the other two, the two foreigners, were men."

"What name the American man? Wouldn't perchance be Kranitz?" Castang reached for the telephone.

"Tall, heavy-built, something of a belly. If no hat then hair fair, pale, going silver, slicked to one side."

"Had hat," apologetically, "but the rest matches. I think the name maybe did begin with a K."

"And the German?"

"Big and dark but names – sorry."

"All right," said Richard.

"Long gone anyhow. Düsseldorf – is that Köln, or separate?"

"Köln is Bonn: the other's separate. The cops there will be rather less sleepy, but we've no possible grip, on what we have. Unless the bullet when we get it turns out to be a seven-sixty-five fired from a Walther, but Kranitz couldn't be that much of a fool: I saw his gun and handled it."

"He'll have ditched that," Richard pointed out. "However sleepy the cop was here they'll have gone through the detector, even on a non-commercial flight. Even only to Germany."

"Ring that clown again, to check?"

"No. On the one hand, if your woman was nixed in the parking lot it's a clear alibi. On the other it's an insolent message. See what I can do, she says to you, and how nicely I can time it. Whoever she'd employ, for a job like that, would be a good class pro. From your account it *was* a good class pro."

"Catching whom," said Castang glumly, "our chances are roughly those of catching Martin Bormann."

"Now there you make me think," said Richard. "But I'll have plenty of time to think by the look of it. Let's go see your judge. Fausta!"

Since every affair definable in the Penal Code as a crime is studied by a judge of instruction there are a good few of them. In Paris there are eighty-six, or should be. In Castang's city there are eight, where there should be a dozen: they are very overworked. The government dislikes judges of instruction. They have too much power, and show too much independence. Why, they have even been known to inculpate important capitalists, for trivial matters like the death of workers after the security regulations were found to be costing too much.

The judge Rombout was a decent man. He worked hard at his profession, was good at it, rose in it. His dossiers were models of conscientious, neatly-finished exactitude. He would sit at them through many hours of overtime, but never too long, for he believed in spending time with his family. He was ambitious, for he had three daughters with the Ursuline nuns and a son with the Jesuits: they cost a great deal of money. A strongly militant Catholic, he wouldn't have any nonsense about right and wrong, but his justice was tempered with a great deal of mercy. He liked being a judge of instruction. You didn't have to send people to prison: it is a deplorable thing, sending people to prison. If people were better parents, one wouldn't have to send their children to prison. He gave his children's Latin the same care as his own homework, and worried about being dense at maths.

He knew Castang well. It wasn't enough, to send in these damned written reports and verbal-process transcripts, and then a formal cut-and-dried ten minutes in the Assize Court as witness. A Serious-Crime commissaire should take his crimes seriously: Mr Rombout liked him to come in and have a chat about human aspects. Castang was a decent man. So was Mr Richard a decent man (a little over-sophisticated). We are all decent men, insofar as our jobs and our lives allow of it. It is an extremely difficult business, being a man.

"Well, Castang. Monsieur le Divisionnaire, this is a pleasure," standing up. "Please; please," pointing at chairs. The same politeness to a prostitute as to the Advocate-General.

However much tact, or 'sophistication' Richard (Castang kept his mouth shut) could bring to the matter in hand, consternation was writ large in the pen, the spectacles, all the things a judge has on his desk and fiddles with when disquieted.

"Oh dear," he kept saying. Politics.

69

There are only two ways of coping with politics: to worry about them or not. Worrying about them – thought Mr Rombout – is fatal. That way leads the Independent Syndicate of Magistrates, being Left Wing; fierce clashes with the prosecutor, the Chamber of Accusation, the Appeal Court: worse, with the chancellery at Paris, upon whose good opinion depends the career, the children's education, one mustn't handicap their future, the mortgage – everything, in short. We can deplore the vanity and the greed, and the corruption too alas, of politicians, but when they are placed in Authority over us, the gospel recommends humility. And charity. The Minister of Justice is at heart a decent man. He must be held to be acting according to his lights. No one more than Mr Rombout could deplore, and more vivaciously – there should be no place for virulence – this lamentable new law of the Minister's, so maladroitly, he must not say cynically, entitled Security and Liberty, which so notably diminishes liberties while increasing insecurity. But himself could hardly be thought an unprejudiced judge in the matter. Did not the project seek notoriously to diminish the functions and authorities of the instructing magistrate – to wit himself? And is it not the foremost principle of this judge that he should instruct *à charge et à décharge*, seeking neither to disculpate nor to incriminate? Let the judge who has never, no never, allowed his emotions to get the better of him cast the first stone.

Monsieur Richard, in brief, made little headway. Left wing, right wing . . .

"My dear Commissaire . . ." Fictitious attempts to discredit rival politicians seeking electoral office . . . A government lending comfort (albeit tacit) to such manoeuvres . . . No, no. Meddle with pitch . . .

"My dear Castang. Here is the rogatory commission of which you stand in need in order to elucidate a crime: crime there undoubtedly is. In that pursuit you have my support. I do not insult you by urging diligence upon you: I will not dangle clichés about fear or favour: both alas are widespread in this unhappy world. Bring me a suspect; it is my rôle to establish responsibilities. But do not, I beg of you, bring me persons of straw as a sop to public opinion, while telling me that the real authors enjoy immunity. That will only cast discredit upon us both."

Time to go: the judge's secretary had come pottering in and out upon phony errands, to shift them all.

70

"And no press conferences." Not shouting; he never shouted. "I won't have the instruction vitiated by any of these accidental-done-on-purpose press leaks."

Along the corridor of the instructing judges at least one was working late: a sad fellow in handcuffs polished the bench between two yawning uniformed cops, being talked-to by his lawyer. A very pretty young girl, but Justice stands with a foot upon the tortoise, and will she still be young and pretty when you get to court? The serenity of the magistrate is a time-consuming business. Ah, if by punishing the wicked one could protect the children of the poor . . .

"Well," said Richard, "it was a foregone conclusion but it had to be tried. All that prudery is his way of saying he's not going to be left naked in the cold wind. Too many judges of instruction flagrantly insulted in public by every notorious crook sitting in Majorca, laughing; and what is the Keeper of the Seals doing about that?"

"All right; what are we going to do?"

"I don't know about you," said Richard, "I'm going to do a whole lot of the things he keeps telling me not to. Go home, Castang, and see me tomorrow morning."

Castang didn't go home. He went to see one of his indicators.

A tricky business, this of the indicators, the Fingers. The word is pejorative: no cop wants to use it, nor to talk about them. It doesn't consist of handing out bottles of methylated spirit to clochards, nor protection of the weaselling bartender. Nor does the famous secret fund for bribes amount to much: police forces are administered with parsimony. You can of course take bribes, and pay them back where they will do most good. Since cops have little to do with justice, it is the fear and the favour which come mostly into play. Mostly the latter, since people in general are on the make, that's how you wangle them. Make a dollar for me, I'll make one for you.

Maximilienne Charlotte, an improbable name, and always known as Maxie, was a whore. They are all indicators in a small way: it is natural; in return for not being pestered. The police – it is a cliche – could not survive without whores. Maxie was quite good at both her professions.

She succeeded by having energy, enterprise, originality; in this as in any other business. She had some humour, rare in any profession.

In short she was a sound businesswoman: Castang was an investment, and she protected it. On his side, it was much the same. Thus, they got on together.

71

Too, they found each other good company. Enjoyed one another. Had fun together. Neither cops nor whores get much fun, nor much company they enjoy. Maxie might not have many brains, but she had lots of sense. Even, it could be said, they respected one another.

There was a time when they went to bed together: not since he had married. Maxie understood this; it increased her confidence. She might get cross, and show him her behind a bit, to tease him: it did not diminish their respect. Since there was nothing either to hide nor to confess, he did not mention her to Vera.

She made plenty of money; lived in an expensive block, spent freely. Went to doctors a lot, and laboratories, and spa towns for the water cure, to which she was addicted. She liked clothes, and her creature comforts. She was also a careful saver, investing cautiously, Frenchly, in real estate. This combination of frugality and generosity was attractive: to the poor she gave without strings.

She was lion-coloured, and had a loose lionlike stroll. If her bones had been less heavy she would have made a good dancer: if her features had been lighter she would rank as a good-looking woman. As things were she looked striking, filled the eye nicely, and did comfortably, thanks. She had avoided undesirable protectors: anyone who tried found himself in an unpleasant glare of publicity over his income tax returns. On her side – she was such a sympathetic listener – her knowledge of affairs was wide. In the expense account world there was remarkably little discussed or planned that she could not fit together. If the deal was made she knew how; if it fell through she knew why. It's a smallish world after all; a ghetto: in all but the very biggest cities no more than three hotels, six or seven restaurants, golf club, tennis club. They dislike the company of other than their own kind. And of course, they're all prostitutes together.

There was rarely much in this world to interest Castang directly . . . most was passed on to Massip, the chief inspector of the PJ whose speciality is Economic Crime; a type of cop nobody writes stories about. But one of the characteristics of this ghetto is that they all wear a Star of Nixon: in polite terms it's a right wing milieu.

"Hallo Henri."

"Hallo Copperbottom," as it swayed away in front of him out of professional habit, in search of a good cigar: this was also one address where he got Glenthingummy whisky, which he much liked. Wasted on all those frightful little bankers, but a good truth drug.

72

"Ever hear of a woman called Alberthe de Rubempré?"

"Heard of, yes. Never laid eyes upon – she's very rarefied. If mentioned, talked about with bated breath."

"What context?"

"Big shareholder in the pharmaceutics place. French thing but subsidiary – American owned. Said to have a controlling interest in Jeangeorges."

"That's the electronic thing?"

"That's right, very speedy. Government defence contracts, awfully pally with Arabs. Talking of Arabs what's this stuff about you being shot up – you do something to vex Colonel Qaddafi?"

"They weren't Arabs, or if they were I'd be very much surprised – so she's multinational?"

"Very much so. Said to be madly rich. Said to be les, which means nothing save that nobody ever heard of anyone getting any. Got a fairytale place out in the hills where nobody's ever been."

"I have," succumbing slightly to the truth drug.

"Really? – tell."

"No, you tell."

"Don't know any more. One of those computerised robots from Holland, takes a lot to impress them – they have practically ambassadorial status. You know, too stiff to go to bed: want to sit enthroned and have it brought to them with decorations round the dish. Type that takes its trousers off and looks first for a hanger so's they won't get creased. Fascinated with anything les – it's to cover their own impotence. There's a terribly sweet young girl downstairs whom I phone up – Indochinese so the colour contrast goes like a bomb." Castang would normally have been laughing at these professional insights but was bored today.

"This mean anything to you? Name of Kranitz, known as Stan. Polish American."

"Lousy picture."

"Yes, it's a photokit mockup; I haven't got a real one."

"It does and it doesn't, which might not mean anything. Can I keep it a bit? Light might dawn and I could ring you: I'll try it on Alissa, that's the Vietnamese gorgeous. Japanese you see are magnetised here like iron filings and stand bowing and hissing for hours on end, while Poles are like Germans, want couscous with lots of harissa."

"Hence the name?"

"That's right – vague connotations of hot chili pepper."

"What are they saying about Marc Vibert?"

"You mean about his mistress disappearing? He's their great hero and the general consensus is that it hasn't done him any harm. Two schools of thought; that he did it on purpose because she was an embarrassment, a bit too outspoken and extreme: alternatively that he was pushed into it by his wife who hated her guts and has been raising hell. A put-up job either way but fairly adroit: said to have been stage-managed by a cunning old fascist schnok name of Joinel."

"Where d'you hear that?"

"A gang of merchant bankers actually. I could have told them, but forebore, that Doctor Joinel is an occasional but valuable regular . . . no no, far too smart to have his brains picked: when he's here talks of nothing but symphonic music which is his real passion."

"We found Madame Kranitz today. Dead. In an underground parking. Shot in the back of the neck."

"Wow. I haven't had the television on – I don't like it at breakfast. Bouh . . . well, I am damned careful whom I accompany anywhere and especially I might say in underground parkings. Ah – that of course is where I heard of your Polish pal – that must be the husband."

"Right, and still no light?"

"No, it was something oblique – but now this . . ."

"Yes, it'll be the number one subject tonight and tomorrow. That's why I came: I want you to be extremely alert."

"But who did it? – I mean was it Colonel Qaddafi?"

"Whenever there's anything extreme, like a political assassination, the Colonel will always be a handy whipping-boy, with nods and winks from the wiseacres? It's like harissa, makes the rice taste more exciting. I've no doubt but that the bar of the Hotel Metropole will be buzzing with tales about Arabs. If not Corsicans. An attack, you see, upon Monsieur Vibert."

"You mean you want me to get my ass over to the Hotel Metropole. Mother," making faces at her watch, "this is the crack of dawn."

"All in a good cause," said Castang.

Vera greatly disliked television sets but put up with having the thing in the kitchen, like a tin-opener. It was an objectionable but sometimes indispensable tool, and all one asked was that it should function properly. Rarely now did she get into real rages with it. Even the sicking noises with which she greeted announcer-girls (whose whory clothes and ways make Maxie look like Mother Superior) had become largely mechanical. They ate supper together in silence, looking at the eight o'clock news. Monsieur Marc Vibert was greatly in evidence, very greatly shocked and pained. A spokesman from the Ministry with the face they put on for Pilgrimages to the Graveside promised that no stone would be left unturned. I most solemnly Pledge; meaning I'll answer no further questions.

"Poor you," said Vera.

"Yes . . . mostly poor Richard, but poor me too, by definition. The Controller on our necks; Ottavioli and the whole band."

"It's bad."

"And looks even worse. We couldn't find her, and now we couldn't stop her getting chopped. Deport everyone unable to show sixteen quarterings of pure French ancestry. Starting with you, and leaving the President in his underground atomic shelter, maybe a few admirals, and Alberthe de Rubempré."

"Why is she important?"

"It's what we'd like to find out."

The black eye . . . but there had been so terribly many lately. Beating up harmless bystanders (shooting a couple 'pour encourager les autres') seemed always to have been endemic, but of late the venality, brutality and homicidal imbecility of the Guardians of the Peace had been setting new records. The consolations, of being told what went on in Moscow, Dallas, or Rio de Janeiro, were meagre; not to say inadequate. We keep telling everyone how Civilised we are . . . one has to keep looking around, and telling oneself that this is not after all Paraguay. Who are we telling?

How limitless are our capacities for self-congratulation?

Not so very long ago the most famous newspaper in France told us to be ashamed of ourselves, finding it necessary to use some tart phrasing. The Minister of Justice found this wound to his vanity so unbearable that he attempted to take legal action – for defamation so please you – without even noticing the pitiful figure he cut in the eyes of the entire world. He did not even have the excuse of being stupid.

Castang sat slumped in his kitchen chair in front of the television screen, covered in black shame. He was too young, by a few years, to remember the time forty years before, when the majority of the people had welcomed a fascist take-over; even one conducted with force of arms by a foreign country. A shame that has not yet been wiped away.

Commissaire Richard, however, was not too young.

Richard was where you would expect to find him in the early morning; sitting at his desk, conducting the day-to-day affairs of a regional service of the Police Judiciaire, one of the half-dozen largest, and weightiest, in the country. Except that he appeared to give the day-to-day affairs small consideration, for his desk was empty save for his glasses.

Fausta had looked up when Castang came in.

"The instruction is to let you in, and no one else." A highly unusual instruction, to say the least. "I don't know," she said drily, "and I'd rather not guess." She went back to her typewriter. It was to be concluded that Fausta was running the day-to-day affairs: of course some people said that she always did.

Castang stopped, to see if he had any cigarettes. It didn't do to smoke Richard's cigars. Yesterday the Judge of Instruction had fallen into the trap of accepting one. He'd been too polite to say anything, but kept taking it out of his mouth and looking at it, with a face in which incredulity and nausea were nicely balanced.

"He's in a very bad mood indeed," said Fausta without looking up.

"So'm I," said Castang.

"Close the door and siddown," said the Divisional Commissaire. There was a nasty silence lasting thirty seconds. One heard the serene noise of the clock on Richard's wall; a pretty, antique clock with a soft fragile chime. Don't give me any chiming clock when I retire, he said: I already have one. As for old men with beards carrying scythes, that is me.

Richard's room was soundproofed. The door was padded, the windows double. It was not to suppress screams; there were never any screams.

"When this affair started, I recall saying to you that none of it was to go any further. Does it? Has it?"

"No. Nor is Orthez a talker."

76

"Somebody is. As I learn from my one-time colleague and present superior, Monsieur Ottavioli. I'm wasting no further time on it, save to remind you that Madame de Rubempré very kindly offered you a job. She may have other people here. We have a tendency to believe that infiltration is something we do. It's standard everywhere including here. Understood?

"You of course I've known a fairly long time.

"I have occasionally taken risks in my life: you are aware. You also know that I haven't taken any major risk in twenty years, the time roughly that I've been sitting in this chair. The occupant of said chair being – you are aware – not paid to take risks: he has people to do so for him. Like you.

"Further, to get things clear before I start, you know very well a fact never mentioned in this office: because I had an excellent Resistance record and am a Companion of the Liberation I had an early and rapid promotion. Whereas since various old friends, we needn't name them, quitted the vale of tears it has been obvious to all that I was on the shelf. I belong in brief to a time that has gone, and of which nobody now chooses to be reminded." He relit his cigar, which had gone out.

"You may or may not – I don't care in the least – be surprised to hear that behind these twenty years of blameless mediocrity subsists a medieval concept of personal honour.

"Don't think me paranoiac. Nobody's stabbing me, because nobody would take the trouble; nobody would think it worth the effort.

"Quite a lot of people have come though to the conclusion, independently of each other, that I'm not a person to rock boats, being an old cunt hanging on for his pension. The principle of public life in this country being cowardice and fear, there is no reason to suppose me an exception.

"Incidentally, I haven't carried a gun in thirty years, and don't propose to start now. It may relieve your mind – this is not John Wayne coming out of retirement to save the nation. I don't give a fuck about the nation. Nor do I care whether the Unknown Soldier buried under the Arc de Triomphe, assuming there's anything there at all, was black, white, or Jewish. Clear?"

"Yes."

"I got into touch privately, last night, with the managing editor of a French newspaper, and I'll leave it to you to guess. I proposed that he send me a good reporter. Self-evidently, I can use their sources of information. They, it might be thought, can use mine. He won't touch me and on thinking it over I don't blame him. He's a little older than me. He's been a journalist since 1937. His attitude probably – I haven't asked him – is that any official source is being treated by him as dishonest until proof to the contrary is furnished. Concretely, this entire affair is tainted, and myself along with it. I don't deny that such an attitude, from such a man, wounds me profoundly. I had not realised how much, until I got up this morning. Haemorrhaging," with an abrupt finger towards his solar plexus, "here.

"My personal attitude clear?"

"Yes."

"Then let's sum up the matter briefly, as far as it has gone. A few political manoeuvres, of the sort one would normally greet with derision, have reached a stage where somebody dies, by violence. Nothing new in that. What else was the assassination of Broglie, or the suicide of Boulin? They got mixed up, voluntarily or not is irrelevant, with crapulous affairs. They died and were they pushed? Not my business to attempt an answer: I'm not a choirboy. Assassination on political grounds has been a feature of public life since a good while before Alexander.

"Do you perhaps recall, Castang," in a sudden pleasant return to his natural manner, "the passage in Dumas wherein a candidate to become General of the Jesuits must prove possession of an important state secret?" Richard as General of the Jesuits would certainly have induced the giggles in normal times: not now.

"There's a witch-word going the rounds – destabilisation; and I'm not talking about a few colonels in Bolivia. You and I might find our so-called advanced liberal society somewhat reactionary in practice. Or so most people conclude. Now if you were extremely dissatisfied with that state of affairs, how would you go about pushing public opinion?

"Quite. Vibert's their man. Popular, good-looking, dynamic, a good speaker, pronounced authoritarian and reactionary views. Looks resolute. With Viviane as his Egeria, everything seemed to be going nicely.

"Who knows if your little Murielle hadn't decided on personal grounds that she'd had enough of Viviane, things might have gone more smoothly. However, Vibert shied off. Call it an excess of prudence, or call it a streak of honesty, what you please. The kidnapping by wicked terrorists was a bit too phony, also badly stage-managed: it didn't come off cleanly. Instead of playing it dramatic and emotional Vibert goes quietly home, makes things up with his wife, behaves in general as though he were really rather pleased to be rid of Miss Viviane. And that leaves them up the pole. Since the government, nothing if not prudent, refuses likewise to dramatise the situation. The press, which has started rather too many hares of recent months, isn't taken in by all this, orchestrates it rather as a domestic tiff – Viviane acting up in the middle of the night, probably drunk – and with Murielle threatening everyone with libel actions nobody created the scandal anticipated. Vibert, perhaps soundly counselled by the excellent Doctor Joinel, does an ostrich act. Irresolute? I'd prefer to believe that the man has rags of personal decency left, as well as loyalty to his wife.

"He realised perhaps too that it wasn't just putting a marriage ahead of ambition. The man's not a fool. He realised – or Joinel did ahead of him – that allowing these people to use Viviane as leverage on him would be delivering himself bound into their hands."

"Which was what they intended."

"Who's they, Castang?"

"Madame Alberthe de Rubempré has lots of friends. Some in Germany. I'm hoping the Bundeskriminalamt can tell us something about that."

"You do, do you? Let's just finish by seeing where we stand here, before we go racing to the Germans. If you were 'They', in your opinion is chopping Viviane a clever thing to do?"

"I'm not they. Speaking as a cop I'd conclude they'd no further use for her, found her an embarrassment. Hysterical perhaps, liable anyway to talk. They can't keep her in a dungeon somewhere. Not after I turned up there at the château. Chopping her creates a shock. Reinforces the hypothesis of a Red Brigade. Mobilises – or so I suppose – a wave of emotion. Sympathy for Vibert – this dastardly stab at his private life and honour, etcetera. Besides a bash at the government, whose crooked and incompetent police forces are incapable, etcetera."

"Now we're there. What makes them so certain that the police forces are incapable, etcetera?"

"They – I'd rather call it Rubempre – must feel bloody confident in their friends upstairs." Richard wasn't grinning with approval. His mouth had disappeared into a tight hard line. His face was as grim as the Eddystone Rock in a force-eight gale. He was nodding slowly, repeatedly, and it wasn't in friendly agreement.

"Which I'm not about to take lying down. Very well, I'm at the end of my career. My house is my own, I've money saved, I've no children dependent upon me. Whereas you . . ."

"I don't altogether get this," said Castang slowly. "We've a homicide. A public prosecutor agrees it's a homicide. A judge of instruction delivers us a commission for interrogation and enquiry. Nobody has actively forbidden us to proceed in a matter like that. Are we that paralysed? We can't just go arrest Rubempré, sure. Is it certain we can't even get anybody to bring to trial? With a chance of establishing a link, maybe even getting grounds for a conspiracy charge?"

"The good Mister Becker, who – you're aware – is the head of the Bundeskriminalamt, made one of those deliberate gaffes recently that the Germans are adept at. The French police, he was quoted as saying, do not inspire confidence. The reputation of France as an asylum for so-called liberties is abused by undesirable elements, towards whom the French police show a tolerance and even apathy amounting to complicity. Now who was he talking about? Hardly Klaus Croissant, whom we extradited with the greatest promptitude. Nor the three Red Brigade girls who were found in a flat in Paris. Nor – we may presume – all those Basque terrorists sitting comfortably drinking beer in Hendaye, who so greatly embarrass the Spanish Government."

"We enjoy embarrassing the Spanish government, whereas we're too cowardly to pull the noses of the Germans."

"Not the point, boy," said Richard patiently. "Mr Becker was pointing out, not too obliquely, that if fascist groups commit outrages in France or elsewhere, it is with the complacent complicity of the police. Meaning me. If I – or you – ring up asking what his computer has to say about Viviane Kranitz and her friends, I'm likely to get a very dusty answer. Telephones ring in Bonn, long faces are made on the Quai d'Orsay, and Divisional Commissaire Richard is placed on indefinite sick leave."

Castang looked joylessly at Richard and said, "I could do with a drink."

"It's a robber baron's castle," said Orthez.

"Right, and pretty well protected. Only two ways in, both into

80

this village below the gates. Which is full of medieval retainers, all forelock-tugging to Madame la Comtesse because say what you like she's a sure source of income, a good deal of it tax-free. Eyes and ears everywhere. We post people down below, even just to record the comings and goings, how long is it before it's noticed – five minutes?"

"There're these paths behind, in the woods," puzzling over the map. "Woodcutters and such."

"Come on, you're a country boy. Look at the contours, look how steep they are. A Land Rover maybe, a Citroën on mountain suspension – you might make fifteen kilometres an hour in second gear. You going up there, disguised as a woodcutter?"

"No."

"Well then?"

"I don't know; place is isolated. Vulnerable on that account, no? You go there to repair the phone wires, you dig a bit, find the main electricity cable, and snip."

"Lovely, except they've water there running down the hillside enough to power ten thousand houses. Manorial rights – own turbine, own generator." Orthez, whose tastes ran to Skorzeny exploits, preferably including a company of parachutists, was feeling wistful.

"A few over the back, no Land Rover, just afoot, simultaneous with a good strong diversion in front . . ."

"Who d'you think you are then, the Emperor Bokassa? You can be first whichever way; there's a Great Dane and he'll bite your b—" The telephone rang.

"There's a dotty woman asking for you, Castang."

"I know so many."

"Says she's Marilyn Monroe."

"Put her on . . . you can talk."

"I don't know whether really it's an awful lot of good," said Maxie's voice, "but you did say, concerning the lady that was under discussion, even if grasping at straws, you know, a friend booked in to the Empress Eugenie."

"What sort of friend?"

"This is hotel shoptalk, porters and the like. Brazilian, evidently wealthy, travels with a maid, the reservation was made by your friend, seems at home in financial circles."

"Maid? – woman then?"

81

"That's right. Four guests this evening, very discreet: meal to be served in the suite. That's all I could gather I'm afraid: I didn't want to seem eager."

"We'll do what we can," said Castang, who didn't want to seem too eager either. "And the name?"

"Arabella de Serta."

"Arabia Deserta? Spell that . . . and the financial circles?"

"Vaguely, Paribas Bank is the best I can do."

"All right."

"Who's Marilyn Monroe?" asked Orthez innocently.

"She's a friend," said Castang, "of Napsabadzsag."

"Is that you?"

"That's the Big Chief Goblin."

"All right, screw him and tell him so from me."

"Difficult," said Castang who was getting into a better frame of mind, "it's the Hungarian Communist Party."

Disguises are rather frowned upon in the PJ, as tending to be more trouble than they are worth and leading to entanglements seldom to be justified: however . . . Castang went to see Massip. Chief Inspector Massip, the head, meaning all there was, of Economic Crimes, was a grey individual, so colourless he needed no disguising, but Castang, mindful of injunctions, was going to keep Arabia Deserta an unknown territory.

"Supposing I wanted to make an approach to banking circles?"

"You couldn't; you can't talk the jargon."

"No, it would only need to be very tangential; just some sort of credential to establish a bit of faith." Massip thought.

"Can you do a Canadian accent? Québecois? At a pinch then . . ."

The lab made no difficulty about forged documents: those are common coin. A business card was produced in florid copperplate. Harold Greenpeace. Attaché de Direction. The Bank of Nova Scotia, Paris.

"Does it exist?" asked Castang dubiously.

"Better than that – highly thought of. As tax havens go it's cool, and by comparison Switzerland is talkative: you won't need to utter at all."

If you do it at all, make sure it's done properly. Commissaire Richard, without access to the Westmore Brothers, produced a wonderful old lady who had been a Westmore Sister, who for a modest monthly retainer kept her hand in from time to time. She studied Castang's dark go-to-meeting suit, kept in the office for funerals, official receptions and Prefects.

"Something financial, for a meeting in a hotel: that's easy enough."

"Has to get past the hotel help," said Castang, "which has a sharp eye and a good indexing system. It doesn't see me often, but I wouldn't bet on non-recognition."

"Sharp but stereotyped: we'll alter this bookmaker's look. A haircut – who does this usually, your wife? The eyebrows, the ears. Fill out the cheeks a little; you don't look well-fed enough. And bleach your skin for a pasty citified look."

"God," said Castang looking in the glass, "I could even sell life insurance to myself."

"With a bit of lift in the shoes. These glasses – no, even the best contact lenses take some getting used to . . . no, tortoiseshell is wrong, try these. They'll distort a bit, but it's only for two minutes in the hotel lobby."

The 'Empress Eugénie', built in the heyday of that lady, had been like her a handsome and elegant structure of much dignity and charm, a little over-decorated but very nice to look at. It had been knocked down, exactly like Euston Station and in consequence of the same mentality, and been replaced by an unhandsome, inelegant slab of no dignity and less charm: the French do it too.

In an effort, partly conscious, to compensate for dinginess without it is all beastly luxury within, with a multiplication of servile attendants and electronic gadgets: trilingual secretaries and porn video cassettes: telex to Tokyo simply whizzing away and a computer terminal to the Bourse. Businessmen with little plastic labels herd into conference rooms and mutter furtively in hideous little groups, picking at calculators (if yours is bust the porter will lend you one free). Eavesdrop – frowned upon; bad form – and you might learn that small boys were cheap today, cheaper-than-yesterday: down seven-sixteenths and causing much agitation.

Of the Empress Eugénie there survives only a bad copy of a full-length portrait, probably by Winterhalter, which is thought to give tone; surveying this mob with benignant bewilderment: I must ask Louis who all these Japanese can possibly be, and what can they want?

Castang bustled over to the desk with the haughty nauseated look of people who lend money. He wrote on one of his lovely cards 'A.

83

de R. will serve to introduce' and said, "Kindly have that given to Madame de Serta," before going over to sit by himself wrapped in a veil of prophecy. His shoes were his own, and always kept very well polished; one indeed of his few extravagances. The briefcase on his knee was Richard's (who never used it): pristine thus as well as grand. A copy of the *Financial Times* had been added for local colour.

In a very few moments there was a menial by his chair saying,"'Mr Greenpeace? If you would be so good," and working the lift for him. Even if it is only one flight bankers never walk. One of these days we will see sedan chairs reappear, with powdered-wigged footmen, and a security man disguised as a linkbearer. He kept his hat and glasses on, though he could scarcely see an inch: the menial was there anyhow for the faltering footstep.

The first floor of course is suites: noiseless air-conditioned passage. There were actually little black boys carrying candelabras, but they were only painted plaster. The menial held the door of the sittingroom for him. There was nobody there. He took the glasses off as well as the hat; now at last he could see something. There was nothing much to see bar the usual bad copies of Empire furniture and Manet's 'Déjeuner sur l'herbe' which decorators think is vaguely contemporary as well as sexy in a well-brought-up way; though nowadays it's used as a Campari advertisement, which rather spoils things. The exterior-marks-of-wealth (like his briefcase) were scattered about. He stood and looked out of the window (there were three to choose from) on to the interior courtyard, in summer bedizened with geraniums, icebuckets and gipsy violinists; now nothing but old newspapers and empty bottles: all the beautiful people had got under cover. Castang wondered how good an actor he was and whether he knew his lines. A door opened and Madame de Serta appeared. He forgot his lines.

He had never known anyone who travelled with a maid bar Bianca Castafiore, for whom see Tintin books, passim; she leads poor old Irma a devil of a dance, and everyone else too. He had expected indeed some such type, bejewelled and bebosomed, much sharpened as to nose and voice, and fearfully condescending. Whereas this was a very good-looking young woman in a velvet housedress. She had beautiful dark brown hair looped on either side like George Sand, and looked much more like the young Eugénie than the portrait downstairs. She had no jewellery but a square

84

Cartier watch on one bare brown wrist, exactly like the one above Castang's freshly-manicured hand (attention had been paid to detail). He kissed hers, bowing properly and beginning to recall lines.

"Do sit down then," in French: he understood why it had been clever to be called Greenpeace. His English was a bit music hall; his Spanish mostly obscenities. This test he could pass.

"It is good of you to forgive being importuned."

"Oh, for a friend of Alberthe's . . ."

"A friend is a little too much to say: I have papers for Madame de Rubempré's signature, or that at least is the purpose of my present errand."

"A drink?"

"From anyone else I should refuse," with heavy banking gallantry. "A small one, dear lady, with pleasure." Christ, a tumblerful of Scotch; there were now two good reasons for getting carried away. Richard's ghost, dressed up as a Calvinist dominie, appeared at his elbow: how does one go about a good seduction? In Nova Scotia, Castang, they wait for Eskimo Nell, who comes once a year when the fleet's in.

"Do take a cigar. Well, what about Alberthe's signatures? I'd love to forge them but I wouldn't quite dare," waving aside the property Dunhills.

"I'm in a slight embarrassment if the truth be known – I slipped down from Paris since the estate attorneys give me to understand there is some urgency. Madame de Rubempré's admirable majordomo is of course obeying his instructions. I know her thus to be in Germany, but . . ." he stopped for a sipsip: this was the tricky bit.

"So you come storming in here; very brazen and barefaced of you."

"I am desolated if I have been indiscreet."

"No. I'm teasing. How did you know I was here?"

"Hotel gossip," said Castang with perfect truth, "but you may count upon my silence."

"And did this gossip – I might have guessed it – run to my purposes?"

"Certainly not," with a fervent look, like a Prefect meeting the Pope. She grinned.

"You lie well, and that's your job of course. Alberthe is a cousin of mine. Well, dear man, your objection is easily met with. The

85

lawyers are applying whip and spur I take it, and you have to go racing to Germany, and you're up shit creek because you haven't the remotest clue where."

"At the risk of a loss of dignified pomposity," grinning back "that's it exactly."

"Tcha, I'm in a good mood this morning. But of course you'll go telling everything to Alberthe, and if the filthy papers are really urgent she'd be cross if I didn't tip you off. What day are we? She's staying with friends – no, that won't do; she wouldn't want . . . mm, tomorrow there's a diplomatic party the German Government is giving at Schloss Bruhl – mm, you'd have trouble getting in there. However, the day after she'll be in Baden-Baden. Racing or gambling? – exactly, either would surprise you greatly, so I'll take you off the hook; it's another boring party, the General Commanding, and rather her than me if you ask me, but she inclines to be humourless about these ghastly functions. She'll be home after that I believe – I hope so anyhow because I've no intention of staying in this fearful dump longer than I have to: in her house at least nobody gossips about one's movements." Castang thought it extremely likely.

"So make what you can of that – as it's business she'll probably be at the Kaiserhof, but that's a guess."

"I am infinitely obliged," meaning it sincerely, "but I must not impose upon your kindness," setting the halfpint of Scotch aside with regret: what a waste.

"You needn't run away," lazily, "I've nothing before dinner."

Oh yes you have. A naughty caprice, of condemning a Nova Scotian priss-ass to eternal damnation. The bottom buttons have somehow come adrift, and the luminous legs are atwinkle there.

If he'd had a bit more whisky what might not have happened? If as seemed rather likely she was thinking, like Madame de Chevreuse, what a pleasant souvenir it would be in her old age. Richard's ghost, still at his elbow, was having acute tetanic convulsions. He'd had quite enough Scotch: could be the Reverend Ian Paisley for all he cared, but what very peculiar and convoluted pretexts men can produce for not doing what they want. Almost as far-fetched as the reasons (numerous and excellent) for falling upon this ripe apricot like a steaming bull. The thing was how to get out of the door without appearing ridiculous. He got to his feet and staggered around a bit.

"As the Englishman said, 'Thank-you-thank-you, but never

before sundown,' " arranging the seat of his trousers, which were feeling uncomfortably tight.

"Really? Is that the rule in Nova Scotia?" grinning evilly.

"The chief rule in Nova Scotia is to take the next plane, I should think."

"You're not thinking of breaches of fiduciary trust, are you?"

"Oh I am, I am. In the extreme background of my mind," putting the glasses on as a precautionary measure against all that tit, and taking them off again for fear he wouldn't find the door. For the love of Heaven, or the Code of Criminal Procedure, or Something, keep talking. "I've never set eyes on the place, somewhat to my relief. Codliver oil and whisky," shaking his finger at her, "half and half, is the most violent and rapid aphrodisiac known to man."

"Speaking as a woman I'd hate to think of their breath at the time."

"Life is full of missed opportunities," clutching the briefcase to his chest like a lifejacket and wondering frantically where the hat was. "I keep the kindest memories of Brazil," putting the hat on like a dunce's cap. Or, he thought hurrying back past all those grinning black boys holding torches, like an extinguisher on a candle. At least he'd succeeded in making her laugh; she wouldn't be feeling too vengeful. He thought of the four men round the dinner table that evening, and started to laugh himself. Wondering uneasily about Buggins' Turn Next.

The extreme of hypocrisy would now be to go back and rape Vera. Since he had a strong inclination to rape somebody he went back to the office, where everyone had gone home but Richard, who burst out laughing at the sight of him. Laughed more at the story; said wearily "Thanks for something to laugh at." Men laughing together greasily; big jolly hawhaw at all the innuendo, pathetic.

"It's sundown," said Richard. "Come on, I've earned a drink."

"Did you ever hear of Tallulah, Castang? No? American actress, in my young days. On being asked whether she ever had lesbian tendencies replied, 'No, no, dear, even when playing with myself I always think of a man.' What d'you want, more whisky?"

"No, a beer: this stuff they serve here isn't whisky."

"Two Belgian beers," said Richard. He relapsed into thought and then said, "Baden-Baden" in the tone of someone trying to recall a forgotten fact.

"'s in the Black Forest," said Castang helpfully. "Big French

87

garrison, ever since the occupation days. Our Bulwark against the Russians. They never dare fire a gun off, because ammunition is too expensive."

"Yes," said Richard patiently, "and what would be the distance from the border about?"

"Not far I should think. Without a map . . . I dunno; less than a hundred kilometres." Richard was being jolly pensive: a thing enforced, so to speak, by general cluelessness.

"President Truman said, Castang, in words to the effect, that reading history was the only really sound guide to decision. He was quite right, you know." What was this, more Tallulah? Richard had only had one beer; hadn't been drinking in the office surely? – he never did.

"Baden-Baden," said Richard, appearing to be falling asleep. With great suddenness, in a crisp, rapid, level delivery, he showed himself Nero Wolfe: all that was missing was that his lips hadn't gone puffing in and out.

"Napoleon got it into his head that any surviving members of the royal family were a threat to his throne. There were a few in England, but fat lazy stupid ones, could be disregarded. Of the Orléans or cadet branch, the highly ignoble Philippe-Egalité had got chopped, to the regret of none. Remained, in case you need reminding, the House of Condé, closely allied, and of as we may recall great military reputation. Represented by a young man of eighteen, the Duc d'Enghien, then living, in common with a large number of aristocratic personages who had emigrated to avoid getting chopped, in exile just across the border in Germany. Handily placed to come back should things turn out in their favour. In – funny to relate – Baden-Baden . . .

"As is further well-known, and forgive the pedantic disquisition, this is the one irretrievable crime that Napoleon never managed to shake off. He attempted to put the blame on Talleyrand, but we don't know, I think, exactly who had the idea. They whisked across the border with a troop of cavalry, kidnapped the young duke on his way to a party – perhaps back from a party – got him to Paris in a couple of days, clapped him into the Château de Vincennes, trumped up a conspiracy charge, and a day or so later, without bothering about time-wasting things like trials, had him shot. *Jawohl!*" which was about all the German Richard knew.

"Wasn't it then that Talleyrand said, 'Worse than a crime: a mistake'? or have I got that wrong?"

"I rather think that was Fouché. What Talleyrand is supposed to have done is to look at his watch and enquire innocently 'Is it really eleven o'clock? Then the House of Condé no longer exists'. Words to that effect."

"Wouldn't this be a mistake too?" enquired Castang.

"If we're coining aphorisms, one mistake deserves another and the same applies to kidnappings." Richard felt in his pocket, produced coinage, and paid for the beers. "Let's go sleep on it."

"Sleep with me," said Vera with abruptness, a few hours later.

At the Police Judiciaire, it was a day like any other, occupied with current affairs. Wheels turned, the outermost slow and ponderous, with reference to numerous well-known metaphors concerning millstones, God, Justice and so forth. The innermost wheel, meaning Divisional Commissaire Richard, was turning very fast, perhaps freewheeling.

Another nasty precedent had occurred to Castang in the night.

"What about Colonel Godard?" Back in the days of all the fuss about Algeria this gentleman had been the Chief of Staff or something of the OAS. Some bright spark in the parallel police, perhaps another history student, had taken a gang, whipped over as far as Münich, rolled Godard up, put him in a van tied-up-hand-and-foot, and left him blatantly parked on the Place de la Concorde, or somewhere equally public, with an insolent message to the official instances saying If you want it come and get it. Words to the effect.

Richard took his glasses off.

"You're worrying, Castang, about the illegal combined with the immoral. If I may say so, you're rather young. And you haven't understood. If you'd been here in 1940 you would have been faced with this problem before. If the government to whom your allegiance is sworn acts in both an illegal and immoral fashion, what is your position?"

This was clearly a rhetorical question. Castang merely blew his nose and wondered how long it would be before his eyebrows grew back.

"You can acquiesce eagerly," said Richard, "so as to cash in, there being plenty of opportunity both for quick promotion and a nice slice on the side, as reward for Zeal. You can give lip service, as a rule out of complete and consummate poltroonery. You can pretend to give lip service and sit on the fence, with a vague notion of keeping your nose clean, looking after Number One, and a general guideline of insisting on written instructions, while never yourself putting your name to anything likely to compromise you.

"You can stay put," quietly, "with a good many sincere protestations of devotion while dragging your feet and even acting in contradiction to your orders. To last even a short time at that takes more talent than most of us possess.

"You can fuck off out. And at this moment it is timely to recall that it is no longer 1940, that we are no longer eighteen years old, that there is no General any more, and that Fuhrerbefehl is no longer what it was. Because all those characters had a sort of courage, that at least of their own convictions. Our beloved rulers don't dare give a direct order, openly. They prefer to Let Things be Understood," cuttingly. "Enough said?"

Air services between European cities, where they exist at all, are notable only for their ridiculous expense. For the price of crossing a frontier you can go to New York: Castang would have preferred that, on the whole. The advantage – there were few – of a rogatory commission signed by a judge of instruction is that within the context of a judicial enquiry the government will pay your fare. It might even run to a self-drive car. In the present instance it might be more prudent if your movements were not too closely docketed, but paltry as the secret fund is it should be able to serve some purpose, or so Richard said.

Then there is this vexing matter of disguises. Being the Bank of Nova Scotia for any length of time is not recommendable. The sound rule where masquerades are concerned is to appear as something as close as possible to your genuine persona. A policeman is never more convincing than when acting and talking like a policeman. As for credentials, the lab can whip you up more elaborate things than a phony calling card, but there was no real need. Richard's youthful excursions into clandestinity, or was it mere prudence? – had given him, one could only guess, a taste for boltholes. He produced a warrant card which looked genuine precisely because it was genuine. It belonged to a gentleman who had retired, was all he would say, but what's retirement? In a foreign country, moreover, a slight polish is lent to the performance when you belong to SDECE. This unpronounceable acronym stands for the splendidly named Service of Documentation and (an afterthought, as it were, and in parenthesis) Counter Espionage. It means the Company in French.

Suppose, this being not beyond the bounds-of-possibility, you meet a real SDECE man on your travels? He might ask the computer who the hell you are. The computer will reply that you are retired, at which he will retire too: foxed.

There is a further factor, unmentioned by Richard but occupying a small black corner. People thought prejudicial to the interests of the State have been got rid of, now and then. Nobody, even high in the confidence of the Elysée Palace, was going to get in a tangle with the Service of Documentation, bearing the fairly high rank of a Chief of Studies: over-liable to find himself rubbing his own funnybone.

"A certain amount can be spent upon clothes," eyeing Castang's corduroys "The smell of horsedung that follows you about . . . the funeral suit will do until you get one of those very Bavarian lodens. Hurry up now. Orthez will drive you to the airport – and I'll call upon Vera; you need have no anxiety about her. It might even be nice if she had a little holiday. By the way, don't take any guns. I'll bring yours with me, at the appropriate moment."

Köln airport – one hasn't anything to say about airports anywhere that could lessen their tedium. Just be grateful that they didn't take you on to Frankfurt on account of fog. And who needs self-drive cars? For anyone wanting to get to Schloss Bruhl it's practically next door. The Pope can keep his helicopter: Cardinal Castang takes a taxi.

Government buildings in Bonn were never lordly, are mostly shoddy, not to say shabby, and even shitty, despite efforts over Green Spaces: and not having Berlin any more, or grand official buildings vaguely associated with Frederick the Great for entertaining important personages, Schloss Bruhl is really awfully handy: a smallish, pretty, pleasantly situated baroque pleasure-palace, most agreeable to look at, and containing respectable Art and furniture some of which is genuine.

Its origins, loosely episcopal and reeking of nepotism, tyranny and the selling of indulgences, are only vaguely scandalous nowadays: it has no really low association with dreadful people:

Napoleon, Hitler, Henry Ford or whoever. It is well worth a visit, which is more than can be said of most government palaces. Since it is the place for the really classy government piss-ups the tourist is liable to find his rambling severely restricted by Security. This nightmarish modern obsession has reached such proportions here-abouts that the tourist half the time can't get anywhere near the place, because of worries lest the Security be Insecure and needing a great deal more private security to make it so. Bundesamts for this and that proliferate like rabbits. Being German and efficient they take pains over the public relations, not wanting at all to be called Fascist. Castang, in his capacity as a security-person, caused no comment at all and got matey with a highly jovial fellow whose job was to reassure no matter whom. These people had such (thinly-disguised) contempt for a French police official that they didn't even bother checking on him. Being patronised in this good-humoured fashion, a thing that had aroused Richard's fury nearly as much as Alberthe de Rubempré's tolerant assumption of his total impotence, had aroused the Commissaire pretty fundamentally. But Castang found it handy. Made things easier.

"Now who are you interested in? Ah, die Frau Baron; all is now clear."

"Valuable person in the eyes of the French Government."

"To be sure, to be sure. Well I can reassure you totally; she's on my list. Here we are, Frau Alberthe de Rubempré, one chauffeur, one footman, bodyguard naturally, but people like the old forms; cardinals with Domestic Chaplains."

"Transmitters in the breviary, and exploding rosaries."

"That's right, hahaha. So you needn't worry, not only has she hers but ours, and ours is the best there is."

"You've descriptions, photos, of the driver and the guard? Like to compare those with our records."

"Sure: they don't get inside the perimeter of course: separate filter. But all that personnel is handpicked. Can't even let you through the perimeter, unless you want to go through an extremely searching interrogation."

"No need," said Castang, in what he hoped were airy tones.

"As a courtesy to a colleague, take a tour round the kitchens if that would amuse you. The grub is the one French thing there is around here, hahaha."

Now if one were working on a scenario for a flaming great

terrorist raid on the West German Government, thought Castang amusedly . . . A Mission Impossible if ever there were one, on the face of it, but put some damn thriller-writer's imagination to work…. He was free-wheeling now: he'd got, at least, what he came for. Even as he was, blindfolded, forbidden to make an X-ray, with nothing but the sensitivity in his fingertips to guide him to weakness or fragility, he knew he had found one. For no security system, however sophisticated, is foolproof. There is always a key, and a man who holds it.

The reason for the kind offer to 'show him round a little' was now apparent: the security man loved food. A glance at the kitchen was certainly a pleasant and skilful piece of public relations, and it was also a nice pretext for picking. While jovially passing a buttery time-of-day with cooks the fellow was dipping his finger in pots and licking them. A double weakness, in fact. While the shiny eyes were distracted by greed the man's mind was not on his job, and hankypanky could be both planned and rehearsed (there was a television camera watching them but there are ways of distracting them, too) and furthermore Castang knew, having been in restaurant kitchens before, that the cooks hate this behaviour.

They weren't saying anything: get on the wrong side of a security man and you can very easily lose a good job. But a cook's eye does not glitter with greed, but with a suppressed wish to take hold of that fellow and shove his whole head in the pot. Much like the royal brother in Plantagenet times, who after a career of unparalleled double dealing was finished off by being plunged head down in the wine barrel he was so fond of sipping from.

For anyone interested in food, and Castang was (had even made himself by perseverance into a fair imitation of a cook) it was both a fascinating and a frustrating place. Nothing but the best. A special plane flew in each day straight from the Rungis markets with the finest and the freshest of everything. Extremely simple process. By basic premises of geography and climate the soil and the sea of France is the most generous, the most varied. The best is sent to Paris, for there they pay the highest. Pay more than anybody else and there you are. The simplicity as much as the vulgarity of this logic appealed to him.

You need not imagine that the guests of the Federal Republic are hereby assured of the world's best grub: it is rather *la grande bouffe* than *la belle bouffe*. Too many traps along the way. Castang was reminded of an acquaintance, larder chef in a starred restaurant and so much in love with his raw material that he was accustomed to say wistfully 'We turn out lovely work, and those damn cooks make shit of it.' The security filter between the kitchen and the diningroom isn't going to help either. But the biggest drawback is simply that it's banquet food, and all banquet food is horrible. By trying to please everyone you hit a common denominator of dullness, and worst of all you've got to keep the beastly stuff hot. By the time the wretched guest actually gets something on his place it's soggy.

The only remedy to this is to eat straight out of the pot, as Castang's new friend (food accelerates intimacy) was busy doing. He was in fact making a hearty meal. Not content with polaroiding everybody coming and going, counting silver coffee-spoons, generally making an infernal pest of himself, he had appointed himself Chief Taster. He should have a splendid robe, thought Castang (working painfully back from Abdul the Damned up to Suleiman the Magnificent – nobody can ever remember all the Sultans in between), made of innumerable skins of some delicious-tasting beast; not ermines for they surely would be rather nasty. And an immense turban, higher than any cook's toque. Bright scarlet perhaps like a fire extinguisher. And carry upon his shoulder, processionally, a soup-ladle two metres long. And never forget that the Chief Gardener (the indoor servants always look down upon those from the mere Outdoors) is also the Chief Executioner in his spare time. And that all those Eunuchs are mighty handy with silk bowstrings.

If only he stuck to security . . . but this delightful dallying – plainly a daily occurrence – had made him a self-appointed expert on the Bouffe.

"Oh that nice stuffing – that's for the quails," in a helpful aside. "I never can resist that – hm, not quite enough shallot."

Castang was watching a magnificent salmon, sadly, as the beautiful animal was flung on the bench and brutally slit along the backbone.

Finding out what Madame de Rubempré, lucky her, would have in her stomach that night (he hoped for her sake she had sound digestion but felt sure she'd sound everything) was however less important than a few things Commissaire Richard was anxious to learn. Hard work. He got quite hungry.

"The really sad thing," the man was saying, putting a few *petits*

94

fours in his pocket for when time hung heavy in the office and one fancied a bit of a nibble, "is that nine out of ten of the pigs don't have the remotest clue what they're getting and would anyway vastly prefer a lump of *eisbein* and a glass of beer."

Castang had lunch in a pub. He got lentil soup and a big sausage with rehydrated instant-mashed-potato, and drank apple juice.

The policeman was thinking back to the animal he had seen on the big metal table, being very clumsily butchered, with a lot of waste. It had been perfect; any scars bring the price down. No gaff marks, thus netted. Never got further than the estuary. Unless my marine biology is much awry some must get up the river; isn't that where they fertilise the females? Probably there's a marine biologist counting them. You stupid cunt, you've caught a breeding hen. Look, Castang, go back to Nova Scotia will you, and wait outside the cannery door.

Else do what everyone else does: go to a restaurant, and wait your turn for a little titchy bit tarted up with spinach leaves and chervil costing a hundred and fifty francs: or go without.

The most unpleasant feature of this entire affair was not being able to mention it to Vera. There'd been nothing in his life he'd had to hide. He'd never told her lies: there'd never been any need. There was no cop's life – was there any human being's life, anywhere? – without smelly corners, but she disinfected them. There was nothing at all that she was afraid to face.

This business would worry her very badly, and she would be quite right.

Like any woman at all who thought, Vera was going through a crisis, which had already lasted a year or two and whose end was not in sight: a woman can no longer allow the men to make existence into the butchery it has always been. Time has run out. The woman cannot take man's place, do the man's work. That will not alter anything except yet again for the worse. Instead of endlessly submitting . . . Clumsily, painfully, the women were groping everywhere; trying to get a grip on their new responsibilities, understand their new role and act upon it. Painful for them; for the men likewise. For six months Vera had sat quietly at home with her baby, but had been getting increasingly acid. He could not understand – did she wish to go out and work? (ridiculous; how could she look after the child, how could she paint?) No, of course

95

not, she said impatiently. Then what was it she wanted? 'I haven't got it all worked out yet' she said, enigmatic; infuriating; unsettling. Not happy. She had been oddly pleased with the gunning of the old flat, with the move. 'I don't want to go back'. Then where do you want to go? 'I don't know yet; let me think'. It was not the smallest of his worries.

And this wasn't the moment to worry about it, any more than it was to think about salmon. Karlsruhe, and time to concentrate.

It's a funny place, Baden-Baden; designed with much care, and loving attention to detail, for the comforts of old ladies and the well-being of invalided gentlemen. This gerontocracy has frozen it in time: more than anywhere else here are the vulgar luxuries of Edwardian cheesecake. It is impossible to see, or to imagine here, anybody poor, ragged or hungry: anybody vagabond, dirty, or a card-carrying Communist. The young (there are a few) have been deloused, trimmed up and as it were sterilised. Marx, Lenin, or Adolf Hitler (perish the thought) have never been heard of. That old horror Sigmund Freud has wormed his obscene tentacles in all right: Oedipus and Electra gibbering at the doorway of every tomb; and there are a great many. There are almost as many shrinks, faith-healers and assorted charlatans as in Beverly Hills, but they're awfully discreet. Hare Krishna might pop a yellow shaven head out but would get the door banged on it. The police force is almost invisible but highly efficient: create the slightest disturbance and your feet won't touch the ground.

A stage-set, in which all the old ladies drinking coffee and eating cake, both with lashings of cream; all the old gentlemen hobbling into the apothecary's to get the new prescription filled; are one and all the uncles and aunts of Frieda Lawrence, cousins with every schloss in the Danube Valley (Patrick Leigh Fermor's hospitable hosts) and looking forward greatly to the next visit of the Prince of Wales – no not that one, nor the one before – who on earth IS Mrs Simpson? – nor the one before that, so nice-looking in his midshipman's uniform. No no, the Real one, with all those well-bred, well-behaved, well-brought-up mistresses: dearest Mrs Keppel. Vulgar man, the Kaiser, and what does he want a Kiel Canal for? Prussians . . . tedious people: they probably piss in the washbasin.

Castang was struck first by the physical stage set. A dear little valley, with dear little hills on each side, rather steep for bath chairs, even those with rubber tyres and a sturdy-legged page boy, and the horses will quickly get winded. But along the little valley health-giving strolls are pleasurably taken. The dearest, cleanest, quietest tiny river tinkles plashingly along with a wee fall from time to time. This is lined by park, with many manicured bushes, labelled trees and a great many flowering begonias: and numerous neoclassical temples housing mild good-mannered art. Terraces, where you can eat ices while listening to concerts: soloist Fraulein Holzenbein in a long black taffeta frock. La Belle Hélène; both pears in chocolate sauce and Offenbach too.

The automobile is the great worry along here. It's the one feature of modern life allowed, along with the sad tidings that help has to be paid a great deal of money. However, there is a sort of agreement that nobody should ever mention unions, and that they should behave like real Servants.

Castang was contemplating all this with something of a long lip. In these two or three narrow, cramped streets the appearance of a Rolls Royce would cause no comment, but moving at anything more than a majestic footpace called for wings, which would be conspicuous. A busy bustle, like an Aberdeen terrier at a rabbithole, was also to be shunned.

This was plainly a job for the Master Criminal from Spectre, chloroforming all the chambermaids and making a getaway in a jet-propelled bathchair: a job taking a month to plan and six to rehearse, and depending on about forty people doing exactly what was expected of them; Richard cast as Fu Manchu, and Orthez and himself as Arsky and Krutch. Anyhow they didn't have six months: they had until tomorrow evening.

So you ring up Richard and say the swing-on-creepers act is not on. Where the hell did the French Army belong, around here? The answer to this one was discovered back down the road a piece, where a dreary little suburb stretched out what seemed a very long way in this narrow creek bed before turning into something called Baden-Oss. An infernally difficult left turn across a narrow bridge over the railway-lines, and then there were helpful little military arrows pointing to things like the Sergeants' Mess, so that the Russians shouldn't lose their way.

Well what did French military transport do; all the trucks loaded with mobile military brothels and vino? Good, there was a shortcut back to the autoroute, but this seemed to be the only way out.

Germans, it is said, like to make very careful and detailed plans

97

for things. The French, again, are good at improvising last-minute schemes in which a free-for-all panic suddenly resolves itself into a spontaneous entertainment of charm and delightful sparkle. This had better be true.

The really tricky aspect of all this was the extreme difficulty of finding things out without tipping his hand. An appearance hereabouts of Inspector Machecoul from Renseignements Généraux, worrying about security, would simply alert some eager little aide de camp to the need for same. What we had here was a private citizen being entertained to dinner by a general; a very grand general living in that elegant schloss up there on the hill. A fairly formal but unofficial party: despite a military liking for pomp, for a section of something dressy like Chasseurs Alpins, bulled up to do the Military Honours, this would be a relatively quiet affair. Nor was it like Schloss Bruhl, where special arrangements were made for the flocks of drivers, bodyguards, secretaries, interpreters: here there would be no army of briefcase-carriers. Military drivers would be off on-the-scrounge at the officers' mess cookhouse: the Frau Baroness' servants, too toffee-nosed to pig along with corporals, would likely sit and suffer with a sandwich. If they didn't something would have to be invented, but Castang was aware of the value of making no plans at all. String, remarked the Duke of Wellington, is better than wire.

He only made one telephone call, to the hotel on behalf of Madame Arabella de Serta, to know when the lady was expected. And to Richard, who had arrived in Strasbourg.

As was to be expected trains this late at night were few and far between, and nothing to Strasbourg before ungodly hours, but he couldn't risk a taxi. He managed eventually with a tufftuff to Kehl which is the border town, and walked across the Europa Bridge, where Orthez picked him up. Together they took an interest in the frontier controls. The French and German guards were very thick together, and took liberties with national sovereignty: there was a German cop on the French side. True he only stood and stared, while the oppos stood about languidly and a Customs person, faithful to tradition, indicated with his hands in his pockets that the ranks of this fine body of men have not been increased since Napoleon the First, and he was going-slow-in-protest. On the German side official zeal had slackened too, this late. Nobody had glanced at Castang, who walked humbly along the pavement and noticed that foot passengers didn't even exist. They were checking perhaps one car in five, apparently at random, just to keep the computer happy. The rhythm would be much the same by day: there would be a lot more grey-green uniforms, but there would also be a lot more cars. One thing nobody gave a glance to were the FFA numberplates of the French Army in Germany.

"Yes," said Orthez, "I got a couple faked from the Strasbourg Military District. Wouldn't want the car searched and asking what we wanted with all these missiles."

"We're not going to have Richard dressed up as a Colonel in the Dragoons surely?"

"No no no," said Richard crossly. "A fine thing that would be: they've all got one another's graduation years and class numbers by heart, because of pecking order. As long as you haven't been creating any complications, Castang."

"I've done nothing at all except have a bloody good look at the terrain, which is difficult. Mustn't spring anything at all till the last possible moment."

"And? . . ."

"I'd advise very strongly against any sort of assault. The fragmentation grenades and the paralysing gases are right out. In or around the hotel," unfolding his maps in the cheap hotel room, "can't we get a stronger bulb in this lamp, Orthez? a snatch is impossible; the way out's too slow and congested. On the way to or from the party – too public, the alarm would be given too quickly: we'd be stopped at the bridge. To which there's a slow, awkward access with lots of traffic lights. There are other crossings both north and south but there we'd be noticed. At this one we'd be unperceived on condition that no alarm has gone off. So doing it actually at the party is best, provided that the military is perfectly satisfied: we don't want any sort of civilian against soldier confrontation." Richard was nodding approval.

"So three points. One, how to neutralise the driver and the guard. They're hers, they go with her. The security at Bonn is very good: here are photos and descriptions, and she has a car, Lincoln Continental, lent her by this chemicals pig she's staying with. She may have the same one here, she may not, but the car's got to be got rid of so as not to arouse comment. Back in the hotel garage would be best.

"Point two the lady herself. We've nobody remotely resembling the descriptions and if we had she's not likely to be either drunk enough or sleepy enough to be foxed for an instant.

"Third point the bridge. We've got to be able to get back here without a whiff of suspicion: whatever story has to be good enough to keep the soldiers quiet for three quarters of an hour: likewise the fellow-guests. If the Bundeskriminalamt gets even a breath of anything funny afoot it'll be on the computer at the crossing and we're gone geese."

"That all?" enquired Richard. "Quite enough too, so let's get some sleep."

Carried away? Dazzled? Euphoric? Castang didn't think so: these swimmy states of mind were not that frequent. Carried along might be nearer the mark. The planning and the execution belong almost entirely to Richard. One rarely sees a Divisional Commissaire at work with his own hands.

There is a simple reason for this. The master cook, the one with the 'high bonnet' who spends his time out front buttering up the customers, is seldom seen at the stove. He might burn the tarts and crack the cream. Then he'd be laughed at by the little 'prentice boys. And that would never do.

Put it another way. The fundamental fault in bureaucracy is the avoidance of individual responsibility. The departmental head who will go to extraordinary lengths to avoid even signing his own letters is known to everyone. In his small way he is on a par with the minister, who when pressed to answer yes or no replies that on balance the results are globally positive.

Richard was not only standing at his own stove but washing up his own pots. As for being launched upon an enterprise criminally illegal in the worst possible way, you'd think he'd been doing nothing else his entire life.

As early as breakfast next morning a personage appeared called Machecoul (did this extraordinary name just arrive upon the tip of his tongue? Was it plotted in the wakeful reaches of the night? Nobody would ever know.). A Commissaire too. It is always wise to disguise oneself as something one closely resembles anyhow. Castang's masquerade as the Bank of Kerguelen would not have withstood the slightest scrutiny, and Richard was prepared for scrutiny. The military establishment is bone-headed in the sense of narrowness and rigidity, but isn't necessarily thick. While still drinking coffee he had struck up confidential relations with the fellow who made the wheels go round in the General's personal household; an excellent laddie called Staff-Captain Ailleret.

Machecoul had a frightful voice, straight from the sixteenth arrondissement, fluted and precious with a rise into the soprano register at the ends of phrases. The burden of his polished discourse was as follows. A conspiracy had been uncovered for an Attempt calculated greatly to embarrass the Republic (the other republic too while they were at it; the Federal one). It was at present a little obscure who was nourishing this conspiracy. No, not perhaps the Red Brigade. More likely the Guadeloupe Revolution Front.

It was obvious, wasn't it, that everything must be done to avoid embarrassment to Republican Government, including the military establishment. Very. Commissaire Machecoul would be in touch. He would give himself indeed the pleasure of calling upon Staff-Captain Ailleret a little later in the day: telephonic communication is always indiscreet. Very.

Wasn't this horribly risky? enquired a nervous Castang. Yes, highly. If however obliged to take risks, take horrible ones. But suppose . . . No: characters like that love sealed secret orders. Alberthe is well guarded, and these guards must be suppressed without attracting attention.

"How'yre going to go about that; put a mickey in their beer?"

"I think it likely they don't drink. Heavy dose of valium I think in the hamburger."

"Comes in these capsules – probably got a horrible taste inside that gelatine or whatever."

"Or turn the hamburger bright green," suggested Orthez.

"There's that. Need a sort of pharmacological person."

"Sherlock Holmes had the same problem only then it was opium." Orthez had gone to bed with a Paperback Classic.

"What did he do then?"

"Put it in curry."

"Excellent. Old Indochinese hospitality; give them curry."

"Suppose it fizzes, or creates a horrible smell?"

"Shut up, Orthez. These nineteenth-century techniques are much the best."

"Suppose they say they don't like curry."

"Shut up, Castang."

101

"Now, having got two sleeping gorillas, what d'you do with them? Slap them in the guardroom saying these two clowns are a bit pissed?"

"Ring up and find the right dose and how long it takes to act. Get them back in the car, then you get rid of car and all."

"Suppose there really was a terrorist attempt. Sentries and stuff, all bulled up. Look at Buckingham Palace. Given two machineguns, Christopher Robin and Alice would go through the whole Brigade of Guards like a dose of salts."

"Scotland Yard will have thought of that – the IRA. Civilian persons lurking about, and that's us."

Richard was heard a little later on in his bedroom singing while shaving (the walls were thin). 'South of the Border – Down Mexico Way'. Detective work told Castang that this delectably abominable ballad must date back to the thirties. Jesus, he thought, the old man's regressed into childhood.

"Right," said Richard. "There was some guff too about her kneeling down to pray, in a black lace mantilla, exactly like Marlene Dietrich in the Garden of Allah. It's how I see Alberthe – does she look like that?" hopefully.

"No."

"Pity."

"She's seen me incidentally. And she has a sharp eye."

"We'll work on that – pass in the dark. The mouth a bit – ears sticking out – long black greasy hair – your own mother wouldn't know you."

"Suppressing Alberthe; without a lot of struggling or yelling. She's bright: the moment she sees the guards are changed – and she won't be duped by any tourist bullshit. By the way are we from Strasbourg? Anywhere round Baden-Baden a Bas Rhin numberplate wouldn't attract attention . . ."

"See to that, Orthez, would you."

Castang padded in cheek and lip, with ears like Jimmy Durante and hair like John Lennon in his Rasputin period, was fit to give anybody the giggles. Richard, with the wisp of hair pasted across baldness common to every senior French functionary, alopecia being the natural consequence of chicanery, was even better. It wasn't just clothes and a voice. The hands were made white, podgy and hairy – front as well as back, said Castang. Orthez' tendency to make bad puns (Staff Captain Ailleret had already become 'the IRA man') was extinguished under a hairpiece of a frightful metallic blond, odiously curly.

"You look like Lawrence Olivier as Hamlet," said Richard. "Three and a half hours in a blond wig and nothing to drink but poison." A large parcel of sandwiches was packed: they were all three to agree that the charcuterie Alsace butchers are so proud of is disgusting.

The giggling, like three children on New Year's Eve, was due to the knowledge that if one tiny detail of this kindergarten performance went wrong, was even seriously challenged (Staff Captain Ailleret might be a careful man, not content with a real police identity card presented upside-down) it was next stop Paraguay: three jobs as male nurses in Doctor Mengele's clinic.

It was just another police-judiciaire operation. Legality didn't enter much into consideration. You have, let's say, a group of bandits. You know – you have even proof – that they are planning a hold-up. But this is unsatisfactory. Under law you can only charge them with conspiracy, association of malfeasors. The penalties are piddling; a year or two in jug. Catching them *flagrante delicto* is another matter. If there is 'commencement of execution' that will fetch ten or twelve years and you haven't wasted your time. So you make a stake-out, and you wait (in circumstances generally of great discomfort since the bandits know about this trick as well as you do) for the fun to begin. A dangerous business; one in which lives get lost.

It was carried off by Richard with such aplomb that they never doubted it would work. Not even Fausta, who knew him better than anyone in the office, had guessed Richard would be so good an actor. Just getting out of the car . . . a mincing, important little walk. The phrases turned with protocolaire elegance that Staff-Captain Ailleret, though far from dense, never even thought of querying.

"Now these are suspect personages. And an incident upon German soil, you understand . . . Under the peace treaty this is military terrain and the Property of the Republic. But has that diplomatic status? – like an embassy? Has it ever been challenged in a court? No, and we don't want it to be. As for any incident involving the Military Government – I think you'll agree: not even the General should be told of this: it would worry him unnecessarily. I rely upon you. And I think I can promise you that my report, which goes to the Minister-President in person, will show up well on your confidential records."

Laid on far too thick, thought Castang anxiously, before realising with stupefaction that the more brazen, vulgar and impertinent mendacity becomes . . . will people swallow anything? Why not? We are living in a world, he thought bemusedly, where staggering quantities of information are stored in a silicon chip, instantly retrievable to every Jones or Schmitt who troubles to breathe on the button. The Secretary of State picking his nose there in Japan is beamed within a microsecond by satellite to the admiring gaze of Nuala O'Kennedy in Lisdoonvarna, while the ignorance and credulity of the world is unchanged since the day – 1240 or thereabout – of Pope Innocent IV – splendid name for Christendom's most egregious crook. He choked slightly, seeing Orthez' expression when sat down to dinner in the servants' hall and faced with a generous helping of curry . . .

Upstairs they weren't eating curry. Highly elegant spread, judging by the smells drifting in betimes from the kitchen next door, where a high-powered cook brought in for the occasion was dishing out the goodies, all arched neck and distended nostril like a fast-paced trotter. Was Richard dipping his finger into all the silver timbales like that clown up in Bonn who had discovered that gluttony compensated somewhat for the tedium of security?

Apart from the necessary passage of time (the dosage had been the subject of much argument: how do you go about enough-to-lay-out-a-buffalo without sending people off into dangerous coma?) Richard had foreseen a tricky moment when the dinner party broke up. Other guests had chauffeurs too – altogether a lot of eyes capable of indiscreet curiosity. Luckily the gorillas were a surly pair, disinclined for post-prandial conversation about automobile motors such as Orthez was ready to provide, or guff about security, his own charge. They shuffled off to play cards in the car. And the important gentlemen had come from their villas outside Stuttgart and Mannheim and Ludwigsburg: a tedious drive lay before them, and they were well-oiled as well as buttered. Off they went with a skittering of gravel while Richard's little delaying tactic came into play: Ailleret had been sent for a whisper in Alberthe's shellpink ear. 'Madame, there's a government official waiting outside who begs the favour of a brief word before you leave.'

Having made her goodbyes she appeared in the bright light of the

104

front steps. Castang, hovering, had to strain to overhear. The lady had not had too much to eat or drink – highly alert and plainly angry. Though in perfect control of herself there was a little line jumping at the corner of her nose. The large beautiful eyes, pale in the electric light, were observing Richard with chill scepticism. Castang belched – damn that curry – and held his breath. Ailleret, bowing and walking backward, ran quickly up the steps to wash his hands of these troublesome civilians. Richard, cool as an Arab sheik playing bridge, sidled towards her confidentially. She made a few steps, her satin skirt rustling in the stillness. The two gorillas were in a heap in the back of the car: quite safe; Castang had been feeling pulses.

"These two men have been drugged," said Madame de Rubempré, furious.

"I think it only too likely. As I told you, I suspected they'd somehow been got at. That enquiry however had better be left to Captain Thing – we don't want to embarrass the general."

"What is to be done?"

"By good fortune I have two excellent men at my disposal. The attempt is probably planned between here and the hotel. In my car you will be quite safe, and my man is armed. I think it best to allow this one to go back to the hotel as planned: we'll see whether any hijack is attempted. Parpaillot here can drive it."

"But if an attempt is made . . .?"

"These people, believe me, will be prudent. They will observe that the chauffeur has changed and smell trouble. Certainly they will withdraw – not at all anxious to attract the attention of the German police."

"But have you notified the German police?"

"Madame, believe that the French government would not be grateful for my doing so."

"There's sense in that." Richard bowed and opened the back door of the Citroën. And she got in. No miracle really, though Castang had been ready to imagine anything, down to asking the General for a motorbicycle escort.

"Follow the other car," loudly to Orthez, "at a discreet distance – take it away, Parpaillot." It is occitan for a Calvinist: Castang deplored this *nom-de-guerre* while admiring the invention.

He drove pompously back to the centre of the spa and into the hotel garage. The night man looked at him, though not mercifully into the back. Castang handed him the keys.

"Madame la Baronne will ring in the morning." The man nodded, reassured. It was a long difficult walk back to the Citroën, with nerves jumping in the back of his neck. "All well," he grunted, getting in beside Orthez.

The car turned. The woman in the back said nothing. Had Richard's piece about 'Imprudent to remain in Germany under the circumstances' been sufficiently persuasive? Orthez drove soberly enough until the turn for the autoroute, when he gave it all he had. For that sort of road there's nothing any better. It has an injection motor and five forward speeds, and at two hundred kilometres an hour sits as quietly as a nun riding a bicycle. They would be at the border in half an hour.

Castang had difficulty in sitting quiet as a nun, though Richard apparently had none. If that night garage man got fed up with his comic book . . . or if (a thing frequently observed and described) the smell of tension hanging round Castang's body as he handed the keys over alerted a subconscious alarm or unease, so that he got up and walked about . . . and flashed his torch in the back of the big Lincoln . . .

There was nothing to draw attention to the Citroën, but if they had a mind to the Germans could close that border post in no time, to anything up to a thirty-ton tank, an item of equipment they had omitted to provide.

They could still bluff through, presumably, on Richard's official card which being genuine should draw bows and salutes from any pisspot computer, even the dreaded machine in Wiesbaden. If the alert was given would the German cops be sufficiently impressed by French government credentials? 'A debatable point' had said Richard in a light, dry tone. 'I think that we should all be asked politely to wait while these unlikely tales were checked with the maximum of Wurtembourgeois exactitude. Nor, I think, would stories about the delicacy of our diplomatic mission make much dent in zeal. That is not the bovine rural constabulary, and the moment they hear of a terrorist alert the fastener goes zip. It's well-known that the Red Brigade sits in unobstructed comfort in France.'

'What would we do then?'

'Jump in the Rhine,' said Richard cheeringly.

Moreover there was the inconvenience of a passenger who far from serving as an extra diplomatic passport might start telling the Herr Wachtmeister to get her the Reichs-Chancellor's private number: that would never do. This dressed-up dame in the satin frock and the ermine fur; you couldn't just anaesthetise it and stuff it in the luggage compartment. 'Can't stand the smell of ether anyhow,' said Orthez. Richard's eye, lighting on the thermos of coffee accompanying the sandwiches, rested there in thought.

'Nineteenth-century methods are the best,'he had said, again. 'If you read old-fashioned adventure stories you learn that ingenuity is boundless.' And did Richard's literary tastes . . .? (New surprises every minute.) 'Oh yes,' mildly, 'when I was a boy on night duty.' He had a memory of something, of a totally loony melodrama involving Hanaud-of-the-Sûreté (perfect delight; hardly a model for the young and ambitious policeman but neither is Maigret: Hanaud is anyhow lots funnier). There was a young girl, wearing moreover a satin evening frock, who had to be brought across a border – Geneva to be pedantic – without her alerting the defenders of Swiss republican liberties. A gangster lady had quite a bright notion: balanced on her knee in the car she held a thermos flask – like this one – loaded with acid: how d'you like that, very 1900. But efficient, very, at enforcing mild-mannered silence from the young lady while the passports were being examined.

'Oh come!'

'What d'you mean Come? She's not to know there's nothing in it but coffee.'

'All we can do now,' said Castang despairingly, 'is hope that Miss Marple never gets to hear about this.'

'You wouldn't really,' said Orthez admiringly.

'What you want me to do?' patiently. 'Keep the nine-millimetre Walther bored into her ribs while the Germans conduct a body search?'

Castang admired Richard's way of showing them that once one began to Imagine things, there was no limit to fantasy. Madame de Rubempré, safe in the arms of the French Government, didn't welcome the curiosity of officialdom any more than they would . . . It steadied everybody's nerves. That empty thermos was still there in the door-pocket, stopping him from getting nervous giggles when he thought of it.

Orthez steadied the auto on the way into Kehl – the sort of road tempting one to go faster than the limit; fertile terrain for radar traps. At midnight? Unlikely, said Richard calmly, but respect the red lights just the same, my boy.

There wasn't a solitary soul on the German side of the bridge. No machineguns, grey-green uniforms, nasty-looking dogs: even the computer was sleeping peacefully, unlike the purse in the fairytale which screamed out 'Help! Master! Thieves!!' when touched. On the French side of the bridge was a glass box containing a cop sheltering against those draughts off the river, and yawning fit to break the windscreen, who looked at them with watering eyes and went 'Circulez' with the finger which, said Orthez, he scratched his crutch with. A German policeman would never scratch in public, even sitting down: we must be in France. There to prove it was the notice telling you helpfully which way to go to Join the Foreign Legion, especially if in a hurry because the cops were after you.

In France. They could no longer be pursued, tapped unobtrusively on the sleeve or taken openly by the collar. They had won. All three at this moment thought that what they had done was mad, wrong, silly, and they'd live to regret it, but nobody said so. First, the relief of tension: the two in front lit cigarettes without thinking. Richard, patting pockets for the tin box in which cigars lived, muttered something about Shortest way home Or – and bit it off into a mumble about turning left to avoid the city.

Alberthe hadn't thought much up till then but she hadn't fallen asleep despite a good deal to drink and the swift motion: too sensitive not to be affected by the tension in the car. It must have appeared normal to her that the Red Brigade would find her a plummy catch. Most people after all would have said nonsense: what interest could they possibly have in me? Richard had counted on this vanity, which had been basic to his entire plan. Most people too would find it difficult to believe that RG officials – it is not a body devoted to being Helpful to the Public – should be taking so much trouble. But there, she was accustomed to plenty of servants, to being well protected, and to having officials at her beck and call. She was in fact thinking of telling them where to go: she had plenty of friends in the area with hospitable houses. One would stay a day or so while the mishap was sorted out.

"Do you know Benfeld?" she said decisively, "That'd be nearest, I think." Really, they shouldn't be smoking without asking permission – that cigar was disgusting (she was not the first person to have this cross her mind, and the Citroën's ventilation leaves a lot to be desired). It was only half past twelve. And the story made rather a good one. Arriving in the middle of the night, wearing evening dress, looking regal, escorted by cops. Everyone would be entertained; 'it takes Alberthe' they'd say. She was imagining Jean's face when she said she'd come for a day or so's shooting. Her business in Germany was largely finished, too, and hadn't gone badly either.

No answer: she turned to Richard, deciding to be tolerant about that appalling cigar.

"Commissaire – I'm sorry; I forget your name." So had Richard.

"Moschenrosch," he said amiably. Autoroute nearly all the way, but it would take a few hours, and when would they get some sleep?

"Do your men know the way?"

"Oh yes. We're taking you home, you see. It's more prudent."

Slight frown: this did not quite fit the scenario, would take some time even in a fast car, and would create a small problem.

"No, I think I'd prefer – you see, I have of course no things by me. My friends will be delighted to give me what I need; but I shall of course have to arrange for my luggage to be collected."

"We'll see to everything, Madame." He wanted to keep her quiet as long as he could. The car had threaded its way through industrial suburb, turned out on to the Colmar road. Mulhouse to Beaune through the Belfort Gap, formerly a weary drag, would go smoothly at this time of night.

"I'm afraid I've made up my mind: will you be good enough to give the necessary instructions?" They'd be past Jean's village any second.

Well, she might as well learn that winter had arrived.

"My dear girl, I already have." Now at last Orthez had the car properly moving again, and it was freshly tanked. One saved public funds by tanking in Germany. It could of course be argued that this was cheating the French tax-collector; the thought amused him.

Alberthe was slightly speechless.

"Listen, friend, you have no doubt rendered me a prominent service and you must not think me ungrateful, but this is now an excess of zeal."

"Oh yes, very much so," letting the window down to throw the cigar-end away: Castang up in front there coughing pointedly.

"Then will you please do as I ask?" Puzzled still, but getting there. The old lady who saw something nasty in the woodshed, and tyrannised her entire family for years on the strength of it, had trouble too in realising when everybody decided enough was enough.

"Driver, stop," said Alberthe ringingly. Nobody budged. "Account for yourself," tigerish at Richard.

"With pleasure. You are sought as a material witness, and possibly you will have more to answer for, in a criminal investigation of a homicide and other matters as yet unexplained but certainly connected. You are being taken into custody on the authority of the magistrate instructing the affair. The means by which this has been effected were irregular, I agree, but there is reason to believe you anxious to evade explanation. Not the first time it's happened," cheerfully.

"But this is monstrous! And who are you anyway? – you're a masquerader."

"Taking that bit by bit, yes it is monstrous but amid so much else that is monstrous don't worry, it'll hardly be noticed. You will be there, you see, to confirm that in fact you came with me quite voluntarily. No more monstrous in fact than kidnapping little Viviane. As for who I am and the remark about masquerades you are led into error: I am a duly accredited agent of the law and so are my collaborators. Take care," as she put her hand on the door, "if you jump out you'll certainly kill yourself." It would be a day later that, refreshed by sleep, Castang remarked that this was a quotation, from the moment in *The Three Musketeers* when Milady is arrested. She won't convert me with psalmsinging either, said Richard, after due pleasure had been taken in this classical allusion. For the present he only added as an afterthought, "If you do jump out, that will of course save everyone a lot of trouble and would even be a sort of justice."

Alberthe said icily, "I'm going to make you regret the day you were born."

"Yes, they all say that. It's what the shrink calls a transference, meaning that you foresee the same emotion, if you aren't already feeling it. It passes. One comes to make the best of it." She decided to. She stayed still awhile before fumbling for her little handbag on the seat between them. She hadn't made this furtive, and Richard merely said, "You might just give me that. I don't really believe that you'd take the tiny gun to visit a general, and I wouldn't even think it was your style in day-to-day behaviour, but one takes reasonable precautions." There was nothing in it of course but her lipstick and a handkerchief. "Hanky?" he asked politely.

"May I have a cigarette?"

110

"Certainly. Not one of these? – no. Castang, have you got any?"

"Castang!" she said suddenly.

"Correct – you've one old friend in faithful attendance. You'll get to know both of us better. Only Gitanes, I'm afraid." She smoked it in silence.

"Do you intend to treat me with humanity?"

"That will be a matter entirely for you to decide but had better wait until we get in. Meanwhile think about it. Cooperate and so will we. You'll have to accept realities for once in a while." This time the silence was shorter.

"I put the question because I have a personal problem."

"Oh, I see," kindly. "The answer to that is we all have the same. In exact terms I can't let you out of sight hereabouts and don't wish for any scandal at wayside service stations. We'll stop on the embankment – look for a good place, Orthez – and we'll all get down in the field." The car drew up on the verge. "Not looking," busying himself.

"It's a small lesson," when they started again, "which you might ponder. There are laws: we respect them when we can. Governments in general show us an extremely poor example. So do you. Likewise there are laws of humanity. Despite a generally bad press we respect these too when we can. We do not seek deliberately to humiliate you or to hurt your personal dignity. You had better understand this early that it's a position that can arise. It will be entirely up to you. Once more, you and your friends haven't been respecters of human rights. A working man is very vulnerable in his dignity. You've always been protected. If now for a while creature comforts are missing, that's dura lex sed lex, meaning you never thought of that before but now you're going to."

"You'd torture me, would you?"

"Would you like to answer that question, Orthez?"

"Can't remember how to put it in Latin, but you bet!"

"Castang."

"We've all been to school in Montevideo."

"Let's see if I can remember any German – oh yes: Arbeit macht Frei."

"You're a sadist." To which Richard made no answer. When passing Besançon – the autoroute skirts the city – he remarked, "There was a boy here of sixteen shot by the Germans. They weren't sadistic about it. Let him write a letter home – childish, and

111

very good, of perfect dignity and nobility. It's fresh in my mind, the text. because it was quoted in the press. On the thirty-seventh anniversary of his death his mother committed suicide: that's just the other day. Evil goes on. Alas. My own first introduction to sadism was at the age of eighteen – the usual corporal in the army."

More time passed: Richard was feeling the desire to doze off. Alberthe, sensibly, had gone to sleep. She looked very nice.

"Won't be quite as tough though as she thinks she is," he muttered. "You asleep, Castang?"

"Yes," said that gentleman, who had taken his wig off to get comfortable.

"Stop for a coffee, Orthez, and when Castang's had a kip we'll change places."

While falling asleep himself in the vacated front seat Richard had another regression into the backwaters of youthful memory: this time a series of boys' adventure-books popular with the soldiery during the war years. The Saint! The Robin Hood of modern crime! The French child recognised that this was simply Arsène Lupin over again (the constabulary is perpetually bewildered) while failing to appreciate the Wimsey get-up, the silly-ass line of chat and the excruciating archness of dialogue; but amused by the fantasy common to this period of fantastic athletic feats while perpetually chain-smoking: by Bulldog Drummond out of Raffles, inspired by seeing Noël Coward in a dressing-gown.

Forever capturing villains, and giving them a good boot up the behind to teach them not to be beastly. Fond of floggings too, and greatly given to clonking people over the head so that 'presently they slept'. Presently Richard slept too, but his sleep was uneasy.

Castang did not sleep; neither did he dream. His job was to stay awake and this he did, humourlessly, professionally, unimaginatively. He had had enough of a doze in the front to keep his eyes from getting gritty. The most he allowed himself to think was that this job was far from being done. Anything else was too difficult. What Richard thought was presumably what a high-wire walker in the circus thinks, which is not about falling, whatever else it might be. What Orthez thought nobody ever knew: for long it had been popularly supposed that he never thought at all. This had been disproved by experience; he was good at keeping his thoughts to himself. At present he was sensible enough to hold himself on the level of technical concentration. One is not supposed to exceed a hundred and thirty kilometres an hour on a French autoroute. The drivers who do not respect this create a certain number of problems, made more intricate by the rather fewer in number that do. Beyond that, he felt pretty certain, Orthez was saying to himself that he had a day off coming to him, and driving this damn car all night meant he bloody well deserved it. As for the lady in the back seat, she was a parcel. To be tidily wrapped up, her contours well contained in enough string, addressed, franked, and posted. Next please . . .

While Castang had this flaw in his character: he was not able to bottle up. Ideas had to be spoken, thoughts pushed across to somebody else in order that something should be made of them. If something worried him he spat it out. There had to be a perpetual dialogue. No doubt of it, a grave weakness.

Richard who had slept neatly, like a cat, awoke as neatly on the outskirts of the city, said nothing, was his usual self-contained, urbane and wary self; as though the last twenty-four hours had been a dream, as though workaday reality had never been altered, as though the escapade had stayed where it belonged. One made a wish, in an idle moment. As in fairytale one got one's wish: it was then that the problems began. But no, all was as usual.

As for Madame de Rubempré she had woken too, as noiselessly, and was looking thoughtfully out of the window, as one does at a town never before seen, arrived at by night, signalled only by the growing clusters of unsleeping lamps, the slowing of the train and the joggle at the passages over points. One's eye is caught by figures bicycling through the empty streets. Where are they going at four in the morning?

Orthez put the gear softly down into third, into second as they reached intersections where the red traffic lights had been switched to wink yellow during the quiet hours. Made his turns as careful as forty hours before, when Richard had said laconically, 'Strasbourg'. They were home.

Orthez held the door politely for Alberthe, who managed her long legs and wide trailing skirt as neatly as though he had been the Ritz groom, stepping out as the carriage drew up. Dignity she did not lack. She said nothing. Whether the Duc d'Enghien said anything, getting out and stretching his stiffened legs at the Château de Vincennes, seems not to be known to history. This was a lot less ominous, being only the PJ offices. On the street side they look it is true most forbidding, for most of the windows are barred and masked by wire screens which collect dirt. But on the courtyard side it is a building like any other set of offices dating from the early nineteenth century; solid and calm, looking out upon a few trees through large well-proportioned windows kept fairly clean by the early-morning scrubwomen. She looked up at a window; by coincidence the same as that from which – how long ago now? – not long – Castang had gazed idly out at the blue hour of twilight, and seen Orthez, and wondered whether it was a wolf.

At four in the morning the PJ offices are not exactly a hive of activity: what staff there is makes coffee in the communications centre, puts its feet on the table, reads Saint-books and Batman-comics, the odd time getting through some neglected paperwork, the very odd time boning up on a legal textbook. The little orange lights on the phones and the telex and the computer terminal burn peacefully. The duty officer glanced up idly at the sound of footsteps, saw Castang and Orthez engaged in some nocturnal business – none of his, thank God – and through the glass panel of the reception-desk the top half of some biddy with long fair hair and a fur coat. Dropped his eyes again with complete lack of interest, missed Richard, whose presence at that hour might have prodded him. He was reading all about how they sank the Bismarck; finding it rather dull.

An unspoken agreement led them all to Richard's room – pretty well the only one where there were four chairs to sit on: Richard said first "Sit down", then to Orthez, "Do you know how to work Fausta's coffee machine?", as an afterthought, "Is there a can of Coca Cola in her fridge?" and then sat down himself, a simple action which transformed him from Captain Blackjack back into the Divisional Commissaire, instantly recognisable by the way he pulled a drawer half out from the desk, put a foot on it, and levered his body in the sprung chair back into an Ivory Tower.

There was a moment's silence: Castang found a packet of expensive Virginia cigarettes in the presentation crystal box on the table, and offered one to Alberthe, who was looking, for the circumstances, not a bit dishevelled, quite ready to go on to a nightclub if the gentlemen felt that way disposed. Himself he took a cigar of the sort kept for official visitors: the occasion seemed to warrant it.

"Two courses of action are open to you," in a routine drone. "The first is to express yourself willing to make a complete statement in

114

response to the questions I or Monsieur Castang will put to you concerning the disappearance and subsequent death of what was her name again, Castang?"

"Madame Viviane Kranitz."

"Just so, in which case it will be taken down in shorthand, typed up into verbal-process form, you will be asked to read it and sign it, and everybody can go peacefully to sleep: does this appeal to you? No? Well, you can reconsider your position at any time. In that event you become a non-person, you are held pending enquiry at my disposal. In a very old-fashioned-sounding phrase you are '*au secret*' which means that you see and communicate with nobody, present company excepted."

"If I am correctly informed, Commissaire, you have the right to do this for no more than twenty-four hours."

"And as-much-again with the approval-of-the-Proc, that's what the law says," drinking Coca Cola. "You're an outlaw, my girl, in the hands of outlaws, and I'll keep you here a month if that's the way you want it, and in the psychiatric ward at the end of that."

"You cannot withhold my right to a lawyer and a doctor."

"And an Indian Chief. Detention cell, Orthez."

"Coffee?"

"It'll wait." Silence.

Orthez returned with keys, chinked politely like a concierge waiting for a tip, said "If you please . . . along . . . down . . . through there . . . stop," unlocked a door and stopped himself, puzzled: he had never before had to lock up a woman in a long evening skirt carrying a little bag. Job for one of the girls, damn it. He went back to the cupboard at the end of the passage, found an overall and slippers.

"Can't leave you in that stuff. Change into these please. Call me when you're ready," found he'd forgotten the form for listing personal possessions, went back for it. "Bag with contents: one lipstick. You can keep the hanky. Sorry – regulations. Watch please. Rings. Ear-rings. Hairpins. Sorry – anything capable of doing yourself or others an injury. Night hours – you can make your bed. Here, blanket-sheet-pillow. Better get some sleep while you can: you'll be called to wash when the day shift comes on. Okay? Light out," suiting the action to the word. Does the old man really mean it? plodding back.

Castang had just asked the same question.

"Every last word of it. All right, Orthez, take your day off . . .
three hours' sleep, Castang? I'll give her one. And I guarantee you
I'll have your case for you inside six."

"What are you going to use on her, electricity?" Richard put the
coffeepot back carefully.

"You don't like it?"

"Physical abuse? – no."

"Then go home, if you can manage on your left leg."

"Meaning?"

"Your right arm and leg have gone into this already, so now if
you're feeling limp . . ."

"Look, the kidnapping can be covered. You wouldn't have done it
if you couldn't cover it. Fair enough; we're stopped in a lot of things
only when we can't cover them. To quote you, dura lex sed lex. Now
you've got her. Present her to the judge. It's as far as we go."

"Don't you ever use your brains at all?"

"I don't have any: you're the one that's bright. She's a stinking
fascist: we lean on her to make her spit it. What does that make us?
Puts us squarely in the boat with her, and that's where I don't want
to be."

"Castang," said Richard softly. He looked of a sudden very old
and tired. "You realise what you're saying. You're putting me in
with the Indochina colonels, who were sent out to Algeria and told
they were defending the soil of France. True, heaven knows. I didn't
understand them then, though I feel I do now. I was your age. I
thought them a pack of bone-headed barbarians, mouthing slogans
about the crusade against bolsheviks. Now, I understand something
of their bitterness. They had seen so many of the young – and always
the best – senselessly massacred, watering Vietnam with blood so
generously given – and what for? To please a handful of United
States Senators.

"Which of us is the wrong age? Myself, plainly. You are the right
age – how old were you in 'fifty-six, 'fifty-seven? So you grew up in
peace. I am to you a ridiculous figure. You have had a certain
entertainment in watching the old fool act a comedy part, recapturing
the glorious past. Resistance hero boring all the children stiff
gassing on about the good old days while sitting by the fireside.

"To you it's all clear. The world is worthless, and meaningless,
because what is right nowadays, and what is wrong, and what do
these words mean? – do they in fact mean anything?

116

"The enigma is that violence breeds violence, so that to reply to violence with more of the same is an inevitable escalade, and can never be right – isn't that so? I spent some years in trying to find the final, definitive illustration of this. Judith found it for me, because being Spanish she feels the problem touches her pretty closely.

"You aren't an operagoer, no and neither am I: I suppose policemen seldom are. There exists a work by this old chap Beethoven, yes, we've just about managed to hear of him. It's a simple story, unlike some. A man is put in prison – medieval Spanish fortress – and kept there many years unjustly through the malice of the prison governor, whose various crimes and extortions would be laid bare were this man at liberty. The man's wife, in a hope of finding a means towards his escape, disguises herself as a young fellow, gets a job as assistant jailer, and by being bright and willing arrives on the inside. Never mind the artificial contrived sound of all this: it's a stylised concept.

"Right, the news arrives suddenly that a high official is about to arrive, to inspect the prison conditions. This throws the wicked governor into a panic, the inspector being an old pal of the secret prisoner. He resolves thus to cover up by assassinating the chap.

"Orders are given to the chief jailer to dig a secret grave. Who does he choose as confidential assistant – the disguised wife. The grave is dug, down in the dungeon, the governor arrives, draws his dagger to go queek, the woman jumps up, puts a pistol to his head and says 'I am his wife!' Collapse of wicked governor, because at that moment the inspector arrives and all is betrayed. End of story, with happy wedding bells."

"I don't quite get the point."

"Neither did I. Judith came home from seeing this, crying very much, very wound up indeed, and after battering my eardrums a great deal – it seemed to go on for a week – said that what worried her was the girl's pistol. To come you see to the help of her man was perfectly right and proper, but to point a pistol at the villain's skull at the moment his dagger is upraised – that is violence. Therefore wrong. It takes Judith . . ."

"Women's reasoning," said Castang rather lamely.

"Quite so. You may as well go home, Castang. I'll do my own dirty work – including the digging of the grave," showing his teeth.

"No. Be too easy. I say I don't want to have anything to do with that, because it offends my delicate digestion, that would be like all

117

those intellectuals complaining about the Indochina colonels. Either I help you dig the grave, or I put a pistol to your head telling you to stop."

"And which is it to be?"

"There's something wrong with this logic somewhere," beginning to laugh. But Richard did not laugh.

"There's nothing wrong with it. We always break off, don't we? We can always find a joke, a pirouette, a play upon words – instinctive to us. We're servants of the state? We accept the familiar get-out? The all-too-notorious Reason of State? No. That is precisely the way the woman downstairs justifies her little conspiracies. A Committee of Public Safety, stepping in to save the state. When Goering became Minister of the Interior what was it he told his police functionaries? – 'I don't have to worry about justice.' All these reasons of state are the same. The State is corrupt, and does not deserve saving, but we are obliged to defend our concept of the state."

" *'Au nom du peuple français, justice est faite,* " quoting the executioner after he pulls the string.

"He used to say 'Make way for the justice of God'. Sentimentalism can't apply in this job. There's no liberal way out. You know, Simenon said he'd spent fifty years trying to make people understand that criminals didn't exist."

"He was right too, as all your experience and mine goes to show."

"He was only very nearly right. There are no criminals, but is there no crime? I am sometimes tempted to believe that the reason of state is the only one there is. It's lawful, is it, to go out and kill Germans, when the legally constituted head of the state says so? Faced with that one, back in nineteen-forty, I found it easy: I was just a boy. Now I wouldn't go to fight for my fucking fatherland and nor would you. Fight for the defence of your home and your family, would you? If the little green men were raping your wife you'd stand by and say you were a Buddhist? When they shot up your flat and sent you a kidnap threat on Vera you were anxious to believe it was all psychological warfare: how d'you feel now?"

"Caught," said Castang wearily. "All right, let's go down and get it finished with."

He went home that evening. Home to Vera. Home was an apartment, a tent, a wagon on the prairie. Home is where your heart

118

is. Your woman, your man, your child.

Vera. This young woman. Pleasant young woman, useful adjunct, complement, what-have-you, in the cop's wearisome and generally boring existence. An alibi. A comfort mechanism.

She was quite an advantageous young woman to have about. The advantages were balanced by a corresponding number of handicaps, yes. But on average . . .

He found himself looking at the young woman for the first time. She was shown, yes, in a grim, pretty unrewarding light in this stinking little apartment, worn by the fatigue and anxiety of the last days: he had known everything – well, all there was to know. She had known nothing. She was wearing the uniform of all young women, jeans and a pullover: the pullover was in need of a wash, and so was her hair.

As a young girl she had been beautiful in an exotic way, and an enterprising reporter had named her 'orchid' – 'Cattleya', that was it, inspired by the dashing colours chosen for the gymnasts' leotards that year. The half-childish face was piquant and pretty, but most of the beauty was in the unusual harmony of the bodily movements. It had been the time when girl gymnasts were still chosen for this quality, and not entirely for their childish fearlessness and 'short segments' – before the era of odious moppets who could do nothing but fly through the air with-the-greatest-of-ease. Nothing female allowed; no breasts, no hips, no bottom. Vera, already much too female, had only got on to the team as a replacement, even then.

It hadn't lasted long. Only a year or so later had come the accident, the broken spine, the paraplegia, the long harsh struggle for a basic human liberty; that of putting one foot in front of the other. In dealing with Vera – in thinking of her – one could not lose sight of the basic, bedrock quality of this life. Reduction to essentials; *dépouillement*, the absence of all unnecessary lines. Like all Frenchmen he was a complicator: she was a simplifier.

Childhood in a peasant family; hard work from the very beginning. Enough on the table, a bed in the loft with a sister, a great deal of love; and that was all. At five it was noticed that she could dance, at seven that her coordination and equilibrium were unusual. The village schoolmaster said a word to the authorities. Nothing unusual about that: they're on the lookout for girl gymnasts and boy ice-hockey players as early as they can get them. At eight she was taken for training by one of the big clubs, sent to boarding school in

119

the city. Kindly treated, and given to understand that a career of promise was possible. In the city there was a good art master: she saw for the first time drawings. At eleven there was talk of the Gymnasium made possible by a state grant: her parents were told that their sacrifice was a small price for this signal honour. At twelve she was being considered for the national junior team. A meteoric career. Bright, ambitious, hardworking child: everybody very proud of her. 'Your parents are nothing' they told her. 'The state is everything.' She felt, instinctively, unhappy about this. She loved her family, and she was fifteen when the Russians arrived. Next year she sat for the extremely severe entrance examination at the School of Graphic Arts – in later years she would wonder whether she would have been accepted were it not for being taken that year for the senior team. Had there not been another Vera – the splendid, the all-conquering Caslavska? Had not the great Larissa Latynina herself, after watching her on the bars, said 'Worth watching'? The village seemed very far away. But sixteen is an age very dangerous to girl gymnasts who grow too fast. The dread word 'morphology' got bandied about and all the trainers were beginning to look to smaller, younger girls . . .

At eighteen she was taken to an international competition as substitute – pinch-hitter for a possible team third placing: swamped anyhow by the Russians and Rumanians. She made a pig's breakfast of her balance beam, and angry words were spoken: obliterated, and by a pack of East Germans . . .

There was one reason – and the ostensible – for her running away. A dudgeon; a fit of childish pique. That year, however, was to be remembered for a good many children of this age throwing off passivity, angrily rejecting the hypocrisies of their seniors, denouncing the manipulations designed to make them patient, obedient cannon-fodder. What good were these parents, preaching their snivelling code to which they themselves gave the most superficial lip service? Vera's instinct had been to reject carrot, as much as stick. It cost her a great deal to cut herself from a home she loved (her parents cast her out, angrily condemning her wickedness and ingratitude) and a country whose soil had nourished her fibres. It was as much of a defeat as a victory. She turned to a man, the first personal relationship she had ever had, the more hungrily, eagerly. It is a compliment, thought Castang, to be given a girl's virginity, but it's a strain too to be told that you are the only one; there will never be

120

another; and to know that 'there's my blood on the bargain: never break it.'

The accident, then: the long weary months of helplessness and total reliance upon him. A university education. Female stubbornness teaching itself to walk, while teaching itself to draw, teaching itself English; and to be a wife. The wish for a child, masked behind a variety of 'jobs' – the work as an illustrator, the going out as prison visitor, which she was good at: was she not in prison too? The unselfishness with which she gave everything she had: under a self-control that compelled the respect and admiration of everyone who knew her was, too, the girl he loved. A happy girl of great simplicity and spontaneity. The girl who could not cheat on anything, who could not tell lies; quite literally incapable of saying an insincere thing or a false.

When she became pregnant, carried the child to term and bore it – in her words – efficiently, he was very happy. For himself, because the male does few constructive things, and the policeman on the whole does little better than the average. For her: now she would see that it was all worth the effort; that nothing in her long struggle had diminished or withered her; that the frost in May had not prevented the blood from flowering, fruiting. He looked forward to a serene and happy time of fulfilment.

It hadn't quite worked that way, what had gone wrong? Something biological, endocrinological? – earnest consultations; does having a baby do something odd to the nature of the beast? Why had she become so much more silent – severe, intolerant? What was this new puritanism? – there had always been jokes about 'Czech stalinism', but this . . .

During several months in which he told himself it was a passing phase a new, disturbing Vera had come increasingly into the foreground, and he wasn't sure he liked it. Hostile? Aggressive? – no, these were not the right words. But alarming, yes. However, he had been very busy – the Lasserre scandal, the upset in the usually comfortable routines of what is for nine-tenths of the time only office work. His promotion, which at first he had been happy with: he was less sure now. The need to introduce a new dimension of thought and care and activity. It is not only that there are now three-of-us where before there were but two: a baby is a time-consuming energy-sapping object, even viewed impersonally, and the first baby is always something of a tyrant. The worry about the flat being too

121

small. Lately there had been a good many things that would have to be thought about tomorrow, and increasingly a feeling of anxiety; that unless he began thinking about things today he might find it too late.

This wolf time had come at a bad moment. It was distracting his entire energies. And was taking an increasingly difficult turn. He wanted badly to have a day to stand back, to try and distinguish lights from shadows; to make sense of it. Events had followed too quickly upon the heels of one another. He had been pushed and harried. Increasingly, and accelerando, in a direction he hadn't wished to take. He had lost all control over his own actions.

That was something which happened to most people who tried to take any action following an event, instead of merely filling in forms about it. The sense of *engrenage*, of cogs catching the sleeve or the scarf and dragging one in, was inherent in a legal process, and what else is a criminal enquiry? But he had come slap up against politics. That is not a wolfpack. In this twilit jungle one cannot distinguish wolves from wild dogs, jackals, hyenas. Capitalist hyenas . . . ordinarily he would have been laughing at this wordplay, but he wasn't.

In the muddle of police work, which has so little to do with morals (the underlying paradox of all police work is that it is supposedly dictated by the Code of Criminal Procedure, or the Judge's Rules, or the Supreme Court's decision in the Miranda case: you might as well say the Book of Deuteronomy) Vera was of good counsel. He, and she, had made their minds up at the start that there were no hard and fast rules about bringing work home, or confiding worries. It was loose. He avoided dragging her into squalor, rubbing her nose in anything dangerous or, much more frequent, boring her with long tales of deplorable decisions reached . . . she would be the first to say 'Don't batter me'.

But she was there when he needed her. Was he not there when she needed him? They did not keep accounts of what each owed to the other. He needed her now. And he choked at the idea of even giving a hint of the day's work. There was a wedge driven between them.

Anyhow, the first thing that happened when he got home was a blazing row.

"Oh, you're back? It has doubtless not occurred to you that for the last forty-eight hours you haven't even deigned to give a word of apology or reassurance." How had that happened? It had totally –

but totally – slipped his mind. And how had *that* happened? He was taken quite off balance. I forgot . . . how lame did that sound. Unconsciously perhaps, but had he deliberately forgotten? All those whores in his life, and no wife.

I know I'm in the wrong. But why do you seek so assiduously to put me in the wrong, to keep me there? Why so unforgiving? Why was the tirade so bitter?

"A wife – am I a wife? Safely doormatted at last – now she's safely anchored, now there's a child to keep her busy, now she can be honey and sweetie and a tin of golden syrup, and open her legs wider because she was so happy to have a baby, and can't wait to get another stuffed up her fan?" Why so vicious? And it was most unfair that he was never able to get off the defensive.

"Gangsters came and shot me up, though that of course is simply public relations, the Corsican Liberation Front thumbing its nose at the police, but they of course are much more deserving of sympathy than this Czech drag-ass: I'll just keep my chin bravely up and say shining-eyed that I'll always follow whatever my man decides will be good for me, and if it's good for me to have a cop outside the door they're watching over me, and I have to be grateful."

"But what is it you want? That's what I keep asking, and never getting an answer."

"Want, want, that's all a man ever has in his skull, baby wants titty," furiously wrenching her bra open and snatching a startled child out of its nest, "baby have a good shitty, heigh-ho, that feels better; men, nothing but a pack of squalling babies wanting nice wifey to wipe their bottom for them." If only she wasn't so angry . . . "Go on, break a few glasses, an ashtray. Get drunk. Oh, she's so exasperating. Oh, such a tiresome woman." Castang did the first of these things, went and got a dustpan and brush, much tempted by the second.

"But it's never happened before, or at least hardly ever, and surely you realised that this job – it was very sudden too, I'd no time for more than the office toothbrush and – you must understand that a worrying time is compounded and made much more so when a threat was made at you – putting a cop out there, what d'you want, that I buy you a dog; what would you do on the street if somebody just gave you a push, sent you sprawling, calmly walked away with the child, I'm not doing it all for enjoyment."

Bed: sour: not talking to one another.

"When you can't speak rationally there's nothing for me but to keep silence, that way at least I'll say nothing I'll have to regret later." It wasn't an atmosphere in which he could purge himself of Alberthe de Rubempré.

Richard had been calm-voiced, detached.

"You are in the hands, Madame, of the Red Brigade. As you are aware there are a great many, of every type and tendency. You can call yourself a hostage if it pleases you. These affairs can be carried out for publicity, or defiance, what does it matter? One extracts what leverage there is. In your case there is information, to be extorted, by whatever means I think fit. I can blindfold you, isolate you, give you salted food and nothing to drink, strip you and turn the heating off – it will be in the day's work. It would be the simplest affair to tie your arms above your head until the circulation fails, and repeat that. I shall not stop short of inflicting pain upon you, if that is what it takes. Above all I can keep you here for as long as I please: a month or a day is all one to me. You will be missed? Enquiries set discreetly afoot? I am indifferent: there is no way in which you can be traced. After your release, you will make a claim that you were kidnapped by the police? The claim would not be welcomed; nor would it be believed. I can furthermore arrange for you to be given as a present to a real Red Brigade. They'd be delighted to have you, and would doubtless enjoy setting a high ransom.

"Make however the affair brief, and it will be of more comfort to you. You have something to say? . . . What I want is simple. I want the names of those responsible for the capture and eventual death of Viviane Kranitz, and the evidence to make it stick . . . because make no mistake: this is going to be answered for. If this puts you in a position of self-incrimination, that will add to your griefs. I am concerned with nothing but rapid results, and the means to check the information you give me. If they are less rapid, the verifications more difficult, the delay will turn to your undoing. You will be woken at hourly intervals," said Richard, turning on his heel and walking out. Castang took a look through the peephole before turning out the light. Alberthe was sitting straight, her knees together and her hands in her lap, the big pale eyes looking straight out before her, resolute.

"Classic technique?" asked Castang when they got back upstairs.

"That's right. I don't want to use physical violence on her if I can

124

avoid it; I'm not a savage. Give her three intervals exactly on the hour, then when she's acclimatised make it half-hour, two or three. Then when she's braced let her have four hours' quiet and repeat the dose," yawning hugely. "Mm, go take a kip. I'll have plenty to occupy me with what Fausta has on her desk. Say about midday you spell me. I'll take till eight this evening, you go off then till tomorrow morning. I'll spend the night with Ladybird. If she sings earlier, then book her and let her sleep as much as she wants."

"I understand."

"Do you? It's got to be the real thing. If she grits her teeth and holds tight, that's to the good. If she starts imagining scenarios, trying to pull the roof in by involving Vibert or the Minister or God knows who, then you know how to handle that."

"Not altogether a novice."

"You'll feel better," said Richard kindly, "when you've had a rest."

"I thought you were keeping that line for her."

"Come come, Castang."

"What about the loose end in Germany?"

"Exactly. When those two wrestlers awake from deep refreshing sleep they should have a considerable headache, a thorough bewilderment and a growing sense of consternation. Quite possibly too some explaining to do: the garage fellow will be puzzled but concluding they were only drunk. The lady baroness isn't in her room? Well, her luggage is, and she's hardly a bad security risk. What do Laurel and Hardy try? They run round to the Army, and find that tight lips prevail all round. They're at a loose end; no instructions, no Alberthe. To avoid creating an even bigger uproar they'll try to behave as though the situation was normal: go turn in that car, pick up their plane, return to base. No? When they do we'll be ready for them: it will have occurred to you too that this pair is very likely of further interest. Wasn't them who knocked off Viviane, but they'll know who else does these little jobs. We should be able by then to use her to verify their statements."

"And Kranitz?"

Richard shrugged.

"Piano, piano. We've all we can handle on one plate for awhile."

There were plenty of places suitable for a siesta, beginning with his own office, and would that be too noisy once the day shift came on? Well if Richard could shrug so could he. He could of course always go downstairs, find an empty detention cell next to Alberthe's, hang a Do Not Disturb sign on the door. It would be nice and quiet down there.

Before falling asleep he wondered vaguely what pretext Richard would find for hauling in the crew of the plane. Mm, it was one of those occasions for finding that packet of heroin under a seat cushion; the one kept in Richard's safe, brought out and dusted for occasions like this. The whole damn plane would be sequestered... he was asleep.

The little alarm on his wrist woke him: he'd unhooked his phone. Richard who always lunched in the office was breakfasting instead.

"Fausta sent a girl to the baker for you." There was cheese in her little fridge, and a smoked fish wrapped in alufoil, and some tomatoes. There were two rolls as well, sliced with ham inside.

"That for the patient?"

"Bring it down when you've eaten. You can be the kindly one. I've been a Nasty Nazi all morning; it's time to change gear on that. Be a bit sympathetic."

"Anybody know she's here?"

"They know someone's there," laconically, "or what would I be doing in the basement all day, watching changes of temperature in the white mice? Fausta will keep her mouth shut."

"No sign of giving?"

"Holding all in one piece, refusing to utter. When she gives it will also be in one piece."

The alternation of kindliness with nastiness is likewise a classic. This much in fact is all common form. What is politely termed interrogation is of course a form of torture. It is the reason why so many people afterwards claim that they were confused. One doesn't have to tell the truth. The police don't even expect it. The truth will come out later, in the quiet room of the instructing judge. But the police want a story. Refuse to give them a story, and they will become unpleasant. There's nothing much right about this system, but finding a better is not easy either. It is like any situation where a business man seeks to gain at least a verbal advantage as grounds for striking a good bargain. One must not sentimentalise the role of the police.

"Hot," he said about the coffee," and still fresh. This bread's not bad either. It's what we eat ourselves ... You refuse? I make a note for the file: offer made and ignored."

He sat down next time, made himself comfortable, lit a cigarette.

"You make the mistake, you see, of treating us like a pack of imbeciles. You might say that was natural, looking at me, but you were a bit too confident, as good as saying outright we were helpless – you've only yourself to thank, now.

"Nothing but circumstantial evidence against you, so nothing that will hold up in court? Error, if you'll take a bit of friendly advice. Once we didn't believe that Viviane Kranitz had been kidnapped by any Red Brigade – your bad luck there that you're hoist with the same petard – odd expression that – you didn't dare hang on to her any longer. Thinking that she was in that case a direct witness against you, once she realised that Vibert had let her down and that she was being manipulated, and plainly she did, you made the further mistake of having her killed. Even there; you've got a damned great piece of land to bury her in. We would have found her eventually, you think. Yes, perhaps. But setting her on the street like that, trying to reinforce the Italian-assassination scene, that wasn't clever. There are a couple of cops left who won't lie down for it, and I'm not talking about Italy. The boss I'm afraid is pretty much embittered about you, and disinclined to be his usual sweet self. The longer you wait, the further it gets stacked against you.

"I'm easygoing myself – I don't want you to have a rough time. But heaven help you, when the boss gets back this evening."

Next time he was quite chatty.

"Well, well, hot news. Those two clowns of yours who got left in the car have been behaving foolishly. Where can the Frau Baroness have got to? – telling the Germans the Red Brigade must have got her. Following upon the dastardly slaughter of Madame Kranitz, yet another ghastly outrage. German police much perplexed, not giving that to the press, but it's sitting on our private telex. Two clowns arrested for possible complicity. That's all for now but have nice dreams. I'll keep you posted with all the latest developments."

Thoughtful and academic.

"It's a very funny thing, circumstantial evidence. I had nothing to do much, so I've been reading up on one of the police classics. Nineteen-sixty-two and it wasn't till '66 that they got it untangled. Set records in police manhunt annals. I suppose the English will have beaten that since, with their Yorkshire Ripper. Probably much the same thing happened there. Was in Boston, the Strangler. The cops had three or four candidates who fitted so damned well that it frightened them. Circumstantially each one fitted the picture down to the last detail. The real strangler of course didn't fit any of the elaborate psychological projections at all. Then there was Doctor Lawrence Shaw. A woman he'd been sleeping with, and boy did he come to regret that little human frailty, felt a bit vexed at his throwing her over. She managed to persuade the entire apartment block, what am I saying, practically the whole neighbourhood, that he was a cannibal sexmaniac. Gave him a frightful time, until he had the sense to go to the cops and come clean. Career ruined. I wonder what happened to him – perhaps he managed to pick up the pieces again in another part of the country.

"Just shows you – circumstantial evidence, especially when fuelled by malice, can be a very dangerous and damaging business. To bring the authorship of a crime home to the satisfaction of the Assize Court, one has to do better than that."

Around seven she spoke for the first time. He had been ready to shut up shop, and tell Richard that they'd have to be patient.

"You'll have to kill me. You won't dare to let me go."

"Which will be the lesser evil? Saying that does demonstrate how little you grasp. There's a good deal of re-educating to do."

Punctually at a quarter to eight Richard appeared, looking exactly as he did at a quarter to eight in the morning ahead of any working day.

"I think a bit of a split is beginning to show," reported Castang: "she began talking."

"The Stockholm syndrome my boy; psychological dependence. She'll be in love with you by tomorrow morning."

"What's that, something for me to dream about? She's beginning to think about being let go, and what will happen if . . ."

"Leave her to me."

"I've been wondering about it myself." Richard's smile was a winter sun on a snowed-in landscape. Still; sun . . .

"Worrying, are you? Where are the witnesses? What will the Army say? Do you see the good Staff-Captain compromising the promotion by telling people there were these two characters, see, making out they were RG inspectors? If there is a German police enquiry, on account of Laurel and Hardy full up with barbiturates, you think the Army will eagerly be saying, 'Yes, actually, we arranged that'– do you?"

128

"And what will she be saying?"

"Really, Castang, I neither know nor care. We drop her off somewhere, in the middle of the night, dressed as we found her, let her make her own way home. If she wants to construct a fantasy about gangsters seizing her for ransom . . . since she dreamed up a Red Brigade earlier who seized Viviane Kranitz she can say they did the same to her. She can say she's suffering from amnesia. Or she can efface the whole thing – it never happened – she's been staying with friends."

"And if the judge wants her, as a witness?"

"You think he'll want her, do you? Well I think I can demonstrate to him that that wouldn't be a very good idea, and I think when he thinks about it he'll agree. If she manages to avoid an inculpation herself for conspiracy, and she's smart enough to plea-bargain herself out of that, then she's a prosecution witness, and will she fancy herself in that rôle? To avoid indictment as co-defendant she's got to sing. I'll explain the facts of life to her. Well, go on home; your wife will be waiting for you."

"Oh my God."

"Oh your God what?"

"I forgot to warn her when I'd be back."

"So she's been keeping the hamburger hot for three days now," said Richard grinning. "It'll taste delicious."

He had woken around four, the bad time; struggling in the grip of black depression. Every imaginable scenario for catastrophe screened itself implacably in the dark room. Real RG inspectors, not nice people at all, had arrived and were quietly taking Captain Ailleret to pieces thread by thread. Alberthe had committed suicide and he had to take her body out to bury it.

A fierce wind gusted on the windowpanes: there was a rattle of icy rain. It had suddenly become a great deal colder. The cold settled round Castang's heart.

The whole situation – the entire business from the beginning . . . Bad, bad, and wrong. From the very first false step, at the moment when Marc Vibert had appeared in his office with a series of tales each more ridiculous than the last. He, Castang, had compromised then, accepting the whole cancered web of hypocrisy, of cover-up and face-save. It was as though every breath he had drawn since was straight from the foul mouth and the rotted teeth of corruption.

Shit all over the wall, and what he had done was plaster it over with more. Cover every inch, telling yourself that that was the way it had always been and now nobody could notice. Worse; that that was the way it ought to look. Looks fine now. Like new. Goes well with the curtains.

Vera, in bed with him, snored slightly, turned over, slept again deeply. She would guess – no; there was no guessing about it. She would know. She knew already there were things he could not tell her, things she must not be allowed to . . . her senses were acute, and especially her sense of right and wrong. You don't make a wrong come right by adding more wrongs in a hurry until the original one is indistinguishable from the rest.

So hide. Hide behind Richard. He is your superior officer. He gave the orders, thought out the tactics, understands the strategies. A senior officer, of immense experience and ability. And he had been to Paris, talked to the Sous-Chef, and the Coordinator, to those more senior still, who understand politics, have a line to the Minister, know what can be spelt out and what can't.

Even if anything came out, even if everything came out . . . Not that it would. He could not be brought down, without dragging down Richard, and Richard would not be dragged down . . . What had they done anyhow? Anything that hadn't been done, and plenty of times, before? In the Vichy time, the Resistance time . . . it was as Richard said, you were freed from your oath. The existing government was too cowardly for anything but compromise, spent all its energies in searching for formulae to save its face. Legal, illegal; moral, immoral: good God, it meant nothing any more.

The more reason, Vera would say. In such a time the rightness, the wrongness, of what you do personally – individually – that is what counts. There is no phony argument about Society accepts, therefore I can . . .

He got up. Nothing for it, no sleep any more. Take a shower. Have a proper breakfast. Shave, make a new face, wipe all this off with strong and strong-smelling alcohol. Cold water today is not enough.

It was not rain, it was not snow. Sleet, bad-smelling, blowing in his face, sticking to his coat. Not cold enough for anything to lie. A viscous, dirty slush, turning to mud on the street. Orthèz would be in today; get Orthez to put snow tyres on the car. Blowing from the north-west like this it would go round into the north. It would get cold.

Richard was in the office, coasting through paperwork, studious and uncomplicated as a bookkeeper. When he saw Castang he drew a line to mark his place, made a marginal note before laying the pen down with a gentle smile, bland and crafty, of the man with the bobtail flush raking the pot in.

"She's had a nice sleep," looking at his watch. "*Tiens*, you're very early. Well," magnanimous, "she's all yours. Asked for you. Wants you. There'll be bargaining to do. We'll let her down as gently as may be. She'll give you no further bother. Orthez'll be in this morning. He can type it all up."

As long as it's over, thought Castang. I don't think I could have stood another twenty-four hours of this.

He installed himself in his own office. It was the day for winding his clock. Everybody should have a country clock. His had an amiable enamelled face a bit chipped around the keyholes and a wide, comfortable brass thorax behind, a rather elaborate pierced pendulum. The glass could do with a clean, the wooden case with a coat of polish. It had a deep-throated Guernsey cow sort of note to its dong, mellow and attractive. Somebody had frigged with it once, turning it on – to his fury – to Summer Time: repudiating all such indecent notions it had literally rung midday at fourteen hundred ever since. Being old and worn it lost seven minutes each week. Much to his pleasure. Like other civilised persons he was contemptuous of the technocratic monomania about gaining time, the illusion of doing things faster and faster, winning a second as though it were a golden guinea, the white-rabbitry of How Late It's Getting. If some kind soul had given him a digital clock, counting him down with nervous jerks (hundredths racing lunatically as at ski-competitions) he would have flung it out of the window. Once, as a young sub-inspector, he had bought himself a Rolex; wasn't that what men of action were supposed to have? Six weeks later, in a reject phenomenon as simple as vomiting, he had thrown it across the room. Unbreakable? – I'll show you. He had learned since to let time pass and like it. Life was too short to worry about dying.

Liliane came in, to talk about a piece of business he had turned over to her upon engaging in politics, it being understood that politics left one no moment for thinking of the polis. She was

131

elaborately over-tactful about not mentioning the Prisoner in the Basement: everybody in the PJ knew it was there, but it belonged in the private safe in Richard's room. There were jokes (centring of course around Fausta's desk) about the Man in the Iron Mask. Shrieks from shuttered room. Bloodstained footsteps in snow. He went to get Alberthe's breakfast.

"Where's Orthez?"

"Don't know; haven't seen."

"Ring his flat."

"Doesn't answer. Ill maybe." Annoying of him.

"*Angine*." Handy French expression for the diplomatic virus: Her Gracious Majesty had a slight cold and will be keeping her room for a day. Feeling acutely streptococcal himself he supposed he could hardly blame Orthez: why should he have to empty a commissaire's pot? Obeying perhaps a healthy instinct if he was spending the morning in some doctor's waitingroom, reading his horoscope of three months earlier in a *Paris Match* with half the pages torn out. I seem to be having this problem with wind after meals.

"Coffee."

Alberthe had her small problems too. He liked her the better for this one; a slightly rancid smell of female in the narrow cell, a rattail look to the long blonde hair. She looked at him with despair in her face and he felt pity. No, another twenty-four hours would have finished me. Orthez is right. She made a great effort over her pride.

"I'd do almost anything for a wash." He nodded. The moment was not one to turn the screw on her humiliation.

"I'll see what I can work out. Drink your coffee," kindly.

Fausta? No, not Fausta, reliable though she was: it would not be fair on her. He patted his pockets for petty cash. He wouldn't get this one reimbursed: was that, in the circumstances, very awful?

Down the street there was a Prisunic. Castang bought a towel, a toothbrush, a plastic dose of shampoo, a packet of tampons, three underpants in a cellophane envelope with flowers on it. Back in his room he mulled a bit, put his own comb and toothpaste in the paper-bag, after a small struggle his own Roger-&-Gallet, remembered at the last moment soap. At the end of the row of detention cells there was a place with a washbasin. There was hot water but . . . He raided the cleaning-women's broom cupboard, found some Vim and Eau de Javel, both badly needed; scrubbed unsmilingly. He checked all the other cells. Nobody there. The two pillars, driver and guard, had been taken down to the House of Detention. Nobody believed they had killed anyone: Alberthe was too clever for that; but a narcotics charge will do to hang any dog for a week or so. He unlocked her door.

"Half an hour: okay?" putting the paperbag down.

Being mean, with his expensive eau-de-cologne (one of his small dandyisms)? Not altogether. He had to balance the rule saying nothing in glass bottles – prisons being what they are, people in them have been known to cut their wrists, and worse – against a notion that it might give her a valuable psychological jolt in the right direction. The criminal lawyer Mr Jaggers (of all Dickens' characters his lawyers are the most terrifyingly real and instantly recognisable) used to wash Newgate off his hands, scrubbing lengthily with 'scented soap'. Castang's alcohol peeled crime off his weary face and eyelids. Perfumes are potent medicine. Bringing her back, momentarily, to the world she had quitted . . . Make no mistake; a day and a night in jail will alter your thinking profoundly. Alberthe had had two.

She had been lavish with it, and in the narrow cell it was potent. The little window high up, quite a big window but shared with the cell next door, shed a bleak morning light, of a grey sharper than sunlight, on a face puffed as though by blows of a boxing-glove, and whose component parts held precariously together. The very good-looking woman in the mid-thirties (Alberthe was forty-one) would be sixty-five come Sunday, and had looked at herself in the glass. She could not put the towel, which was soaking wet, around her head: she'd combed her hair out and let it hang. The regulation prison dress was too short for a long-legged woman; her bra and stockings had been removed according to rule; she sat on the edge of the mattress, clasped her hands over her bare knees and tried to smile. Castang, standing just inside the door, picked up the paper-bag and said, "I'll trash this, right?"

"Burn it," toneless. She looked at him blankly and said, "That man. He brutalised me. He tortured me. You – you at least have not done these things. I must thank you. It's something, to know there's a scrap of humanity and decency left." Castang nodded, stonefaced. A pair of interrogating policemen have been known to spin a coin: which shall play the baddy? It is not a rôle they care for. With exceptions: there will always be exceptions. He had been shocked, a little, by the apparent relish with which Richard had taken the rôle over. He would have been wondering, but for knowing a few things that Richard did not speak of; that Judith, his wife, had spoken of to Vera. But Vera was like that: people said things to her that had been kept silent.

"As a young man he was in the Resistance. Those killed were luckier than those captured."

"He stripped me," said Alberthe. He did not think she meant physically. He preferred though not to ask.

He didn't care about being a good guy to make Richard out a worse guy. Nor did he like this querulous, self-pitying tone.

"His wife," he said slowly, "went as a child through the camp in Perpignan. Her father was killed. At the sack of Malaga she saw her mother . . . and herself . . . fourteen years old. Left its mark."

"I wasn't even born then." No, he thought, you were a sort of victory celebration.

"In the seventeen hundreds they were still burning women for witchcraft. None of us were born then."

"I don't understand."

"Only that the evil goes back, a long, long way. I'll go and get my pen."

Perhaps it was as well Orthez had not come in. It might have struck a jarring note, taking her up to one of the offices, having a stenographer typing. He went upstairs for a pad, a ballpoint, a cassette recorder. Goes back a long way? What had he meant? Goes back to once-upon-a-time-forever, no? Hearing of the incredible barbarities of past times made you think there was some progress. Small but there. Hearing of the barbarities of yesterday – today – no, we are just the same. Is there any way at all . . .?

He sat on the mattress too, the recorder between them.

"In case," tapping it, "we disagree about wording, when you come to read over what I write."

I do things I can't tell my wife. Richard won't have told his wife either. Would he even think 'I won a bit back for you, there'? Of course not; he was not childish. It was necessary: that was what he thought. And that is the reasoning of governments: aha, necessities of state. I am part of that. Remember what Richard said. We are outlaws.

Wolves had been given a bad name. If they ever deserved it, which they did as much as any other animal at all, neither more nor less, it made no difference to them. They were – are – that way. A biological necessity. Whereas we . . . we have souls, though we prefer not to think about them. We have free will, though we'd rather we hadn't: it is so much pleasanter to think along deterministic lines. We can choose. If we choose, it implies a choice, to be made. The word 'moral' is far from fashionable, but can never quite be obliterated no matter how we try to bury it beneath derision or denial.

Vera reading, suddenly reading aloud.
" 'The world turns and the world changes,
But one thing does not change,
   In all of my years, one thing does not change.
   However you disguise it, this thing does not change,
   The perpetual struggle of good and evil.' "
Long silence.
"Yes. What's that?"
"Man called Eliot. American poet."
"Oh . . . lousy poetry."
"Yes, but that still doesn't change the thing."
"No."
When Richard had suggested his simple, neat, compact idea of slipping across the border and gathering Madame Alberthe de Rubempré into a bag, Castang had thought, or more accurately not-thought, awhile.
"Not very prudent, is it?"
"The time is past," grunted Richard, "for being prudent." As though it were a dirty word. Which of course it is.
Sitting one day one on each side of the cradle, rocking it with his foot, a thing Vera found hard to do, she said suddenly, "What sort of world will she grow up into?"
"The same as ours. A hair's breadth better, a hair's breadth worse."
"But more dangerous."
"More? Ah, yes certainly. More? It looks like it. Were we wrong, to make her?"
"It turns, it changes, it doesn't change."
"When one is young one thinks it does. Maybe it does. When one is young is the only chance. And it has to go on. So we weren't wrong, to make her."

135

Vera had quoted then a better poet, Jacques Brel.
" *'Jojo nous parlons en silence d'une jeunesse vieille,*
Nous savons tous les deux que le monde sommeille
Par manque d'imprudence.' "

"I've typed this up," said Castang. "The law enjoins that I read it
to you. Sign each page. And at the bottom there's this paragraph,"
colourless, "stating as you confirm that no pressure has been put
upon you or inducement held out, and that you have been treated
throughout with the humanity the law demands."

"I have to sign that," with a return to the ironic voice he recalled
from their first meeting.

"Just so," said Castang. "Perjury by all means. But the important
part isn't, and that is what the judge will want to know."

She took the pen and signed.

"The English phrase 'helping the police in their enquiries' has
always appealed to me."

She looked at him in silence.

"Your momentary absence from society," went on Castang
rather awkwardly, "is as consistent and plausible as you choose to
make it. You went off to think things over. What else is needed since
the press need never get any of this, unless you choose to challenge
it? We release you to the judge, who takes your cooperative attitude
into account in agreeing to your liberty as the price of your silence
henceforward. You can be home this evening."

"I am tired," she said dully, "I am tired."

"Have a sleep. I'll leave you your mattress."

He went upstairs and rang Richard. The hell with his being
asleep. Let him wake up.

"And with your permission," finished Castang, the wheels now
beginning to grind very heavily, "I'm going to take the day off, or
what's left of it. My wife hasn't been happy with me lately."

"Yes," agreed Richard, "you've earned that and so has she. Take
her out to supper; I daresay one of the girls will sit in for you. One is
bound to say one feels relief – and reaction. I'll have Salviac pick up
these characters: illegal organisation for a start, isn't that the neo-
nazi group that attracted attention in Paris? Possession of arms and
explosives will do to hold them on: these must be your mysterious
persons in Arab costume. Good, they shot your flat up. I think it
quite likely that we can make it a Safety of the State thing, in which

136

case the hearings would be in camera, sparing, possibly, the tender feelings both of Madame de Rubempré and her friends."

"And ours."

"And as you say ours. She's asleep? Where by the way is Orthez?"

"Nobody seems to know."

"Struck down," understandingly, "by the Bangkok influenza, very virulent. Having shelled my own peas I can go cook them, hey? I dare say I'll find a means to forgive him. Question of getting la Baronne out of here, and I'd prefer no further witnesses . . . oh, all right." Castang still sitting there; stolid, stupid, generally unhelpful. "I'll get the judge to meet us on neutral ground, aha, and she must have a maid or someone she can trust, to come and pick her up."

"I'm hungry," said Castang looking fixedly at the clock.

He parked the car. There wasn't any cop in the lobby, nor on the upstairs landing. They nipped in to Vera, who was sorry for them, on the pretext of a pee, looking for sympathy, cups of coffee, and a small relief from boredom: he was not inclined to reproach them for this small laxity in discipline. While yawning and trying to put his key in the lock upside down he heard the child yelling; working up a great head of steam and what was Vera about to let it yell like that? He opened the door and stopped dead. He had found out what Orthez was up to.

Very slowly he walked, upon leaden legs, through to the bedroom. Lydia was in the cot. Holding on to bars and bawling and gulping and in a frightful mess from head to foot. He picked her up, sat down, rocked her and cuddled her and talked to her. There was no point in looking round the flat for clues-and-things. He sat, and held on to the child, and rocked slowly to and fro with his eyes shut until she fell asleep from sheer exhaustion. Gently then he put her down. Needed a wash. Needed clean pants. Needed very likely something to eat. Just like Alberthe de Rubempré.

After what seemed a long time of staring dully at the wall opposite – there were no pictures in this bedroom yet and it struck him how like a cell it was – he reached numbly for the telephone and dialled.

"Liliane there? Well, who is? She'll do; put her on . . . Maryvonne. I'm in the flat. You'd better come over here. You'd better bring an ambulance. And you'd better bring Richard. Yes, I know. But tell him – tell him I found Orthez." He put the telephone down and went on sitting.

Maryvonne was a thin girl, with gingery fair hair. Young, without very much experience as yet. But a fast learner.

"Don't drink. Wait just a sec – something hot, milky and sweet." How had she got in? wondered Castang.

"The door was open. You left it open. I'll get the ambulance intern to look at you. Richard will be here in a minute."

"Is he dead? I don't want any intern. Tea will be all right."

"No. Coma. They think skull fracture; those are the clinical signs. They'll make X-rays, of course. Don't worry about Lydia, I'll look after her. Look out, that might be too hot."

Richard entered. Unchanged in voice, eyes, walk, manner. Looking very old. Castang stared at him.

"There'll be no need to make any enquiry, Maryvonne: in fact I know already, simply from fending off a nosy neighbour, that this is the second ambulance to call today."

"It wants its dinner," said Castang. "You'll find some goo in the fridge. Meanwhile give it a crust to gnaw on. It likes that; good for its teeth."

"The first thing it wants is a wash and clean trousers. Come on, poppet."

Richard leaned down, took Castang's head between his palms, and said, "Look at me."

"One, two, three, infinity."

"What's that?" fairly sharply.

"It came in my mind, it's the title of a book I bought in an effort to understand mathematics. I didn't. I mean I don't, but I understand other things. They kidnapped Viviane. We kidnapped Alberthe. They kidnap Vera. Next stop is ten to the power of six, called I forget what but it's a handy means of expression for you-wonder-where-it-stops. Sorry, I'm all in. Give me some more of that disgusting tea, would you? I must have some cigarettes somewhere."

"I'm not going to fuck you about, Castang. They haven't hurt her. Nor will they. They want Alberthe back intact."

"We were just a wee bit too confident, is that it?"

"Castang, don't roast me on the fire I myself built. It could just as easily have been Judith."

"Yes I know, I'm sorry."

"The best thing for you is to go to bed and get some sleep. Maryvonne will stay here. Are these your pyjamas? Come on kid,

138

lift your arse up and get those trousers off." He was past resisting. He did what he was told.

"I got this pill off the ambulance intern. Don't worry, it's nothing but a sedative, good old classic nembutal. You sleep, you hear me? And have confidence. I'm not totally without resources, as you perhaps don't know but will come to realise."

"What resources? The minister?" with a contempt, and a hopelessness in the one word that said much.

"No, dear boy. Vibert. They've left themselves quite naked, you know. This was pinned to Orthez' jacket." A typewritten paper.

'We bring back the empties – herewith one PJ inspector, slightly dilapidated. We did some shopping. If we decide, afterwards, we want to exchange the goods then this, it has to be understood, can only be for goods in perfect condition and the original packing.'

Vibert, thought Castang aimlessly, yes I know who that is. But it has all got into a state of . . . I've been turned round so often I don't know which way I'm facing.

"Don't do anything to Alberthe."

"Don't worry boy. We'll be very, very careful."

"Don't do anything at all." There was more he wanted to say but he was too disoriented. That word he found; a good word; but the simple words, the ones he wanted, eluded him. It was too much of a struggle.

Dreams? Did he dream, or better had he dreamt? Couldn't say, couldn't recall. Not that I am aware. This is my bed. This as far as can be ascertained is me.

Everything was now quite clear. He reached up and turned on the light. I am clear. I am fine. Slight headache; a couple of aspirins are indicated. What time is it?

Small struggle in disbelief of the hands of his watch. Midnight, not midday. Have slept eleven hours.

It was quiet everywhere. He got up, dressed, padded softly about. In the livingroom soft regular breathing told him that Maryvonne, bless her, was asleep on the sofa.

There was a note on the kitchen table in her neat schoolgirl writing.

'Richard says when you wake up phone him, at the office even if he's asleep. I'll hold the fort here just as long as you want me to. Boss's orders, but I would anyhow. M.'

He felt hungry. Wasn't anything to eat. Staved the pang with a big piece of stale bread. Like Lydia. Gnaw that; good for your teeth. Not a difficulty: find snack-bar or something in the town. But there are priorities.

In the office, same picture as – had it been three days ago when they brought Alberthe in? Duty officer this time frankly dozing. Should shake that bugger up. Suppose Arabs in a small dark blue Alpine arrived to rescue Alberthe? No, they had reckoned quite rightly that the ambulance was easier. Let him do the work.

He went up to his own office. All still along here, and the door to Richard's quarters locked. He knew what this meant. Richard, no believer in sitting up biting his nails, kept an air bed in the cupboard where he hung his overcoat. When – it happened – he spent the night in the office and decided that thought had reached the limit, he lay down on the floor and thought no more. Right.

Castang went back, shut the door, turned on his desk light, rolled a piece of paper into his typewriter.

'*Personal to Richard.*

I'm taking myself – and A. – out of your light. This is henceforward a personal matter: leave it that way. No I'm not round the bend. I've had a good sleep and am perfectly lucid. I don't want any officialdom involved. Obvious, for your sake as well as mine. Leave Paris out of it.

My resignation is effective as from this moment.

I have retained a certain amount of official property which I will return as soon as may be. I ask for your understanding about that.

Castang.'

Downstairs everything was equally quiet. He unlocked the door of Alberthe's cell.

"Asleep?" he asked softly.

"No."

"I turn the light on?"

"Do." She sat up, blinking. "I was dozing. When there's nothing else to do."

"Did nobody bring you any supper?"

"Is it that late? Nobody's been near me."

"I'm sorry: I've had a busy time. Hungry?"

"Now that you mention it." She had made up her mind to be very cool, altogether collected.

"Would you like to get up? I'll bring you your own clothes."

"Are you releasing me?"

"First stage. I'm going to drive you, if you agree. Just me."

"I'll just comb my hair."

"I'll explain properly but to tell you the truth I'm very hungry myself. I skipped lunch and supper too. Concentrate on that first, shall we?" She settled herself and her long skirt in the front of the little car.

"There seems to be no one much about – what time is it?"

"Nearly one in the morning."

"It ceases to mean anything much. Being in jail gives one a pleasant sense of irresponsibility."

"Yes. Good, there's not much traffic," accelerating. "It's not very far."

"Where are we going or mayn't I ask?"

"Quite a pleasant place; a country hotel called the Château d'Izy: do you know it?"

"Certainly: I've never stayed there but friends have."

"That's just as well; if the night porter doesn't recognise you there'll be the less strain on his discretion."

It had come to Castang driving in: a manorhouse place some way out and in deep countryside. Very expensive indeed: this detail, along with much else, was not worrying him.

The great advantage – at the immediate moment – was that the night man in such places anywhere in France is unsurprisable. The car can be a battered and dirty Ford just as easily as a Ferrari. Tall and elegant ladies in evening dress, even when somewhat dishevelled, do not alarm. Neither do preoccupied-seeming gentlemen. Horsy clothes – but have cost money. There is nothing, moreover, out of the commonplace in a pair (at getting on for two in the morning) who ask for a bit of seclusion, are extremely hungry, and whose luggage consists of a plastic carrier with 'Prisunic' written on it. Not if the tip is right. Castang kept money in his desk as well as objects that sometimes came in handy to a police officer in a hurry. They were shown to a room with a double bed, but Castang did not even notice, and if Alberthe did she said nothing.

The night waiter in such places is too snobbish to go Warming Up

141

Food, but he too is amenable to persuasion. He says things like all the food is locked up, and proposes instead a scandinavian plate, which is smoked eel, trout, sturgeon and salmon, and that's all right but when you've had nothing since breakfast . . . well, perhaps there's some leftover coq-au-vin. Castang, hung for lamb, sheep, llama and alpaca too, asked Alberthe if she drank champagne. She did. Then there's no more to worry about. She went off to repair the visage and he found he had no cigarettes left but there were some in a box on the table as well as cigars on the chimneypiece. A place that took care of you.

Rolling table arrived with a lot of napkins and baskets. Sometimes they'll say quite brazenly don't pinch the tablesilver, it's counted, but here they simplified; assumed you did and wrote the price in anyhow. The champagne was Roederer which is nice: a full bottle of Evian which is nice too: three sorts of brown bread and a bowl of salad.

"This is doing me good."

"Me too," agreed Alberthe.

The priestly person came back with the cock in a copper pot and an air of patience about this being a lot of work; the same wine it was cooked in, a Chambertin which is nice; and closed the door politely upon adultery.

"Is it part of the deal," asked Alberthe conversationally, "that I should go to bed with you?" She took a cigarette.

"No." He got up, went over to the chimneypiece and took a small thin cigar: cheap things, he noticed disapprovingly. "I'm sorry; I improvised. Food was in my mind. Shelter, comfort – luxury even. I didn't work it out further."

"I see. I was thinking I was supposed to have established a psychological dependence upon my kidnapper."

"Yes, it's well-known. It must sound absurd – even insulting. It hadn't crossed my mind."

"You seem very vulnerable here. If I had screamed, or something. It would not be at all difficult for me to make myself known in a place like this. Wouldn't you then be in an awkward fix?"

"It's very likely."

"What would you do?"

"I haven't any idea. Go ahead if you wish."

"Are you wearing a gun?"

"I am, yes." He pushed his jacket back and made a half turn to

142

show the belt holster behind his hip. "I feel a great deal better and not at all drunk," in the voice of somebody thinking it will probably be fine tomorrow. "I slept several hours: I don't feel sleepy."

"So did I. What do you propose?"

"Have a bath or something. I have thinking to do. These are disgusting – must go and see whether that man has some cigarettes."

"Leaving me alone? I could escape."

"True. I should have some handcuffs. One wrist one ankle; that's pretty efficacious."

"Something obviously has happened. Your plans have been upset and you are distraught."

"That is true."

"Hadn't you better tell me?"

"No, I hadn't. In the end I will, so I may as well do so now. Since neither of us is sleepy. Your friends, I say 'They' for a convenient definition, have been pretty smart. Quick. Efficient. I got home at lunchtime and found that they had kidnapped my wife. She has a small child. They left that, and unharmed. It would only have been a nuisance to them, but I'm still grateful. They used one of my inspectors to get in, and left him comatose, perhaps dead. They want you back. Quick, unharmed, no strings attached. So now – yes, right, I mustn't let you out of my sight, must I? Precious."

"I see . . . In the circumstances – I mean the previous circumstances – would you really have let me go? Try to answer me honestly? Were you holding out this promise of liberty as an inducement? I can say, can't I, an added inducement."

"Yes, and yes."

"Speaking for yourself, that is. That man; I am sorry but I cannot bring myself to speak of him with all the detachment I should wish. He would have sought pretexts to hold me, on any sort of trumped up offence. You have brought me here as a kind of bait. This elaborately staged scene, in an isolated country district, is a little too good to be true, wouldn't you say?" She pointed to the curtained window. "A man – one of your men – posted out there. If I did take to my heels – high heels, and a long skirt, I wouldn't be very mobile – capturing me would be simple. Or would he shoot me? An inconvenient witness is suppressed, all trace of illegal operations is effaced, a signed confession has been left behind: it ties up all the loose ends neatly."

"Not quite all the loose ends. It's not in any case the expression I choose when I'm talking of my wife. For the rest, I should be laughing, I suppose, if I didn't feel a bit too joyless about it. I suppose too I should be able to demolish this scenario, was that your phrase? Rationally. I'm not even sure whether I'm sufficiently rational."

"You can always try," offered Alberthe, taking another cigarette.

"I'll just go and get some. Give me a chance to signal to the myrmidons. And work up a convincing line of phrase." He came back stripping the cellophane. "It's a fine thing a credit card, especially when it's in my own name. Hot in here." He took his jacket off, discovered his gunbelt underneath, shook his head, went over to the wardrobe and hung both on a hanger. His gun he took out of the holster. He broke it open, shook the shells out on the little writing desk, found an envelope tucked into the blotting-pad, counted the shells into it, put the envelope and the empty gun in the desk drawer.

"Hope I don't forget it there for the chambermaid to find . . . a cop feels, and looks, a little bit less like a cop this way. Thinks, too, more like a human being.

"First off, and this is convincing if you allow yourself to think straight, no cop would look at a notion like that for a second. It belongs in fiction, the sort where a tricky twist has to be thought up every ten pages to keep one excited. It's glib, phony, and over-complicated. Real cops never make such elaborate schemes.

"Dressing up cops as hotel help and guests is out of Goldfinger. Using you as a piece of cheese is another phony, when the simple, obvious place is your own home.

"If you're a bargaining counter you're a good one, and cops would take care of you: they wouldn't promenade you round like this where you'd be seen, and remembered.

"For me you are a bargaining counter, if I keep my head. The only one I've got. My only chance to use it is to bring you out into the open and hope that by showing it I can persuade my wife's captors that I ask for nothing. Isolated country district as you say. I'm vulnerable as you say. I'm hoping they'll see it like that. A trap is nonexistent; I am helpless. Indeed they could take you, keep my wife, and use her as a squeeze to obliterate any evidence we may have extorted from you. They'll be thinking, you see, of their own skins, as much as yours and more . . .

"Richard you haven't understood. He captured you, and he

144

pressured you in the certainty that you knew what he wanted. Both illegal. Cops do illegal things because they have to if they're ever going to show results. It's known, and sometimes it's proved, and that's the end of them, to save face for those higher up. So you must remember that they – we – avoid it as much as we can. Why did Richard – he's a very careful man – make such a chancy gamble when he'd done his utmost to avoid all involvement? For whatever the government disapproves or dislikes, he's the scapegoat. Because killing Viviane Kranitz under his nose broke the rule of leaving his face intact, and left him no choice. It was a very foolish thing to do, and my guess is that you had nothing to do with it because you would know how politics work."

"That is so," murmured Alberthe.

"It's not just rats that bite when driven into a corner. But having gone out into total illegality, which he defends on the good ground that the whole Resistance Movement was no different and being sanctioned by public opinion has no bearing on one's conscience, Richard's not going to stand in the open boasting of it: like most cops he has nothing but his pension to live on. He has to get back into legality and stay there.

"For that you have to understand the law. If the judge of instruction knows that the law has been broken he claps Richard in jail, and me with him. He will, and he's not to be blamed, do his damnedest to avoid any such knowledge. Give him a lawful case to make, redounding to his credit, and his face is safe. He wouldn't have charged you with anything at all, knowing well that the legal talent in your defence would run rings round the prosecutor in court. Knowing this, knowing you'd guess it and bank on it, Richard didn't have any choice. He had to hammer you, and use that to bargain his way out, in case the judge who is painfully conscientious should think it immoral to charge your friends with a homicide and see you escape even some catch-all item of the code like association-of-malfactors, or non-assistance-to-person-in-danger."

Alberthe did nothing: she didn't even nod, or sigh, or show in any way that she had heard. She didn't even seem to be listening. Slowly at last she gathered herself up, stood, and said in the most banal voice, "I think I will have that bath after all."

"Don't think I'll interfere with you. Until morning there's nothing I can do but sit in the lotus position and repeat mantras."

145

"And then?" with her hand on the bathroom door.

"Try and establish some communication. If you'll agree to talk to some third person who'll know where to get in touch, then they can rescue you, and take me along too, in exchange for my wife." She turned without a word and went on into the bathroom. When the taps were running she came out again and spoke.

"I am, all this notwithstanding, helpless should you offer me violence, as helpless as when I was in your basement cell. I don't want you to use any violence on me. So I'm leaving this door open – will you take advantage of that?"

"No."

"Is that a rule, or a tactic?"

He looked up and managed a sour smile.

"You're an attractive woman. Somebody may be thinking that, this minute, where my wife is concerned." She nodded then, and went back into the bathroom.

He got up to look for a different kind of cigar, knowing they'd all taste the same. There was a glass of wine left too. He might as well drink it: it would make no difference.

In a few hours, if he had not already done so, Richard would find his note. What would he do then?

He'd be extremely annoyed, that's what. Granted, and what then? He'd regain control of himself very rapidly, first because he would anyhow, secondly because he had to. No Orthez, now no Castang, and no Alberthe either. He'd read the situation, and he'd take steps to get both back. How much time do I have?

Alberthe appeared, statuesque and egyptian in hotel towels, sat down in front of the dressing-table.

"I hesitate to ask the management for a hairbrush: I'd be doubtful whether it were really clean."

He looked at her and went Urrr in a sourpuss way.

"I could of course ask for a nightdress: it would be by no means unheard of."

"This is bad enough," said Castang harshly. "Making a Man–Woman confrontation out of it would be that much worse."

"My dear boy, that's exactly what it is."

"I come over and give the towel a jerk and everything will be roses from then on." She swung round abruptly to look him in the face. Eyes like a painter cat.

"Do you take me for a whore?" stinging.

"I take you for a woman that is more of a man than most men."

"And more of a woman than most women. It would entertain me," with a sarcastic emphasis, "to seduce you? A momentary sensation if not of pleasure then of power? It would perhaps surprise you," lashing him across the face with it, "to be told that I've never been touched by a man – or woman either – outside my own marriage, which has been for five years dead?"

"No, it would not surprise me. My own wife is just such another."

"Very good. You will thus allow me to stay wrapped in whatever rag of dignity is left to me. I am pleased that you should realise it. You could of course – as you put it – give the towel a jerk. I could not stop you and would not try. There would be no advantage taken. Either way." She faced back again, towards the looking-glass. She examined her reflection, as though facing it down.

"Presumably," with her knuckles clenched on either side of her jaw," you have concluded that I, in cold blood, gave orders for having little Viviane Kranitz' throat cut. A way like another to make sure her mouth stayed shut."

He made no answer.

"These people," harshly dry. "Who are bargaining. To have me back. With what end – I am asking myself – in mind? Having been in your hands. Confessed to you? – they have no means of telling. The same treatment, they may very well conclude, I quite probably merit. Whatever their decision they will not hesitate for very long in making it." She put her palms across her eyes and held them an instant. "I am not going to withdraw from that decision. It would not only be too late. It would do me dishonour." She turned towards him again, and again pressed her ears back.

"Your Mister Richard did not torture me. He made it clear that he would go as far as he had to. I recognised that. I am like that myself. There was a moment at which I felt respect for him. I felt, moreover, that he would keep his word.

"You – when I saw you first, I thought . . ." Her voice trailed off; picked up.

"I thought then – later – that you were a weak sister. Forcing me, by whatever methods; your heart was not in it. The legalistic mind; you would feel it due to your piddling conscience to release me, in exchange for my signing your absurd document. I felt, indeed I feel quite certain that I could find means of repudiating that even were I unable strictly speaking to prove that it was extorted under threat of harsher methods. It seemed to me that I could use you.

"You brought me here. It seemed clear that you were going to rape me contemptibly and oh so typically. I was grateful that you did not. In gratitude, it occurred to me that I could offer you my body without debasing myself and without wish – believe me – to debase you. I was glad to have found a man less ignoble than most. I wish that I could give you back your wife."

"Did Monsieur Richard rape you?"

"He did not. I wished that he had. A mean satisfaction of a mean desire. It took away some of my fortitude."

Castang who had lost so much of his own fortitude was glad now of the extra drink.

"Alberthe?"

"Yes?"

"Stand up, would you?" Looking a little surprised, she did.

"Pull the towel." Unsurprised, she did. He walked slowly towards her. She shut her eyes. He walked past into the bathroom.

As he had expected there was a towelling robe hanging on the hook. He held it out.

"More comfortable. And less damp." She turned her back, regally, so that he could help her on with it. She turned round then, tying the sash, but there were no sentimental tears. He was looking himself for a phrase that would be just acrid enough.

" 'Naked as September Morn and a lot less coy' " he quoted. She smiled then.

"Who was that?"

"Carmen Sternwood but you won't have heard of her."

"It wouldn't have done."

"It wouldn't have done," woodenly.

" 'On her left breast a mole cinque-spotted, like the crimson drops in the bottom of a cowslip.' "

"And what's that?"

"That's Shakespeare, peasant. Appropriate for making love in."

"Yes. What's a cowslip?"

"*Fleur de coucou.*"

"The cuckoo, that's me."

"Right or nearly so. Oh word of fear, Unpleasing to a married ear."

"That more Shakespeare?"

"It is."

148

"Yes, well, keep the rest for some time we're in bed together."

Alberthe gave a great peal of laughter. That was more attractive than her being naked, and vicious.

"Who d'you think I am then – one of these great big rugged crocks of shit who takes girls to bed for therapy? And are there ever a lot looking for therapy!"

"We'll do better now," said Alberthe seriously. "You were very rude and insulting, but I deserved that."

"We'll do better now," he repeated thoughtfully, "but I'm not very used, you know, to grand bourgeoise ladies. Exalted spheres. I'd have been more likely to say Hey Missis, can I take hold of your tit, and start counting."

"Leave it, Castang," she said seriously. "Don't pretend to vulgarities that don't become you."

"I don't really make much pretence to understand you, you know that?"

"You don't? You mean – you want me to explain."

"Yes, do."

She went and sat down, on a straight chair; straight-backed. She took a second to concentrate.

"Listen to me, Castang. You know what it was, that the General said?

" 'All my life I have had a certain idea of France.' "

"Yes," nodding. The huge pale eyes held on him like lamps. "That. Exactly that. And since then, what have I seen? The most abject and pusillanimous flight from reality, from decision, from manhood. Disguised as cleverness. Cleverness! Being clever, thought of as a substitute for statesmanship. Kowtowing to all, while prevaricating over everything. Opportunism, masquerading as policy. Every word said," fiercely, "recalling the phrase about falling back upon strategic positions previously prepared. Which were invariably in Bordeaux. Arrogant young cowards, fat old cowards, but all of them with one thing in common; all infernally talkative."

Castang listened. What else could he do? What else was there to do? He had heard it all many, many times. From the rich; fluently, forcefully. Let me tell you something, old boy: just yesterday I was lunching with one of the best business brains in the country and you'd scarcely credit it were it not for hearing it from his own lips . . .

From the poor; pellmell, inarticulate, mean-to-say, in phrases

149

with no beginning and no end, but perfectly clear. Soft on niggers – they got the oil, you see, they got the uranium, the raw materials, right? the strategic stuff. Soft on Jews – they got the brains, they got all the circuits, look after one another, it all goes by word of mouth. Greedy, see – they never got enough, never give up tugging, look to extract that little bit extra. Fella with a little business they'll trickle a bit to him here and there, always hold it just beyond arm's length, as long as he'll keep running and work his gut out, and the moment he's milked dry . . .

From his own sort; the cops, the petty functionaries, the ones trained to put in writing. They knew sentencing and paragraphing; knew how to present a spaced and reasoned argument, but their minds like their wording could not find expression save in cliché. Tramlines yes, worn smooth by trundling a lifetime to and fro; but the ruts were carved so deep they could no longer see out over the top. The witchword and the catchphrase mouthed and chewed and dribbling out in the thin tasteless gruel of non-thought.

This was the pure juice. The voice clear, carrying, pitched below stridency, accustomed to dominating a room. When a woman is once utterly determined, nothing will stand in her way. Her intellect is formidable, her persuasiveness unwavering, her obstinacy immovable. Interruptions and objections will only stimulate a whiplash, devastating, of repartee. In one phrase, in one breath, she will be more seductively charming, and more shatteringly rude than any man. A man has limits while the woman knows none. The reasons for this phenomenon have been the subject of much well-meant biological speculation.

He knew no way of coping with this. Dulled and crippled as he was, out of hope and out of courage, he felt dimly that if this woman were to push the knife in his hand and give him a friendly little pressure in the back he would trot off in an obedient shamble to do her bidding. A tiny wire twitched still at the back of his brain, carrying him a message. In no urgent or agitated voice – in whose voice? – a tranquil and gently feminine voice that said, 'You see, boy, don't you, that a third, even a fifth of what she wants if carried out means simply civil war.' These small peninsular countries of Europe, France, Italy and Spain, are they not Salvador, Guatemala, and Nicaragua?

Another voice, harsh and jeering, said to him, 'You understand now why the Pope, at once sinister and pathetic in the dim obscurities of his mind, is so frightened of women, poor little lad, so like an English Public School Boy.'

Bewilderment. His eyes were slipping out of focus.

"I'm going to copy your good example; I'm going to have a bath."

There was a tube still of the stuff that made foam, many little pieces of soap in elegant couturier wrappings, sweet sachets of goo, all nicely designed to bring home to one's small daughters to play shop with, along with the pepper-salt-and-mustard offered by the gracious permission of the airline. Why no dinky package of heroin, teeny bottle of Invisible Mixture or Elixir of Life? What, there isn't even a dainty dose of powdered rhinoceros-horn guaranteeing six unbroken hours of MeTarzanyoujane. At my word of command, one, on your back: two, heels in the air.

You could do with a shave, while you're at it.

He found himself yawning in front of the glass. Damn great hot bath had seemed a good idea, and wasn't. Should have had a cold shower or something. Shock, still: boy you're still in shock and you want to keep a careful eye open. Need speed-pill.

He hadn't any. Most cops called upon to stay up all night (for example) would take a pill. He had himself from time to time done so until Vera had found them once in a trouser pocket and thrown them down the lavatory, with a severe lecture to follow.

Shaved anyhow and in clean underclothes. Face anything that way, right up to a guillotine. That's pure sentimentalism (he did not approve of guillotines, but they existed; well: he wasn't going to get paralysed about them). History contained too many lessons of people who had gone singing. In the old days, when they sent you to the block, they allowed you a certain dignity. You were expected in return to show manhood. You could make a speech to the people: a dry mouth was not in order. You put on your best clothes. The thing wrong nowadays is that it's done shamefully, hole and corner. Meanly. Like everything the state does, now. No, ask forgiveness of the people. In return, the executioner asked your forgiveness. You consented, and you went.

Alberthe, he thought, might agree.

She was gone. Momentary terror – how could he have been so foolish? – his eye jumped to the drawer where he had left his gun. A romantic, reckless risk; and Alberthe was a realist.

No, she'd gone to bed. There in the shadowed half of the room was her hair on the pillow. She thought of herself as a realist, but was a romantic at heart. Her fate, she had decided, was bound up with his.

I'm something of the sort, myself.

So there you are boy – you asked for it and you got it. Nice hotel, discretion assured, good meal, very good drinks, a comfortable bath, and there's a naked woman in bed just waiting for you to slip in beside her. It would be a pleasant way, no?, of spending the couple of hours left till daylight.

He stretched out in the chair, and let his muscles go loose. There'll be work to do, soon.

She wasn't a spoonful of jello. You didn't chew a bit of gum together and drink a coke and then say 'wanna fuck'. But disguise it any way you – or she – like, coming out like that in a towel, so that he only had to say pull the string, and she pulled it . . . because ask yourself what Vera would have done and the answer was she wouldn't have got caught in any towel.

Alberthe had dressed it up as a kind of test, to see whether he would 'respect her'. Rubbish; it had just been another whory manoeuvre. Designed to get his mind tangled.

He'd got at last the confusion out of his brain, and knew what he had to do. He went and got his gunbelt, buckled it on, loaded the revolver and put it in the holster. An extremely uncomfortable affair, when sitting in a chair with your feet up: very well then, put them down. This is no time for a kip: think. What was Richard doing?

Commissaire Richard had set the alarm clock of his mind to go off at four. He didn't have any Japanese object on his wrist to go beep-beep or play *Für Elise*. He had arranged his options the night before, decided to sleep upon them. They would not look different when woke, and his mind would be made up. Taking things in order: Castang, Alberthe, Castang's wife. The first had had a good sleep, would be under control. The second likewise – well hell, he suddenly realised he'd left her without supper the night before. No harm either. The human being can survive for three months without food, three days without water, and three minutes without oxygen, and he who sleeps dines.

One had however a conscience; a thing not to be regarded as an alarm clock. Inside Monsieur Richard there was a brief struggle between his conscience and the fiend, reminiscent though not very

152

of Lancelot Gobbo. He stumped off to the basement, lightening his footsteps on the way. Took a look through the peephole, distrusted his eyesight, turned on the interior light, made a little whistle. Mechanisms for allowing one's mind to catch up to the event. Brief, *il ne manqua plus que ca*. The whistle, a tedious and sentimental little tune on a penny whistle, entitled *Perfidia*, accompanied him back up the stairs and into Castang's office, where he found the note addressed to him. The lips pursed slightly more; the little tune, two long notes and eight short ones, danced accompaniment in his ear. He was not angry. He was not, he dared suppose, even surprised. Castang was a good cop but. The wording of confidential reports in personal dossiers of police officers is much the same as that employed for elementary schoolchildren. Needs supervision. Monsieur Richard went back to his desk and rubbed his jaw with his hand. A sandpapery noise resulted. He opened a drawer of his desk and found an electric razor. Put the piece of paper in the drawer. No, Fausta might find it. Got up and put it in the safe. Sat, plugged in the razor, began to shave thoughtfully. Busy bees, damn the silly things, wove meaningless patterns around his head. The lips ceased to purse and arranged themselves into resigned patterns suitable for being shaved. *Perfidia* stopped. Need something here a little stronger. A Funeral March, probably: however, what came when he was next able to whistle was that jolly, bumpy tune of the Drunken Peasants from the sixth symphony of Beethoven. A tiresome affair it can be too; going on and on and round and round. Unless the conductor is a very good one. When it does at last die away it is to the thunder of the approaching storm, but Monsieur Richard only snapped the razor off, abolishing the bees, blew away the dust of his beard. And was ready for the day; it was going to be strenuous.

Castang, going through his pockets the morning before, had found a card, clipped it to a page of his notes and added it to the file. This was the card Marc Vibert had given him, with an unlisted phone number. Access; rather like a credit card: it will buy you things, if your credit is good.

Richard, that same afternoon, contemplating Alberthe's 'confession' and pondering unlegal means of turning this highly illegal document into a form acceptable to those of a legal disposition, had come across this card and thought for some time about Monsieur Marc Vibert. The knot from which all the other knots proceeded.

153

Hm, that ass Castang had cheerfully promised him immunity from further harassments and awkward questions. All very well but he himself was not quite sure about this. There would be more awkward questions, quite a few to his own address. In which case Monsieur Vibert was a handy man to know. If a choirboy is caught feeling up one of the girls it strengthens his position to know that the choirmaster was on the same racket. Who said anything about blackmail?

The catastrophe forced his hand: the card became a playing card. That evening at suppertime he had caught Vibert at home in the embroidered velvet slippers. Now is the time for all good men to come to the aid of Me.

"Divisional Commissaire Richard here, PJ. Monsieur Castang was to some extent in your confidence. This confidence I share. It is of importance – you'll agree – that further people taken into this confidence should be as few as possible . . .

"Why are you wasting my time with all this? It's said in a few words. Keeping the lid on all this – crude expression – was, is, as desirable to me as to yourself. The kidnapping of Madame Kranitz was one thing. Her subsequent assassination squared that. No, please let me speak; this isn't to be solved by talk. Squared and squared again; we're not going to contain this any longer by conventional methods. It's moved into a confrontation phase of open violence.

"The mechanisms of all this we have laid bare, by straightforward police methods: a little unconventional it may be, but the results are what count. I was ready, today at lunchtime, to proceed to arrest. That's right. I do not yet know how, but the group got wind of our preparations, and a counterstroke has been made. The wife of my collaborator, whom you know, yes Castang, has disappeared.

"Monsieur Vibert, are you acquainted with a Madame Alberthe de Rubempré?

"These remonstrations are useless, you know.

"Very well, will you ask Madame Vibert to come to the telephone?

"Yes, I'm forced to put it baldly. Homicide, kidnapping, blackmail and the holding of hostages are extremely bald facts.

"Naturally, my responsibilities force me to consultation with my superiors. It is no longer a thing I can contain at local level. I have no means of stopping the press.

"Well, officially you're the deputed representative in the Parliament for this circumscription. Natural that you should take an interest. There is the matter of your projected candidacy to even higher office.

"Do you mean by that you'd prefer me to go through the official channels at the Ministry? No, I suggest nothing; I put a question. It comes to mind that the business could be better controlled, with more discretion, on a more solid basis, were you yourself to initiate the moves. I'm looking for the word – it's ineluctable.

"These people are armed, and they've already shown a taste for violent melodrama in their public relations. Machinegunned Castang's flat, it was in the press. Lucky they didn't toss a grenade in while they were at it, but at that point they sought merely to intimidate.

"Tell me, have you ever stayed – weekend guest perhaps, in Madame la Baronne's château here in the country?

"The phrase 'Fort Chabrol'? Meeting me up at the O K Corral at dawn, yes? Type of thing that whets the appetite of the media: be lucky if we don't have television cameras.

"Quite so, that's what they're there for and that's what I want. The gendarmerie intervention brigade, right; that's a well-trained crowd and their commander is outstandingly good.

"By all means ring me back, and as soon as may be. This is getting on to night-time, and it'll take twenty-four hours to set up.

"Man, instead of abusing me be grateful. If you want me to ring the Quai with an official report you've only to say so. I'm not threatening you, and don't waste your breath threatening me. I'm sixty years old, I've been a cop for forty and let me tell you in a monosyllable: I don't give a fart. Clear?

"I'll be at this line all night."

Monsieur Vibert, telephoning.

"Alors, chère madame, wie gehts denn? Kissing your hands, naturally. That will be quite delightful and I look forward with eagerness. You might give me your good man if he's around: I don't disguise my preferences but the devil drives, stupid fellow that he is.

"Christian? – Marc. Ma foi, et toi? My dear boy, would I be pestering you at home if it wasn't? I'm very much afraid that your plans for the evening . . . Quite right, not on this line.

"That's perfectly correct, and a development has been brought to my ears by devious ways, and sharing it with you is not just the loyal

155

thing, but in my judgment a state-safety factor is involved which . . . yes, that serious. I'd suggest your office. I think a quarter of an hour would be about right. *A tout à l'heure* then."

They sat in conference round a small conference table. Like a very tiny intimate dinner party. Four frightened people. One took minutes but – perish the thought – no tape. Senior public officials in the Republic are paid to prevaricate in public to the limit of their ability. Nobody anywhere could be found to talk more while saying less. English is a language where intonation counts above almost anything. Such a phrase as 'I, um, don't feel quite convinced' is meaningless on paper, is *viva voce* worth a page of prose, and a prosy page at that. The American language is quite dissimilar. It will produce a single word like 'candyass' worth in itself a paragraph, embedded within volumes of such polysyllabic hermeticism, such thick, black, deathly-boring opacity as to make Henry James kneel and beat his pure marble brow howling against the dirty deck whence all but he had fled. The French, than whom – it's a very than-whom people all round – none can be more vacuously orotund, are (the same ones) obligingly terse. On occasion.

"Who've we got down there?"

"Bordenave."

"S'he any good?"

"I never heard he set the Seine on fire. He'll do."

"Not panicky?"

"Reliable."

"What else are Prefects for?"

"Yes, but the press."

"Send him a very stiff telex."

"Brigade him with a strong –"

"No that won't do. None of our –"

"Right, it must stay local. A bush fire spreading to Paris . . ."

"Circumscribed."

"Let him have the intervention brigade. With a couple of companies of the local CRS. That would stamp it out."

"This PJ inspector; the one whose wife . . ."

"Grab his ass."

"Yes, but this Richard. It's his ass that has to be grabbed: tell Ottavioli."

156

"Not be hasty. Have we considered letting this blow up in Vibert's face?"

"Politically too much fallout. A bomb, but a dirty bomb."

"Show of strength."

"Populace needs reassurance."

"Exactly like the death penalty."

"Firmness is called for."

"I'll draft our opinion accordingly."

And a little further in, where the hum of an agitated beehive was less pronounced. Further gentlemen, more senior.

"A report will have to be made for the President: have you got his diary there?"

"Poland till tomorrow."

"There's this Polish connection – wouldn't do us any harm, in my view, coming down on that."

"Mm, fairly heavily financed from the United States. Strong stuff back there in Pennsylvania, full of Polish miners."

"So is the IRA. All that's on an emotional basis my dear. Two or three senators and a good line to Foggy Bottom back in Washington, but prudence would dictate that Bottom unfogs a wee bit: we're hardly seeking re-election in Valenciennes."

"Likewise this Brazilian connection."

"Correct; the Prime Minister's office advises me that there are very good, very strong industrial agreements pending that he doesn't want to see compromised. And the Germans being exceptionally strong there . . ."

"Quite, but we can deal with it here, if not in Brazil. This de Serta woman – relatively lightweight, wouldn't you say? Good financial mind, but a courtesan thing when all is said."

"Yes, well, the service advises that there was a clash with Rubempré over the German interest." Nobody says SDECE; it's unpronounceable anyhow.

"Rubempré can hardly be described as a courtesan thing. I don't know her well but Egeria, not Thaïs."

"Be that as it may," turning over more papers, "she looks to be fatally compromised here. I've a report about a bogus RG commissaire: the army won't admit it but the fact is that Rubempré simply disappeared, and it points straight to –"

157

"It was circulated to me," impatiently. "That's this PJ chief down there, no doubt of it. Description doesn't match but –"
"Did it cleverly though; didn't upset the Germans. We don't have to disown him publicly. I admit, the impudence of it rather appealed to me."
"Gone too far: he'll have to go. Can't have these Resistance heroes imagining they're back in business."
"So has Alberthe gone too far. Frigging about with a few Franquist marquises in Spain, fine, but the right wing in Germany's hopelessly discredited. As long as she galloped her horse over the pampa and stuck to Moral Rearmament – but encouraging this Polish riffraff . . ."
"Bad luck as much as anything: that woman of Vibert's having been married to that clot from Cleveland. Alberthe lost control over them. Thought they could get away with anything and have it chalked up to the Red Brigade."
"If they could have hooked Vibert they would have broadened their base no end. Couldn't resist the temptation. I suspect that doctor, Joinel is it?, at the bottom of it, fancying himself as an Eminence Grise. I have the impression that Alberthe was genuinely taken aback."
"We're getting no further to the core of the problem. They shot up this PJ man's flat – he was sniffing round the Vibert affair. RG think he frightened Joinel. Now they've kidnapped his wife. Even if that forces this – Richard he's called – to disgorge Alberthe. It's gone too far. She hasn't a hope now of stopping the pot from boiling over."
"So you're inclining towards zap the lot, is that it? Bit over-crude I'd call that: isn't it nuke the ayatollah?"
"You'd suggest? . . ."
"Zap these two policemen; it doesn't seem to have spread any further. Alberthe's had a lesson she's not likely to forget in a hurry. Have this Pole deported back to Cleveland with a stiff note to State. The minor elements brought to trial in camera: as for Vibert we've got him where we want him: in return for silence he stays in line."
"My dear it would take one press man, and in a pre-election period we just can't risk it. Discrediting a cannibal nigger general . . . but Alberthe de Rubempré is one of us."
"The point is well taken."
"Where's the Special Section?"
"Carcassonne; standby; six-hour alert for full readiness."

158

"Ring the bell, would you? . . . now I want maps of this section: satellite maps."

"The mineral-survey maps, sir?"

"I don't care what they are. I want the details of every henhouse, bush and rabbithole in the area, is that clear?"

"Yes sir."

"And get on to Carcassonne: I want the commandant of the Special Section available for briefing: am I clear?"

"Yes sir."

Refreshed by a stimulating consciousness of energetic decisions being taken, the gentlemen could unbutton. Never having seen a shot fired, in anger or otherwise, zapping a few people by-paratrooper-interposed gave them quite an appetite, and a pleasure in reminiscence. Now when Jeannou Lacaze . . . my dear boy that's where he started, commanding the demi-brigade of the Eleventh Shock, at that time the secular arm, so to speak, of the service. Rose to command the service itself. Meteoric: straight up vertically to Chief of the General Staff; the admirals were livid.

Now when we sent the Legion in to jump over Kolwezi . . .

My dear boy, I can't be bothered learning their new nigger names, it's all Congo-Bongo and Heart of Darkness to me. King Leopold the Second, absolutely lamentable and utterly deplorable but one can't help admitting, those were the days. Nothing has changed you know.

I did spend some time as a boy in old Foccart's office but really, you know, I never could muster up an awful lot of enthusiasm for all those Waggadoogoo places: really – Africa . . . Of course the Islamic slice off the top, but that's not Africa, is it. I'll say goodnight to you, shall I? Bless my soul; I was supposed to go to the Opera. Well out of that, at least.

I never do: nobody does but Japanese. Drop in, in the morning; I'll fill you in.

"Now, mon Commandant, let's make sure this is absolutely cut and dried. Here are the maps: yes, well, spare me all the technical witchdoctery. I had Monsieur Lamy here, he's our expert interpreter dug out of bed, and as I was saying all in infra-red, however I'll be brief. No no, man, the large scale one first – you've clearance at the military airfield over here: you'll want a troop-carrying copter, won't you? and what I want to consult you about is if as seems likely they've a cowboy or so on the roof here – Here – is it advisable to have a gunship? Don't make it technical dear man."

"Gunship no, qua gunship."

"I beg your pardon."

"Not to be technical don't want to knock the castle down do you? – no need for all that firepower. However gunship yes as source of light. Pin um down." It was exactly like a conversation between Flora Finching and Mr F's Aunt; the gush of amiable nonsense counterpointed by 'Knock him down and chuck him out of winder'.

"You wouldn't mind explaining?"

"Troop-carrier landing at that moment vulnerable. Troops issuing from doors, before they've a chance to deploy; at that precise moment when at close range. Hold gunship overhead at low altitude, steady. Umbrella. In itself highly intimidating and forceful presence: one. Anybody fooling around, hypothesize existence ground-air missile, something of the sort, firepower's there to knock it over: two. Observatory unimpeded vision all azimuths, direct and coordinate a rapid assault: three. Less life lost that way.

"Four; as I have said, powerful source of light. Can floodlight landing area for your carrier, invaluable at night and especially on uneven, defended or booby-trapped terrain."

"But you're targeting your own men, it seems to me."

"Infra-red," said the commander patiently. "Furthermore powerful searchlight can be beamed on any fortified area – like these walls. Not to underestimate lightbeam power to intimidate and paralyse; never had a rabbit in your headlights?"

"But they'll shoot at your light source, won't they?"

"Like to see um try," laconic.

"I see," quelled for once; in fact himself a rabbit in a headlight.

"What's your intelligence estimate on number and probable equipment opposition?"

"Imprecise," unwilling to admit there wasn't any.

"Ten to twenty? Light automatic arms?"

"It would be as well to count on quite that, perhaps. Armament presumably such as would be suitable for urban terrorism; such uh, as is mobile, concealable, unobtrusive. But they may have heavier stuff stowed away in that fortress. Libyan sources, uh." These dear good Libyans come in handy whenever an unspecified boo-man is called for.

"Thirty men," said the commander. "Arm a section automatic

160

weapons, hold reserve section, bit more sophisticate stuff, 'n case called for."

"Ah," with appetite, "you have these things which make a terrifying bang. Paralysing gases," relish growing.

"All that," tight of lip. "Up to you. You want um stunned, or shot at?" One politician disconcerted, but only momentarily. A firm lead must be given to the military. Rapid recovery was made from the loud bang in the padded office. A man trained to show nothing, even when stunned.

"As I said at the beginning, mon Commandant," – he hadn't but they always say this, implying that your memory is bad, that you cannot hold the thread of an argument, that they are forebearing towards cases of slight mental deficiency, "let us understand one another. Our object is to immobilise. There is a hostage, whom it must be our priority to rescue unharmed. But this is a dangerous band, and may show fanaticism when cornered. Must be," choosing the word, "dealt with. Circumscribed. Surgical strike," a tasty cliché coming happily to the rescue. "Persons bearing arms against the Republic will be dealt with radically." He was testing phrases, trying them out for eventual hearing by pressmen: a loathly, cynical crowd. Not Godfearing.

"Like to make that a little clearer," said the commander, who was manoeuvring towards proper written instructions.

"Clearer, yes. Clarity before all things. Persons bearing arms shall be immobilised by such techniques as you see fit to utilise. Persons on the other hand using arms, ah, who fire, I say, upon you; authorisation empowering you to make use of the full extent, uh, of the means at your disposal." Unbureaucratically, any bugger who shoots, you zap.

"Need clear legal charge," insisted the commander woodenly. "Upon territory Republic here – not in Africa now. Due legal process applies. Gendarmerie in similar conditions – verbal summation to lay down arms – shot fired in air – shoot only to maim and only in self-protection. My men not trained this way. Told to hit, they hit. No protracted conversations in preliminary."

"Quite, quite," impatiently. "Numerous precedents, mon commandant – court would uphold you beyond question. Jacques Mesrine; public enemy; carrying grenade upon his person."

"Make it written."

The gentleman sighed, sat down at his desk, uncapped the gold

161

pen, wrote upon the Republic's paper with much pomp.

'It is for the care of the State, and by my instructions, that the Commander of the Intervention Section has been given a free hand in the execution of his orders.' Cardinal Richelieu, giving the famous piece of paper to Milady that cleared her of any assassinations her fancy might dictate, did only a little better. The gentleman would have felt much flattered by the comparison.

Castang had dozed, in his chair. He woke, and wondered what had woken him: everything was still. Alberthe was not a noisy or a restless sleeper; was lying quietly. No nightmares. Neither had he dreamt, that he could recall. He knew where he was, what he was doing, what he intended. He was not unnaturally strung up. Normal in fact. He looked at his watch: it was ten to seven, and he had woken at the time he usually did, at the start of an ordinary boring working day. It was as though he had had a nap on a train. Where was he going, and when would he arrive? He should be feeling more anxiety about that, and was faintly surprised to find himself so calm. This instinct was surely the right one; he must behave calmly, normally, as though nothing were amiss. His eyes a little gummy, it was true; his teeth needing cleaning. He had smoked more than he should.

He went and washed; he rang for breakfast. Small movements and a quiet voice awoke Alberthe: when he came out of the bathroom she was lying on her side, the large fine eyes open and looking at him. The morning waiter came in with the coffee and a casual good morning; he poured out a cup in this domestic, undramatic atmosphere and brought it over for her. She stretched out a bare arm for it and he recalled without emotion that she was naked. It was simply a fact. He had desired her last night; he didn't, now. Why complicate things further?

"Thank you. I slept; did you?"

"Some." He went and drew the curtains. Daylight gathering upon gravel, a lawn, bushes and trees losing the last of their foliage. Except of course the beeches which clung obstinately to their brown dry leaves. A dull day. Raining. The clink of the coffee cup made him turn.

"Pass me the robe, would you?" She put it on with modesty, covering her legs as she swung them out. "I wish I had something to wear."

"Ring up and ask; there's nothing to prevent you. On the

162

contrary, it's the perfect way to approach the matter. Will your maid be afoot yet?"

"She had better be," a small tart hint of the Baroness back in her voice.

"Here then," lifting the phone. "Give me an outside line, would you?" He handed it to her. She looked at him; dialled.

"Paul? Of course it's me; don't be silly. Put me through to Isabelle, would you? . . . well, are you awake yet? Try not to be ridiculous. A very simple matter; I'm close by. Pack me a day dress and the usual shoes and things – and a coat; it's raining – and fetch them down in the small car. It's a country hotel; Paul will tell you the way. What's all the bewilderment about? – just do as I say." She sat back and reached for a croissant.

Richard would have that line tapped, unlisted or not. He would draw the obvious conclusions, and know where they were. He would intervene or he wouldn't. Hopefully, he would have his wits about him and wouldn't.

But let's hope this doesn't last too long. Or Lucciani will appear, disguised as a waiter.

As long as they realise that I'm not going to put up with any nonsense.

Tedious Old Fool. It was a tenet of faith throughout the PJ that calling the Prefect an ass was insulting to beautiful, charming and noble creatures. Very likely the viewpoint was held also in other branches of the administration, since undoubtedly the Prefect was boring. He was proud of knowing his subject. That was just it: he seemed to know every subject and the applicable adverb was always 'exhaustively'. As a young man he had been hideously zealous, and in middle age he was still wearisomely earnest. Old he was not, but leathery of complexion and afflicted with that steely, curly hair that goes grey ahead of time. He was tall and dignified, with a lumbering gait, and on him the somewhat ponderous uniform provided by the administration (the Prefect is a civilian but since Napoleon has had always a vaguely military air) had the misfortune to look ill-fitting, with a little bulge where his stomach came: all his clothes looked secondhand. He was a throatclearer too as a preliminary to getting to the heart of things, a process listeners dreaded. He had been worrying Richard since early morning, having received alarming messages from Paris ahead of the official mail. 'I feel I'm not in full

163

possession of the facts' was his most frequent burden.

"Nobody is," said Richard.

"Murky."

"Yes, well, it's all the fault of Vibert really. This is his fief as you know, so that anything concerning him hereabouts would rebound twice as high; create twice the echo."

"That is of course evident," said the Prefect, put out at being treated as though he were a schoolchild.

"From then on in nothing is. The only person who could shed light would be Viviane Kranitz, and she's dead, and that's why, to some degree at least. Her fault too. My impression for what it's worth is that she was one of those mulishly obstinate persons who can't be budged and someone finally got exasperated. Will we ever know, now? She was very intelligent, extremely so, too much so for her own good; in that fatally narrow and over-specialised fashion. She was moderately pretty, but had immense charm, and must have been extremely attractive: as to that Monsieur Vibert is not going to tell tales. Madame Vibert . . . but not now that the woman's dead: that has sealed every lip. She was supposed to be used as a catspaw, and realised it, and dug her heels in. How are we ever going to get the responsibilities sorted out – Kranitz – Rubempré –"

"This man Joinel."

"Well, you know all about him."

"Which is nothing. Every imaginable title, and all of them figureheads, while paradoxically the real basis of his power is in areas where you can't get at him. He's untouchable legally – I've talked to the Procureur . . ." Richard felt momentarily sorry for the Proc., an emotion that seldom came his way.

"A bit like Monseigneur Lefevre," he offered. Clouds gathered on the Jovian brow, and he went on hastily. "I mean only an ex-archbishop, that's nothing much, but how are you to condemn him for heresy? – he is old, obstinate, traditionalist and orthodox to the old line. Condemning everyone else for heresy: we've politicians like that, and they Split the Party. Vibert is one of these fence-sitters, a bit right of centre but the area is kept deliberately vague; a pragmatist who dislikes the ideological approach. Rubempré is much further to the right but still in a pragmatic way, representing financial and industrial concepts."

"But," said the Prefect with a shrewdness unexpected, "made more complex and obscure by her Jeanne d'Arc syndrome."

164

"There she found common ground with the Kranitz woman," agreed Richard, "but from what I've seen of her," cautiously, "Rubempré is much less rigid and upon occasion opportunist. Kranitz was the one ready to die for France – that, perhaps, is just what she did," pensive. "Joinel, furthest of all to the right and your pure dug-in reactionary, could make common cause for a while with the Rubempré interests, which are financially indispensable, and shared sympathies with Viviane Kranitz, though it wouldn't last long: to her he'd be a wooden old back number, incapable of moving with the times. Did she knowingly accept the rôle of leading Vibert into the fold? – yes, probably. But accept this scenario of a kidnapping to hold the waverer's feet firmly in the path – I feel certain not. Joinel may have come to see her as a hindrance too great for his projects and decided to sacrifice and discredit her simultaneously. He certainly got Vibert detached with uncommon speed from the entanglement. Did he have her killed? – surely not. That must be the doing of some young fanatic – there's a nasty fringe of young thugs – enrolled under this idiotic Free Poland banner that the man Kranitz is waving, certainly with the indulgent complicity of the right-wingers in the States: I say nothing about CIA support, as was seen in Chile."

"We won't go into that," said the Prefect, firmly. "And those are the people holed up there in Rubempré's country house – if we follow your reading, that is . . ."

"A momentary agglomeration; the bees swarmed in a muddled instinctive way where the queen ought to be, once they found the queen missing. She had a gang of zealous young devotees; traces of them have been seen, disguised as Palestinians, or Libyans, or whatever. Free Bolivia, or Free Guadeloupe – anything you like as long as it's a series of outrages that will harden the populace into believing that what we need is a hardline right-wing government which will Put Down Terror."

Richard thought that the old imbecile must have his bellyful by now, but he was still not satisfied.

"Added to, and hardened, by stray elements from Germany, Spain – who knows?"

"It's conceivable. This house would be a concentration point, clearing house, call it what we please she's a princess, and a *princesse lointaine*; there's a romantic thread twined through all this."

"Now will you kindly explain to me the conduct of your subordinate which appears to say the least shot through with aberrations?"

"It's under control," said Richard coolly, "we know where he is, and where she is: he won't do anything without our – call it guidance."

"But his motives?"

"Are mixed like most people's. But he's a good man, and has two sides to his head. He's out of line, naturally, but we have to recall three things."

"That it's his wife, to be sure, much can be forgiven him but –"

"That it's his wife," coldly, "and that his flat, containing wife and small child, was the one shot up in this simulated terrorist rampage. Further, that he has been the investigating officer throughout and feels strong personal commitment and responsibility. Further, that he is rightly anxious to avoid embarrassment or unwanted highly undesirable publicity to the department – and to your office, Monsieur le Prefet. The woman Rubempré was due to be released directly the agreement of the Procureur and the instructing judge could be obtained. Her deposition – since it cannot be termed a confession – is on my desk."

"Being illegally obtained has no evidential value," haughty, not to say chilly.

"But enables justice to pinpoint the true authors of a kidnapping and a homicide taking place on my territory, and yours, Monsieur le Prefet," imperturbably. There was another flash of intelligence; or was it humanity?

"Tell me, Richard, how did they rumble you so fast?"

"I'm inclined to follow that back to a woman called Arabella de Serta who knew Madame de Rubempré's exact movements, and who was perhaps shrewd enough to detect a phony approach," fearfully bland.

"I see." Richard was saved at this point by the phone ringing.

"For you," said the Prefect. The PJ sous-chef, up in the village below Alberthe's estate.

"Fellow alone in a small car – might that be the parcel she asked for? We've let it pass of course."

"Correct, and noted. If they all go back up the hill together let them pass too, and keep out of sight: no intervention possible."

166

A few moments later it was young Lucciani, who had been hanging about the hotel reception desk.

"Fellow asked openly for Madame de Rubempré; I'd tipped off the desk man. Shown up to Room Seven, drinks ordered and lunch too: making quite a party of it all."

"Why. not? – very sensible of them," answered Richard forbiddingly.

Castang was not surprised out of measure. He had reassembled his gun, loaded it, was wearing it. The man that walked in at the door was good old Stan-Kranitz-from-Akron, with an engaging big smile and a suitcase.

He nodded when he saw Castang, and smiled; a complex expression in which was recognition, appreciation of a troublesome opponent, vanity at a hypothesis confirmed; the move read aright; and some puzzlement too: has the present move more to it than meets the eye?

"Ah – when we met last I told myself we had some unfinished business. No, I'm not carrying a gun. Come to talk, and see if we can settle this business like two sensible men, in a businesslike fashion. But you aren't thinking of adding me to your bag: your wife wouldn't feel happy about that notion . . . To keep us even-tempered and no voices raised I'll say that she's unharmed. Good health and spirits. Hello there, Alberthe, how funny you look." Glancing towards the bed. "Been having a little idyll with the Captain here?" She stood immobile, in silence. She can still call up reserves, thought Castang with respect. She is as tired and bewildered as I am; has the same disheartening sensation of initiative lost and control slipped away, but she can control still her face and voice.

"You've brought me some clothes, have you?" as though Kranitz were a footman.

"That's right, Countess, everything you'll want. Feel more yourself, when you've dressed. But I'd like to get a thing clear. We're back in the old-fashioned world where the men have a say in what gets done. Fact-of-a-matter I'll tell you, the heavy father is on the scene, and he has this corny old line: when Poppa says a thing he means it. Better get that understood, okay?" She said nothing, picked up the case, took it into the bathroom with her.

"Sit down," said Castang.

167

"Thanks, I will. Better. Man to man – that's what has been missing, and might have saved a heap of vexation. Thought it pretty stchoopid myself of the Countess there, letting herself be put in the bag that way. Comes of being managerial, parading about with generals and the like. Didden know what you'd try, myself, but thought it likely you had a punch or so to throw. Pretty smoothly done, too: when I heard about those two idiots sitting there swallowing curry chockfilled with barbiturate I admired your enterprise. You were the fella too who sold this smooth banking line to our little fascinator Arabella: well, well . . . Still, let's get to business: what have you got to offer?"

"You want a woman back and so do I, and then we can start again from scratch."

"You mean you march one up to Checkpoint Charlie and I march one down, and we exchange and bow and go back to playing mahjongg?"

"We're both of us rid of an awkward inconvenient hostage that neither of us really want and that can only bring trouble down on us both."

"Sounds nice, put that way. And at the gate there're all these PJ men of yours dressed up as old women and bank clerks and eager to earn themselves a medal."

"If you think I'm that simple-minded I'll be still more so. You drove down here – did anybody stop you? I've set nothing up. I came here alone with her – a glance around would have told you there's nobody here: it's wide open. I'll drive up the same way if you want, to the front door so you see I'm alone. All I want is my wife back. This minute if you like. You can drive my car, with me in front of you driving yours. Alberthe can ride with you."

"What's to stop me then putting you in the bag along with your wife and saying'Right, now we'll start again from scratch?'

"Nothing at all, if you think that'll get you anywhere. Recall I'm a cop. You'd be asking for trouble and why make it for yourself?"

"It's a point. Let's discuss it over a drink. Be my guest," looking at his watch. "Anticipate that nice invention of yours the good old aperitif."

"Stay for lunch if you want to, and be my guest, but I'd like to see my wife today."

"Don't fancy another night with Alberthe, lad? I can tell your wife you're comfortably fixed."

168

"Scrub all the shit," said Castang in a friendly tone.

"All right, fella, you held a gun on me but I've got all the needle out of my system, I'm not sore. You're right this far, I don't want all these entanglements with women. That was what always made for trouble with Viviane, she'd be forever climbing out of bed and putting on my trousers like they were hers. Opinionated. Each little time an argument, a man gets tired. You're nearer the bell for the waiter than I am. Now then," casting his eye towards the bathroom door and lowering his voice, "I reckon you've been doing more with the Countess than just cuddling up to her: she isn't rightly as imperious as I'm accustomed to see her. Did she get nicely confidential under a bit of persuasion over a few of her projects?"

"I didn't get that persuasive."

"Magnum of champagne, son, you got a Roederer brut? And three glasses. A tray of any little tidbits the bar knows how to whip up. And a lunch menu. Then we can be cosy. I hear the food here's not that bad and I've been living on sandwiches this day or so." Lucciani bowed and penguined it out. I hope to kind Jesus, thought Castang, he doesn't pass me any little notes or tread upon my toe. Do nothing, imbecile: following the principles of the good doctor Coué (the French government has great confidence in these). Everything, in every way, is getting better and better as long as Richard is as intelligent as I hope he is.

"Let's talk about your principle in this," said Kranitz thought-reading.

"And yours."

"Make no mistake, son, I'm my own man, here, there, or back in Washington. There's a lot of people everywhere all thinking the same, that Poles are a romance-flavour strawberry milkshake, kissing the Pope's toe and waiting for Our Lady of Czechotowa to come liberate us. Me and a few boys think different. Sure the Countess is a good friend. No more. Doesn't give me any instructions. Hello, honeybun, we were just talking about you. Come sit down, you're just in time for a drink, and here on his cue is this fine boy with my bottle. Don't you waste that good juice none, son, open it slow and easy, I don't want it to hit the ground running, I like to approach things in my own time. Fine, here's for you and I'll ring with the lunch order when I've had leisure to think it over, right? so don't come worrying me none. Alberthe, I've something on my conscience so I'll come right out with it. These two days while you

169

were the guest of the PJ here, what did you take for subject of the conferences?"

Looks very nice, thought Castang, in that honey-coloured beige dress. That's the way I remember our first meeting. She was offering me a job . . . She is repaired, refurbished, renewed – and anew formidable. A woman might say the dress was a little too formal for the occasion. And I'd say – keeping that to myself – that Kranitz made a mistake. He's showing her he is boss, the way he used to with Viviane. With a woman like Madame de Rubempré that's not always the cleverest tactic. Richard – no, don't think about that.

"Smell of smoke in here," said Alberthe opening a window. "Ask him," coming back and sitting down. "Do it politely, and you stand an excellent chance of hearing the truth; a rarity in your acquaintance."

"Well now, I'm asking you, and that wouldn't be a signal of any sort opening that window? Be a mistake, countess. You should have understood one thing from these boys, which is you aren't invulnerable."

"Be smart to bear that in mind," said Madame de Rubempré, mimicking his accent. She reached for her handbag, and found a cigarette. Well trained woman, the maid.

"The Police Judiciaire," said Castang softly, "has not altered its objectives or interests since our last meeting, Mr Kranitz. We were wondering then whether the disappearance of your ex-wife was in fact a sequestration – perhaps designed to appear so. When we found her dead, in circumstances calling for publicity, using a method popularised by left-wing groups – and is that what they always are? – the addresses in Viviane's phonebook became more interesting. I'd no evidence, naturally, that you in fact came to her flat to tidy up that sort of loose end. There were a lot of questions. Judges want them answered, and they have powers of search, entry, arrest, detention. In this context we questioned Madame de Rubempré. I was not present at all the questioning. You will know best, whether her statements would be liable to implicate you. You should know too that a statement of this kind remains unverified until a judge has an opportunity of measuring it against known or probable facts, and deciding – we don't make those decisions – whether there are grounds for inculpation.

"So you make up your mind – you want to reach for a gun, or a plane, or a lawyer? Too late already for the first two."

Kranitz refilled his glass and said, "Bullshit," succinctly.

170

"The State Department," said Castang, filling Alberthe's and his own. "Don't know much about it, and don't believe all I hear. Must have a file somewhere – must be a bloody big fireproof basement. Electronic retrieval of maniacs, loonies, drunken senators, America-Firsts. Anybody who ever said Nuke the Wogs, or General-Marshall-Is-a-Commie. Your Polish Legion won't even rank very high. But the Embassy will write you off straight away."

Kranitz didn't turn a hair.

"Boy," he said pleasantly, "you pissing against the wind, and all you'll accomplish is to wet your own socks."

"Counting on the Brazilians? French and German governments got some big deals rolling there, and it would be judged inopportune to make a fuss about Viviane? Sure, that will cover Arabella, and in ordinary circumstances it should allay curiosity about the house-guests in Madame de Rubempré's country house. You still imagine this entire business will be treated as a slip up – like when some stinking cop shoots an Arab. Judge of Instruction, you'll just laugh. Seen them before. Enquiry goes on for two years and a half and then the dossier somehow gets lost. Nobody ever did find out who kidnapped Ben Barka. Or who shot Goldman. Or whether the Minister of the Interior did or didn't know about the threat to kill Mister de Broglie. That about the size of it?"

"That," laughing merrily, "is about the size of it."

"Here's where you've gone wrong," levelly. "Orthez is dead."

"Who the hell is Orthez?"

"He's the cop you left with a broken skull on my living room floor."

Alberthe turned her head slowly as though her neck was stiff. Kranitz appeared to be lost in contemplation of the menu.

"Call it a fancy name," he said slowly, tapping it with his thumb nail, "write it in fancy lettering, put as much sour cream on it as you like – it's still cabbage soup."

"That what they say in Poland?"

Kranitz looked up.

"That's what they say here. Lieutenant, Captain, Commissioner – there are lots of cops. From where I'm sitting they can all get wasted – you, and your old guy Richard. You just mentioned that Broglie thing. I know Paris too. A minister was embarrassed. What happened? Your own big boss, the Chief Commissioner up there in the Quai des Orfèvres, got wasted over that one." The trouble with

171

this remark was that it was quite true. Castang drank some more champagne.

"I'm short-circuited. It doesn't affect me, either way. My interest is in human life."

"No need for protest, son, and no need for hypocrisy neither. Telling me that you're no threat but that your pal Richard is, and what a pity you can't do a thing about that, won't buy you a piece of pizza. We'll have lunch, quiet and peaceable, and I'll think over what I think, and when I know what I decide maybe I'll let you know and maybe I won't. I'm in no hurry. Where's this waiter? Don't let these little deviations from routine spoil your appetite."

Monsieur Richard's irritability with the Prefect, who seeing unpleasantnesses manifest and manifold in every conceivable course of action was in the churchillian sense adamant for drift, lessened with the arrival of the gendarmerie's intervention-brigade, which was commanded by a young man, and nothing old-womanish about him. He looked at the maps, and said, cheerfully, "Ach, it isn't Berchtesgaden, is it?"

"Let's have your conclusions in factual and concrete terms," said the Prefect stiffly.

A gendarmerie captain is supposed to grovel before prefects but this one seemed unaware of being thought a bumptious youth. He was used to high officialdom, for whenever some horrible calamity threatens the institutions of the Republic, or worse still stands in peril of making them appear ridiculous, the Prefect will be held responsible, and a prefect is an expendable pawn. The captain had seen many such fussy mediocrities. He felt a certain sympathy for worried elderly gentlemen. Their uniform has more gold braid upon it than that of a station master but the parallel is close. Everybody knows that the station master is the most cocufied figure in France. He replied peaceably.

"I'd prefer to see the ground before answering that in detail, Monsieur le Préfet, but the strategical answer is always the same, that we don't let ourselves get hassled whatever the menace: very quiet, very reasonable, and no show of weaponry."

The Prefect like everybody else was aware that this young man had earned high marks in Paris by his manner of defusing an extremely nasty situation during riots in Corsica. He determined to be quiet, reasonable, and make no show of weaponry.

"Tactically," he said, spreading his hands. Yours is the tactics, mine the tact.

"The same rule applies. I think it was Caesar Borgia who said it: Italy was an artichoke, to be eaten leaf by leaf. The main problem as always is the press."

"Commissaire Richard has adopted the standpoint throughout this entire affair of playing it down even at the risk of losing control of the situation. Politically speaking I concede that his view is sound, but matters are developing –"

"To dedramatise the melo," put in Richard before the Prefect could make a speech, "to unmelodise the drama . . ."

"Originally melos, a song, in Greek," said the captain. "Same root as melody."

"Really," said Richard, charmed, "I never knew that."

"Yes, well," said the Prefect irritably, "before *France-Soir* starts their song. They'll gather round, they always do."

"You actually know some Greek," Richard was saying. "Just shows one. Nothing but maths now, as though that was going to help."

"I'm taking no credit," said the captain. "I like to know the meaning of things. Since melodrama is my bread and butter – so to speak – I looked it up in the *Petit Robert*."

"Most interesting and informative." One tried not to be sarcastic towards subordinates, but damn it, they weren't paying attention.

The only influence that drink seemed to have upon Kranitz was to improve both his manners and his conversation. He had ordered a flashy, expensive meal and rare, elaborate wine: it turned out to be a good idea after all.

Or is it me? wondered Castang. False positions and artificial attitudes have been multiplying around me: every reckless folly that offered itself I welcomed, and the appearance of this clown . . .

Perhaps the pomp and circumstance of an hotel of this sort; the priestly wheeling in and setting up of tables, the flourish with which starched cloths and napkins are shaken out and spread, the mannered hieratic hush, the conjuring-trick act, as though all the paraphernalia appeared out of thin air – plates and glasses are a commonplace stock in trade of jugglers. The whole ridiculous convention that turns a restaurant into a theatre, whereby the payment of large sums of money (who's paying for all this anyhow?

173

– I didn't invite anybody to lunch) entitles the customer to two hours of pretence that he is a prince and these are his lackeys. Even in a Grand Hotel, rightly known in the trade as a palace (the illusion has to be, and it can still sometimes work, that this Is a palace) the chandeliers and pierglasses, the immense windows and high stucco-laden ceilings, the florid curtains and carpets, are there to tell you that this is the Belle Epoque: the year is 1900. You have abolished time. Kings and Emperors are upon their thrones, and you are one of them. The slavery and starvation outside are of no consequence. The immaculate, impeccable headwaiter who bows and takes your coat is an immensely reassuring figure. He is there in the flesh, no mere accomplished actor but a Djinn. The Ali-Baba cavern, transitory but real, is yours to command, for as long as you care to spin it out through your cigar and the second cup of coffee. That other waiter, instantly at your side discreetly to receive the Sultan's commands, will not laugh, not even if you adopt a tone of voice that would make a cat laugh. The most pretentious phrase you could muster – 'A little champagne, before we take a glance at the programme' – will be acknowledged with the head inclined in the utmost reverential gravity.

Order a meal in your room (and every room in a palace pretends to be a suite) and the absence of laughable people at the next table makes it all securer still.

In fact, thought Castang, idly watching Lucciani who had been given the harmless job of polishing wine glasses with a napkin, these country-house hotels give, perhaps, the most successful illusion of all; that you are really 'a guest' in a genuine country house, where even the antique furniture is real (that, surely, is the greatest rarity of all). You want something trivial? – a newspaper or a spill to light your pipe? – ring the bell for a footman.

The procedure might be paradoxical but, decided Castang, the mechanism works this way: the very sense of unreality and a stage setting was what I needed to bring me out of this artificial opium-dream.

Kranitz had dropped the phony language, which had sounded so unconvincing, so completely the Polish immigrant pretending to be a real native-born citizen. In the presence of waiters he was going through the usual travelogue of the much-voyaged businessman while studying a menu: I remember eating this one day in Beirut,

174

and thereby hangs a tale which will entertain you.

He is gaining in confidence, Castang told himself, and that is a good thing, since he will be less unpredictable and less dangerous: so at least we hope. He hadn't liked being caught in Viviane's flat. He had realised that mistakes had been made. Sucking up to Madame de Rubempré, a person who needs none of the sustenance and consolation that headwaiters, and mere money, can provide, was an uneasy business; a valuable alliance this, but a tricky one. Her disappearance had shaken him. He must have suspected some clever, complicated trick. It must have taken courage of a sort to come here and see for himself whether this was all part of an intricate sophisticated manoeuvre. That alone would account for the loud vulgarity of his behaviour. Seeing Alberthe without countenance, humiliated and helpless, gave him a certainty of being firmly in the saddle. Seeing a relatively senior cop reduced to an ignominious beggar by the kidnapping of his wife – a simple expedient, simply and effectively carried out: better still. He could eat his lunch with real appetite. Castang was surprised to find that his own was as good.

"I'd like to try and understand," he said. "Is it just a simplistic crusade, an idea of winning back the holy places?" It was agreeable, encouraging, that Kranitz (a rapid eater) should put his knife and fork down and speak briefly, coherently, it could even be said sensibly. If one was not a policeman, listening.

Let's leave aside the brutish and the blunted, the ones to whom being a cop means only the authority to order people around, the power of interfering and the satisfaction of being feared. Keep, by definition, to those with intelligence, some sensitivity, and dare one say ideals? Very few of these could be called 'left wing'. Because this claptrap about social justice for the poor: mean to say, the poor are bloody awful; they're not just invincibly ignorant, they're disgusting. You can't do anything for them and they wouldn't want it if you did. Boy, you may have gone to the university and be full of psychology, and sociology, and even lord-be-merciful theology, but a few weeks of the routine will knock that nonsense out of your head: look, it's simple; if you weren't a pig you wouldn't be poor, right? The standard of success has got to be material, right? – there just isn't any other. The poor are pigs, and the pigs have to be kept from running wild, right? Leave the rough stuff to the roughs; we've

175

plenty. The way to handle them is with intoxication, and where you can't intoxicate, anaesthetise: boy, just learn; look at the television and you'll see how it's done.

Second lesson, forget all this bullshit about law. The law is based on this antique oriental myth about how Moses went up the mountain, I mean Jesus, that stuff is for goatherds. We keep all that, we've Moses dressed up as a Judge of the Court of Cassation in scarlet with an ermine collar and a funny hat like a cook's; it's to impress the poor. There's two ways of getting rich. Right, you've understood, your job is to hammer the second sort. Law, boy, means order. Keep the order and the law will take care of itself, right? You just look at those communists, and you'll see it's exactly the same underneath all that bullshit about Marx'n'Lenin. Got it? – it's Moses'n'Jesus. The rest stands to reason, mate. Free-enterprise capitalist society, the proof of the pudding is in the eating. Why are we richer, and more of us richer, why are we always ahead of them? Because we aren't hidebound with dogma, mate, 's simple. Hypocrisy both sides but we've less, because why, we're less wasteful with talent, that's why.

It was not surprising at all that at any level ninety-nine per cent of cops would be right wing.

Of the one per cent, the Richards, what could you say? Eccentricity? Individualism? Cynicism? I put roughage in the cornflakes, I put salt on your stew. I'm the pickles on your hamburger. In America the Beautiful, a certain proportion of pointy-heads is necessary: a chicken won't stay healthy and active if you deprive it of that indispensible quantity of grit: that's a biological law. All these libbers actually make the system function: just take it easy, see it as a biological necessity.

The thing about this, thought Castang – and I really mean funny – is that it isn't true; leastways I don't believe it, never have. One way or another I've known a lot of good cops.

Don't like these equations anyway; can't stand this mania for figures and statistics. Or parties – this polarising of people under banners: nothing more wearisomely feeble-minded about the human race than its sheep-instinct. Rather the Golden Horde than the Plastic Herd.

Calling the whole of the right wing fascist is anyway herd-thinking – that's to fall into their error, which is calling everybody a Commie whose opinion differs from theirs. Why shouldn't one know people,

176

and like them – esteem them – with every imaginable sort of opinion? He knew what Vera would say: that extremists of any sort, however deplorable, stir the sheep up, and if you didn't have extremists on both wings, reacting from one another and balancing, the human race would never make any progress. Oh yes – Vera was determinedly optimistic – we do progress. It's too slow for us to see, but historically . . . no, we don't die in vain. Criminals are only extremists, people who seek radical solutions to their problems, and they exist on both wings.

Kranitz roused him from reverie. Lunch, important focus of the businessman's day, was over. His own meditation, born of the marriage between some very good wine and a nice Cuban cigar, must be quickly packed and stowed in the attic, for the time of decisions was at hand.

"I've been thinking carefully," said Kranitz. "I'll have another cup of coffee though – join me?" Alberthe too had been silent, thoughtful; what had been going through her mind? Her meetings with different kinds of extremists than those she was used to had stirred her up too, but she had been keeping her own counsel.

"Gladly," said Castang, "and I'd like to finish my cigar. Not often I get one this good." Kranitz smiled.

"There's no immediate hurry, Mr Castang. Things ripen."

What sort of man was he? One had not learned much The businessman, today's robber baron, is often overtaken by peculiar idealisms. The mere picking of other people's pockets fails to satisfy them. This fellow had built up a successful affair in South Bend or wherever, joined a good country club, played a good game of golf, become a good American citizen, and found it boring. Plenty of talent and energy, and one dared say brains; it wasn't a sheep face. What more obvious way to climb further, and join the councils of the great and the mighty, than politics?

Perhaps his past had influenced him; the time spent married to Viviane?

Did Americans of fairly recent immigrant origin think at all about foreign affairs? – weren't they too busy declaring their loyalty to the Flag and congratulating themselves upon it? Perhaps there were exceptions. The Irish liked sentimentalising about the Ould Sod, but did the Italians give a damn about Italy? But Poles, of course . . . That was it, surely. In these countries of the little European peninsula the old nationalist squabbles of the nineteenth century,

177

which have bled us white – surely anybody, with any notion at all of progress, is disinfected of the appalling old nationalist virus. A politician who still waves flags and yacks about Patriotism is by definition an imbecile rabble-rouser, a cynical manipulator of sheep, a blinkered antique – perhaps all three. He has little real hearing, and if he stands as Presidential Candidate he might get two per cent of the vote: that's all he amounts to.

But in central Europe, mainland Europe, nationalism still means a lot. Countries like Czechoslovakia – Vera had taught him – had the feeling of never having properly existed. Ramshackle federations of Serbs and Montenegrins found it difficult to exist because they were still at the stage of Louis XIII France: dress Tito in a red robe and he'd look just like Richelieu. Poland of all places – it had always existed, but had it ever had a quiet moment of not being greedily swallowed by either Russians or Germans, when not both together? Castang rather thought that while he had no use at all for Patriots in France or Germany (except – hush – Breton or Corsican ones, for we still live in the spirit of Cardinal Richelieu), he could understand and even sympathise with a Polish patriot. The drawback was that unable to parade his private army round the streets of Poznan he's flexing his muscles here in our back yard. Which the Government of the Republic naturally dislikes.

Monsieur Marc Vibert had rather a tendency to vibrate emotionally about Patriotism – yes, one could understand why all these people were anxious to enrol him under the banner. Liberate Poland was a strong factor in the Freedom Bloc.

Castang put his cigar out and said politely that he was all ears.

"We'll go back up the hill," said Kranitz. "Together. I'll pay the account; wouldn't like you to think we don't pay our way. Madame de Rubempré will agree. You took her out of durance vile – you had reasons of your own of course." Alberthe had still nothing to say. Ever since the beginning of lunch she had kept her counsel. Perhaps it was a sensible thing, to keep one's breath, as the English put it, to cool hot porridge with.

"As long as you know what you're doing," said Castang. "I've little enough say in the matter. My opinion doesn't change, I'm talking the same simple language as when you came in. I attempt no constraint upon Madame or yourself. I accompany you of my free will. I hope that thought will have shown you that keeping a hostage is a thoroughly bad idea, puts you in a bad light and can only do you

178

harm. I'll take responsibility for saying that if you let my wife go free, back down with me, you'll hear no more about the episode: no charges will be made or pressed concerning the whole incident. Okay? To show my good faith I place trust in you: fair enough?"

"You haven't any little men planted around here with notions of asking me to come and help the police with their enquiries?"

"No." Hoping to Christ it was true: was that little Lucciani capable of keeping his head cleared of western movies?

"Because – you understand – it would go hardly with your wife."

"I'm aware." Seriously.

"Then we'll go. We'll take both cars. As you remark, you're in my hands and I'm in yours: there's nothing further to discuss."

"And Madame?"

"Well," said Kranitz with his smile on one side, "Madame will decide for herself no doubt as she generally does."

"I'll powder my nose," said Alberthe, getting up.

Nothing outside was in the least abnormal. Kranitz went to the desk to pay, making little jokes while hunting for the American Express card. Right wing or left wing, those with or those without, it's as good a definition, thought Castang, as any of the others. He's pretty sure of himself. What's he been thinking out? There was no sign of Lucciani, who was probably busy on a telephone.

Alberthe shrugged in front of the two cars and said, "I'll take the nearest." It happened to be Castang's, the dirtier of the two but there was not much to choose. Kranitz grinned.

"Well, you know the way, Castang, Or shall we go in convoy?"

"Exactly as you please."

"Then I'll lead the way," with virtually no irony.

Alberthe did not speak during the voyage, sitting quietly with her handbag on her knee. Castang had thrown her suitcase on the back seat: it was cleaner as well as grander than most of the things that went there. Only when turning in at the park gate – there was no sign of any roadblock – did she open her mouth, looking indifferently through the windscreen in front of her at the other car.

"You're a person of your word. As I am."

"Nga."

"You would do well not to trust that man."

"I don't have the choice."

"As I had not? A just return of the pendulum?" He wasn't sure what this meant. Was she talking about Richard saying 'Torture you

179

if I have to, you know: only the result interests me"?

"Acceptance," grunted Castang. "Readiness. For whatever."

"Yes," and she said no more.

There was a welcoming committee at the château: at their approach two characters appeared at the front door carrying guns. Castang's interest in guns, since boyhood never very high, had diminished sharply with the years. He wore his own, and was competent with it, in a disciplinary sense: one could get into trouble for not wearing it. Beyond that – he'd ask Lucciani, a great expert on gadgetry. These guns, he noticed with interest, were modern, well-cared-for and handled in a thoroughly practised fashion. They were also pointed at him, and at five metres the rate of fire and penetration power were marginal questions.

"This is Mr Castang," said Kranitz getting out of the car. "Our neighbourhood PJ man. He's wearing a pistol, as in duty bound." The men smiled: one held his hand out politely enough.

"If you please." Castang undid a jacket button, reached behind his hip, reversed the pistol and handed it across equally politely.

"I'll ask you to keep it carefully. Replacing it would be at my expense." The man nodded. French or not, he had no means of telling. They understood French. Ordinary-looking types. They might be the ones who had demonstrated firepower at the windows of his flat – he was still grateful that they hadn't slowed long enough to toss in a grenade. Maybe they were the ones who had executed Viviane. Mm, they weren't masked or anything. He'd know them again. They went on smiling as though the fact had struck them too, and they didn't find it important. Kranitz had a lot of confidence in himself, and it spread around him.

"The library," that gentleman was saying. "I've a word or two still to convey." He knew the way to the library; he'd been there before. There was no sign of the old boy who resembled Mr Flintwinch. There was no sign of anybody. Kranitz would have more of his private army lurking about. It would take a lot, to make this place defensible. At the front, sure, one boyscout with a catapult: you had a clear field before you and were protected against anything short of artillery. But at the back – those outbuildings; the garden, the orchard . . .

"How many people do you have?" Kranitz smiled. Ready smiler; good open solid face on the whole, not at all unpleasant.

"Enough."

"Enough to liberate Poland with?"

"How many groups like this do you think we have – in Europe, out of Europe?"

"So you get them all together for a Bay of Pigs?"

"My dear Castang, a fella as able as yourself should be joining us, not wasting breath on petty sarcasms."

"Yes, that thought crossed Madame de Rubempré's mind too, but I've never been a great joiner. Appealling it isn't."

"Do you think this is some brownshirt rabble, eager to break the windows of a few Jewish shopkeepers? This is a cadre, Castang; a trained group of thinking men. Madame was kind enough to place her country house at our disposal for study, not just open order on the terrace."

"These thinking men of yours are wanted by the Procureur de la République for kidnapping and a homicide, one which it would be impossible to talk out of an assassination charge."

"Politics, Castang: there's room as well as time a-plenty to discuss it all quietly, and you'll learn that some slight clumsiness – I grant you that – will be found balanced by some excess of zeal in worthy government functionaries, among whom I count yourself. I don't think any sanctions need apply to either side."

"That the message you want me to take back to Commissaire Richard?"

"We won't bother with Mr Richard. Has he sent any messages, phone calls or the like by the way?" The man standing immobile by the door shook his head. "He'll have enough to do contemplating his own misdeeds – like infringement of German sovereignty, hm? We'll conduct our conversations through a slightly less subordinate channel. I'll tell you the truth, Castang: Prefects and the like don't interest me at all."

"I'm properly impressed, and I'll collect my wife if I may and go about my business, and if that isn't yours so much the better for us both."

"No, Castang. I think you both stay here until the situation becomes a little clearer. Everything is quiet, but I'm not totally convinced that your little escapade in the hotel down there hasn't been noticed and commented upon. This local zeal we've been talking about may have escaped the attention of our friends, and I'd better have a chat with Paris, to make sure certain people haven't misunderstood their instructions. This evening, I dare say, it'll all be clear. Your extravagant behaviour in Germany confused things, you see: it's really your own fault."

"If you try to keep me here by force you're destroying what chance you have of diminishing the presumptions already against you. You create a confrontation. It's a silly thing to do."

"Jesus," irritably, "confrontation with what? A few oafs in the PJ and some country maréchaussée. That might do well enough for some dotty farmer that barricades himself in the cowshed flourishing a shotgun."

"Looks to me, mate, as though that's exactly what you are. The Prefect can call upon the intervention brigade and a company of CRS in the woods behind here. You're in a bottle."

"I've talked enough," said Kranitz contemptuously.

"I want to see my wife," said Castang standing up.

"That's all right, son," with a return to Kokomo-dialect. Both were interrupted by Alberthe.

"I've been listening to you talking for quite a number of hours, Stanislas, and you seem to be getting more megalomaniac by the moment. I'll remind you of a few facts. Firstly, this is my house. Secondly, I did not agree, and never have, to the uses you have put it to. Thirdly, you are much mistaken in the friends you seem to count upon to extricate you from the follies and excesses you have been multiplying. Most of the influence you preen yourself upon has been provided you through my agency. Beyond that you have, as nobody knows better than myself, support from industrial and commercial interests in the United States, that would ordinarily assure you a certain friendly tolerance, even some closing of eyes, both there and here. All this, I'm astonished to have to remind you, on condition that you respect the laws and the public opinion of the countries in which you find yourself. You had better sing a little smaller. I'd recommend you strongly to begin by setting Mr Castang and his wife at liberty, as was agreed upon in exchange for my own, and go on from there by accounting to me for the abuses I notice of the hospitality you have enjoyed here."

"I've only one word to say to you, Alberthe. I would have said it quietly, in privacy, between us. You ask for it openly; here it is. I don't altogether know yet how pally you got with your cop friend here, or with t'other ex-Resistance-hero who swept you off your feet over there in Germany. I intend to find out. Why, do you think, should I have gone to so much trouble?

182

"I told this clever chap here that an undue persistence in snuffling around other people's personal affairs might rebound into domestic disturbances of his own." It was Castang's turn to say nothing.

"Finding him with his nose in Viviane's laundrybasket in Paris... I noticed that her little address book was gone. He even came here, as I learned later. So that when you put on this now-you-see-me, now-you-don't performance over there in Germany . . . found myself wondering not so much what to make of it as what I was supposed to make of it."

"Having organised one phony kidnapping," said Castang amiably, "your mind jumped quite logically to the hypothesis of another."

"You're being Clever again," said Kranitz, regarding him bleakly. "Bit given to it, aren't you? Overdid it, with all that dressing-up and talkytalky, to Arabella. Overdid it again, trying to lead me to believe that you had Alberthe here in some cellar, tickling the soles of her feet with lighted matches. So I thought I'd winkle you into the open. Finding a little lovenest in a weekend hotel – have to hand it to you, you've talent. That soppy Arabella snaps at anything in trousers, it's well-known, but this was rich. I recognise your style; impudent enough for a basketful of monkeys."

Castang was wondering whether he really believed any of this impassioned speech. Sly the fellow was. Whatever Alberthe might claim she could be made to appear both weak and false. But she had resources, the proud and haughty lady.

"I think, Mr Kranitz, that to judge of impudence you are singularly well qualified. I can pass your disgusting insinuations over without comment that might lead you to believe they deserved any time or thought. Your greedy cunning is betrayed by your low intelligence and your despicable character, and I have no further word to say to you."

It was surprising that Kranitz had allowed himself to speak as he had. He depended upon her good will for finance, for safe houses, for tolerantly closed eyes in government. Wasn't the whole thing, up as far as the gates of Warsaw, dependent upon the notion that everyone can be bought? Piddling gangs with guns were there to unsettle the populace, to 'destabilise' in the jargon phrase: diplomacy is done with cheque books. And if Kranitz lost sight of that he was a worse frightened man than he dared show.

Fear at that moment gripped Castang's heart. If the man spoke so to Alberthe he meant to kill her. As, probably, he had killed Viviane.

The moment her usefulness seemed at an end she was nothing but an awkwardly talkative and potentially dangerous witness. Had Alberthe followed this chain of reasoning? Was she remembering; in this house it had been decided that Viviane . . .? She had told him she knew nothing of it: he had been content to let a judge of instruction make up his mind about that. But now, the declaration had accents of truth.

Perhaps it had still not entered Alberthe's head that Kranitz would dare threaten the hand that wrote cheques. Now if he's clever he'll pretend to be meek and admit he was bluffing. If he were alone with her: but in front of me, and in front of his fellow at the door – his vanity would get the better of him.

"In our circle, Alberthe, treachery is a thing we fail to tolerate. We shall decide what to do about you. Meantime you can have some explanations among yourselves. Testify, as it were. Mr Castang here is anxious to see his wife. Have a little threesome. The cellar, I think with the other." The doorman opened the door and motioned with his gun. Castang shrugged, smiled, walked with his hands in his pockets. Alberthe plainly did not believe her ears, but her recent experiences had taught her flexibility, and she did not waste breath on argument. She had learned that pride was insufficient; her face remained calm. She tucked her handbag under her arm and followed. Kranitz brought up the rear.

"Not cold," he said pleasantly, "next door the central heating plant. Quite comfortable: we found plenty of old garden furniture in the junk room. Cushions might smell a bit musty, but there's no real hardship involved." He sketched a little bow as the guard set about unlocking the door. "A little patience, Mr Castang: I want to get some things clarified."

Vera was sitting in an old basketwork armchair under the light of one of the small windows set in at ground level. There were bars too of course, but the windows were too small anyhow to get out through. She did not register much emotion, but her face lit up.

"I knew you'd come," she said gently, as he bent and kissed her forehead.

"He'd have come earlier," said Kranitz in cheerful tones, "but for being taken up with an idyll in the company of the lady here, who comes to make it all a social gathering." The door closed on them.

Vera had paid no attention to the supposedly poisoned parting-shot: she grinned comfortably at Alberthe and said "Hello."

184

"Hello to you," said Alberthe, her manners taking charge. "I'm sorry that the hospitality of my house has been taken out of my hands. I'm sorry," to Castang, "that you have not been allowed to keep your word. And I'm sorry about that ignoble remark – there's not a word of truth in it." She had such a lot to say that she stuttered slightly: the light was not good enough in the cloudy wintry afternoon to see whether she blushed, a little.

"I didn't suppose there was," said Vera, simply.

"One moment," said Castang. "Is this place bugged? Would you know?"

"No. I suppose it's possible. You're the expert."

"Oh, perfectly feasible – it isn't important. In any of those electric things, the lamp or the switch or the junction box. I don't propose to go hunting: anyway if they wanted they could shove one on the outside of the door. We might just watch our mouths to guard against anything that might help him out of his present perplexity. Can he phone to Paris for example?"

"You mean would the line be cut?"

"I mean it's certainly tapped and he must realise that. But he might have some radio link, a scrambler, something sophisticated."

"They have a lot of equipment; I'm afraid I don't know what. But what is he waiting for? What can he possibly hope to gain?"

"He doesn't know what we might know or conclude," wiggling a finger to and fro in front of his mouth: "I mean by that what Richard has thought or decided, and he's aware by now of all our movements, and what our intentions were."

"What might he do or can't you say?"

"Doesn't much matter what I say because I don't know, so I can't help friend Stan off the hook. Depends on the Prefect, on Paris, on a lot of intangibles – among them your friends."

"One of his motives in putting me out of circulation was, I should think, to stop me speaking to some of my friends – because if they once withdraw their support . . ."

"Yes, quite: he's trying a bluff in the hope none of this has gone beyond local powers of decision. Hate to disappoint him. And at the worst, he supposes that we all have some value as hostages: he'll try and bargain for silence, immunity, and a discreet exit on tiptoe. He could probably get a plane laid on. I'm telling no secrets when I say his advantages are that nobody wants a scandal, or the press."

"Is there going to be gunfire?" asked Vera exactly as if this were a

185

daily occurrence; a television serial at suppertime, that the children insist upon looking at: boring of them.

"How many men does he have?" Castang asked Alberthe.

"There were only four or five," dubiously. "There could easily be more now: I can't tell for sure."

"Does that include any of your people?"

"You mean the servants?" unselfconscious as only people are who have always had servants. "No. We haven't had anybody living up here since the war. Only daily women who bicycle up from the village. My old man – he looks after the house but I fear they must have got him locked up somewhere, like us. He wouldn't take orders, you see, from anyone but me. The estate men all live in the village. There'd only be my absurd maid, and she'd be scared out of her wits. I'm afraid there's nobody we can count on to take a message, or open a back door or something."

"The intervention brigade," said Castang reflectively, "might decide that it called for stronger means," wagging his finger again. "That might create some delay. They'll try to avoid violence; they always do."

"So that we must wait in suspense?"

"I'm afraid so."

"The preliminary dispositions to a siege," the gendarmerie captain was saying; his mildly professorial manner engaging, "were always traditionally a leisurely affair. Known as investment. There was always a comfortable interlude for bargaining: it was much easier if one could bribe the garrison. Or threaten them by saying that combatants would not be admitted to quarter. Even then, I mean when the ceremonial forms were exhausted, it could be a gentlemanly, rather chevalieresque affair. Louis Quatorze once ran out of ice: the commandant of the besieged town kindly sent him some – didn't like to think of His Majesty going short of ice."

"But the assault," remarked Richard, "could be very nasty indeed."

"Very much so. We try not to have any. Battle of nerves quieter and less bloodshed. Taking advantage of these trees, and the various sunken walls and whatnot, we'll make it as imperceptible as may be. Lucky there's no close woodland. What I'm afraid of is snipers. I'm determined not to lose men, so we'll only start moving when dusk begins to gather. Ideally, close in on them by nightfall and keep them standing to and sweating all night. But I've laid it down flat: at a shot we halt, and only when we're satisfied we know where the shot comes from we start probing forward again on either side. Handicapped by not knowing how many of them there are. The essential is to get close enough to talk. Once one can talk, in my experience there's no further problem."

"What I fear," said the Prefect wearily, "is that these people are fanaticised, and would refuse to talk."

"With respect, sir, that can apply to people who are in total despair and feel that whatever happens they've nothing to lose. Deferring to your judgment I'd suggest that these ones have a great deal to lose."

"Political hijackers," heavily.

"I don't read it that way. More to my mind hold-up artists who have got a sack of loot, and find themselves surrounded. They'll use the hostages, if need be the loot, as counters to bargain for their liberty."

"Your man," gloomily at Richard, "hasn't been able to get them to talk."

"I'm disappointed myself: Castang's good at talking."

"I still feel it was a mistake to let him pass across, especially in Madame de Rubempré's company – increases his vulnerability."

"I think," said Richard dryly, "we couldn't have stopped him save by force."

"We could have conveyed an order."

"With respect, sir – if it were your wife held prisoner up there?"

"I would obey my orders, Commissaire." This was designed to be unanswerable, and Richard was wise enough not to try.

"I feel, nonetheless, that Castang may well have succeeded in introducing doubt into the man's mind. We may be grateful for that, later on. He may be wavering, and we'd be in ignorance of the fact – until we can talk."

"Captain, you are responsible for the safety of your men, and to avoid where possible bloodshed. But if this man accepts to parley, showing his intention to pass with a pistol held to the heads of his hostages, that will be my responsibility – to decide whether he is to be allowed to do so."

"We've got some pretty good snipers ourselves," said the captain, gently.

"He could be quite smart enough to keep under cover and

187

demand a car, and a plane to fly him to Libya or wherever. My instructions are to safeguard these lives." Libya! Richard was thinking: in the old boy's mind terrorists are all automatically revolutionaries.

"Nothing's going to happen tonight," he said comfortingly, "and the morning will bring counsel."

"What have you done then?" asked Vera, and he answered in the very words of Leonora, "Nothing, my darling, nothing." His mind had gone back to Richard's 'enigma'. Leonora had only pointed the pistol at Pizarro's head after saying 'Kill first his wife'. She had the sense to realise that he was quite ready and eager to do so: when you have a grave dug, two can go into it as well as one.

He had indeed thought, a good deal, during lunch and before, of putting a pistol to Kranitz' head: wasn't the first time . . . If he had not done so, it was not because he had become a – total – convert to the preachers of non-violence (a Gandhi in the ranks of the Police Judiciaire would arouse small enthusiasm). No, if he had decided against it, that had been the feeling that the people who had killed Viviane might decide easily enough that a policeman's wife was just as expendable and perhaps more so. These people up here – above my head – may think that they're on the way to liberate Poland, and they may imagine – like the Guardia Civil colonel – that one shoots a few cowardly communists, bellows *Arriba España*, and the entire countryside will arise in enthusiasm. A Show of Firmness is all we need. And they're only women, when all is said and done: shooting a woman is only a misdemeanour anyhow.

The boys upstairs may still be thinking along those lines . . . Alberthe is more use to them alive: I'm a man and a cop: a little thought, surely, and I'll be joining them instead of standing there arguing. (Was this a bit like the thinking of ex-captain Bastien-Thiry, who was still saying, with the greatest confidence,'No French soldier will ever turn his gun on me' while they were leading him out to the courtyard where the firing squad stood waiting . . .?) But if that Kranitz were to decide that a Show of Firmness was desirable, and it was time to chop a few fingers off to send as a present to the Prefect, then Vera would be the person he'd choose. A Czech as well as a woman; who cares about Czechs? Far too many of those pigs anyhow.

His thoughts were unpleasant.

188

The least I can do is to *piquer le dix* – the old prison phrase for the ten small steps it takes to traverse a cell from the furthest wall to wall. It is the oldest of techniques for keeping rust from the muscles, debility from the mind.

"I've been doing that," said Vera smiling, getting up. "Take my chair; it's the most comfortable," politely to Alberthe.

He gave her an arm. He was used to falling into step with her. She walked well now; a slight shuffle, a little dragging halt on the left leg: almost she had conquered the last traces of paralysis. Alberthe watched them together, an innocent sort of wonder in her look.

The cellar, like the rest of the house of which it was the oldest part, was well cared for, dry and airy. The barrel vault of carefully dressed stone had been whitewashed not too long ago. A few cobwebs.

"Is this the front?" asked Castang suddenly.

"Yes, that's the terrace level." He had paid so far no attention to the weather – other things on his mind. A grey, lowering day, but not raining. The light that filtered in from near the top of the vault had an oddly clear quality.

"Who is looking after Lydia?" asked Vera.

"Maryvonne. When I left" – how long ago it did seem – "she was sleeping in the flat."

"That's good. They get on well together." Up and down, the old married couple, unselfconscious, out for an afternoon stroll. Alberthe watched them together, trying to understand.

"Are they going to attack this house?" she asked suddenly, emphasising the word attack as though puzzled, not quite believing in it yet.

"It's probable," said Castang smiling a little. "To my mind certain." As he passed her she tugged at his sleeve, waved her finger as he had done, a small child going 'want to whisper'. He bent down.

"Are you just saying that? To make him nervous?" very low.

"It's for real," in an ordinary voice, not smiling at all. "Viviane was killed, you know. And Orthez. It's not as though I had importance. It doesn't seem quite real to you yet."

"So much has happened that didn't seem real. It's the being here, I suppose. Your cell, in that basement . . . but this is my own house. It's like a dentist's waiting room. Or – or the anteroom to an operating theatre," with the first sign of imagination he had seen in her. "Strapped down. Waiting. The anaesthetist held up perhaps by

189

a traffic jam. The others just waiting. Fidgeting a little. Knowing all the instruments and knives are laid neatly in rows, ready to begin." Castang nodded, knowing.

"Your wife – she's so astonishingly tranquil." Vera dropped his arm, went over and dragged across another of the limp old wicker chairs.

"When he was late, coming home, at the beginning . . . he was a young inspector then, just starting in the PJ. Naturally, he got given dirty jobs. There are always plenty. I was a silly young girl. I used to feel very much alone. I used to wait frightened for the telephone to ring, and I was frightened of what it might say. Nights forcing myself to face it, and say it. And if he is not coming home? And if he never will come home, again? It's what they call facing reality, I suppose.

"And then bit by bit, especially after – I fell, you see, and hurt myself, and that's why this leg . . . – I realised that what they call real isn't, in the least. It's the men's world you know, the one they've made and excluded women from. The women could keep their mouths shut. Fall over backwards and open their legs, when that was what they wanted. Make soup or bandages, nursing the wounded hero, when that was required. I used to think of all those young girls, in 1914. Teaching the blind to move, helping strap on the new tin leg and giving a shoulder while they learned again to walk, being there for Our Boys. Poor silly girls, thinking oh yes, I was well brought up but of course he can pull my knickers down if that's what he needs, and maybe I'll bear a boy who will grow up and go gallantly off – just the same – fight and die for the fatherland.

"And I thought, not me I won't. If I ever have one, because then I couldn't, you see, it won't be for giving away into more centuries of slaughter; the useless violence going on and on. That's not real, that's not what life is about.

"I want to make something new, to change all that. A fine thing, isn't it, ten centuries of so-called christianity and all it's taught us is to slaughter one another and try to get rich at the expense of the weaker. That's the system he's there to support, and protect.

"I knew then that the only thing that is real is the man and the woman, together. Nothing else counts. We are always together. And now, you see, I don't know what fear is. Because I no longer have anything to be frightened of, ever. There's nothing they can take away." Castang had turned and stood silent at the far end of the cellar. The light slanting down caught and sharpened Alberthe's

190

fine classical profile, the huge beautiful eyes, resting on Vera's face that he could not see.

Has she still vengeance to take, upon me? Will she tell a tale as that piffling little Kranitz suggested she should? Mean-minded little bugger, but he saw that her being my prisoner, my hostage, call it what you like, had led us helplessly into a relationship that was sexual even if I did not actually touch her. Who would believe that? She's only got to say that we were there for a whole night together in a weekend screw-shop, and she had been for a bath and was naked wrapped in a towel, and I put out my big dirty macho paw and pulled the towel off and she stood there waiting to be taken, perfectly ready.

She won't, though, because Alberthe is several different sorts of highly powered bitch, but she has her own sense of honour.

Nor did she.

"I do understand, I think." She has never had a real relation with a man. It happens, with these extremely beautiful women. They have been too much desired. Though that is only part of it. "It's these stupid nerves. I've the wind up." She leaned forward and whispered to Vera, "I'm dying to pee."

"They were perfectly fair and correct, to me. There in the corner, that camping thing. Henri," raising her voice, "go look out of the window."

He did. The light was changing. Vera knew a poem that began with 'Now comes still evening on' and he couldn't recall the rest and wasn't going to ask because he was remembering.

The moment it began. The moment at which he had been snatched from the real world and plunged into this pretence, the war-game world of politicians, the world in which they play their ridiculous abstract moves towards power as though the world itself would stop and hold its breath in admiration of that entire barbarian tribe. The world of the light between dog and wolf. Dogday so far, far back he could scarcely recall anything of it, sharpening into focus with the memory of poor Orthez crouching and slinking like a wolf through the parking lot.

I am being unfair to wolves. Wolves are noble animals. The Nixons or the Viberts, they are barely jackals. As for their admirers, the voters, the supporters – not even sheep. And what is a Joinel, who thinks himself cleverer than all of them put together? And who is, by the world's standards. Nobody will ever accuse or inculpate

191

him for anything. Untouchable. That's right, untouchable. In all senses of the word. In the real world we empty our own shit-bucket, and you're not even needed for that, thanks. Tape-worm.

The wolf time. It is Vera who is the wolf, though they will never know that.

The light was changing subtly, imperceptibly, in the winter evening of the sky in the foothills of the central massif of France. Wolf country.

Steps rang, small and unimportant, running across the terrace they could not see, clear but distanced by the thick small panes of heavy old glass, the boots ringing on the pavement but in another world. And much further off a small sound that carried with peculiar clarity, as a church bell sometimes will, very far off and unseen, across a hill and the valley beyond. A small, dry snap, crisp in the hill air, of a dry stick broken across to feed the camp fire. A sound Castang knew and had waited for expectantly.

The two women, catching his tense expression, came towards him, crowding idiotically the three of them by his far window. As though there were something to see. The Pope's aeroplane is in sight, lads. Snap, snap. There again, two. And this time, answering, the far-off crackle of thorns under a pot.

"What is it?" asked the two women together.

"Rifle fire. And an automatic weapon."

"It's here," said Alberthe.

"Yes. The wolfpack has arrived. Circling round the camp fire." She paid no attention to his nonsense, listening urgently, anxiously.

"Unwind," he said, touching her shoulder. "That's not an attack. They make a series of feints and little phony manifestations to sound out, a bit; feeling the terrain, flush any snipers – and focus any panic or confusion that may be floating about in the air." He got a look from Vera to pay him for his war-game. Very slightly scornful, a little pitying, just a bit indulgent. Men, obliged to defend their conception of honour. Combat, boys. Get the wagons into a circle, here's the Zulu Impi.

Another set of feet ran, across the terrace; a command was shouted, urgent but indistinct; Kranitz and his boys standing to. Pull in your sentries and get this perimeter manned. Ach, stop being whimsical. Another automatic weapon, sounding heavier – maybe just closer – sputtered off its whole magazine. Keep your distance chaps, we've got fire power too. They'd probably got a lot of ammunition cached here. The point at the beginning had been – presumably – Alberthe's letting them use this nice cosy estate as a training-ground for all sorts of guerilla-goings-on.

Going blue out there, and beautiful. The light will fade quickly now, vision quickly become uncertain. Did the mobile brigade have infra-red scopes? Very likely they did. Did they have surprise packets suitable for a night assault upon – well, you'd call it a fortified position? He was uncertain, because they were reticent about what they did have.

"Perfectly safe. Even if something hit that glass the trajectory would be well above our heads."

"Is Richard out there?" asked Vera.

"Since we're here, yes." The Prefect's motley forces! lacking only the village fanfare and the majorettes to make it a Carnival occasion. The PJ's violent-crime-squad was in fact little suited to a combined operation (not so long ago there had been a lamentable show down in the Midi, with two sets of plain-clothes cops on two sides of the street and both under the impression that the others were gangsters). They would be thirsting for a rescue operation, but any gendarmerie officer would have said loudly that he didn't want those ruffians under his feet, and Richard would have them tactfully out of sight.

It seemed to have died down – a matter of taking up position. Whoever drove the engine out there was unshakable; not going to risk men against terror-squads, which existed in great numbers and under an amazing diversity of labels; but they all had one thing in common; indiscriminate letting-off of large weapons. The days of cowboy armament were long past: they might have rockets, grenade-throwers, even mobile missiles: the riot-squad equipment would look pretty trivial.

Somebody had been reading his mind.

The unmistakable thrash and roar of a powerful helicopter coincided with a great glare of light that enveloped the whole terrace and brought a lurid son-et-lumière even into the cellar. There was a series of extremely loud shocking bangs.

"Get as close as you can against this near wall." He knew that these things were not supposed to kill one, but people had been gravely injured before now by simple tear-gas canisters. He covered the two women as best he could and wished his back did not feel so cold.

"Oh, my poor house," said Alberthe. Castang had leisure to think that this remark showed the typical bourgeois priority: property before skin.

The helicopter stayed where it was, sounding six inches away. Must in reality be rooftop level. There was some petty firing from automatic weapons, but sounding ragged and cowed. A lot of confused shouting broke out. The feet sounding on the terrace were now of a different sort. Bounding about with a muffled sound, as though the physical training instructor were putting teams through appallingly jolly games with a bouncy ball. He could make nothing of this, except for a ferocious 'Up-against-the-wall-there-You', saying clearly that the assault upon the terrace had succeeded – but what about the house? He was answered by a tinkling crash of windowglass and Alberthe's body shuddering: his wrist was up against her neck.

Suddenly borne in upon him. Jump-boots. Paratroops – Jesus, they had really hit the place properly. Somebody in Paris must have tipped them off that Kranitz thought himself a miniature Marine Corps. And rather cunningly forgotten to tell the Prefect. Ha-ha.

Something else got borne in too, which wasn't at all ha-ha. Unless Kranitz had been caught out in the open he was now cornered, and would get a sell-it-dearly notion of using his hostages. Steps were coming racing along the cellar passage, and they didn't sound like a waiter come to tell dinner's ready.

He staggered away from the wall, oblivious even to the deafening racket of the helicopter now making its landing upon the terrace, resistance being plainly at an end. His legs felt wobbly.

He didn't have time to get behind the door. He might have, if there had been a fumble with keys and locks, but the cellar door was an old-fashioned affair of oak boards secured by a massive bolt, and Alberthe's antique Flintwinch, a great potterer in cellars, kept it nicely oiled. The door swung open while he was still tottering about. Slow, far too slow.

Kranitz stood there, his face blackened by effort and fear but forcing himself to stay relaxed. He had an extremely businesslike gun, loose in his hand, sling drooping and barrel pointed at the ground; Castang was not armed and was ten steps away. Knew it was ten, having paced it a hundred times.

"Out," he said. "The lot."

Castang went to pick up Vera, whose leg had gone numb.

Alberthe stood firmly poised, her feet apart. Very odd – she was reaching into her handbag – she'd never let go of that damn handbag – as though insisting upon fresh lipstick.

Castang stood paralysed midway between them. The doctor would tell him reassuringly that it was a combination of anxiety and fatigue that blocked every reaction and he would nod dully while telling himself that it was sheer surprise.

Kranitz, surely, also. Nobody would ever know. Too late for any earnest technician to moisten electrodes with a salt solution and attach them to his forehead because he hadn't any forehead.

He didn't point his gun. He just stood there with his mouth open.

From her handbag she drew a largish nickel-plated revolver. She gripped it with both hands, dropping the handbag on the floor. She stood planted, square to her target. She took her time, pointing the gun carefully, like a child, with her tongue out at the corner of her mouth. She fired it three times, slowly and deliberately. She said nothing.

The second and third shots went out of the door, probably, for with the first she blew his face off and the power of the impact knocked him off his feet and what was left of the back of his head came up with a thud against the door.

She bent and picked up her bag, and put the gun back into it. Tidy, careful housewife.

"Traitor," she said: no other explanation was needed. The voice was very calm, like that of the President of the Assize Court reading a verdict: 'In answer to the question concerning attenuating circumstances, the vote of the jury, by a majority of eight votes or more, is no.'

It was not Castang's first sight of a violent death. It was, for Vera. He noticed that his hand, upon hers, was trembling the more.

Alberthe looked at them and said nothing. There was blood trickling down her chin. She had bitten her lip or her tongue. Castang had sometimes had to put handkerchiefs in the mouths of epileptics.

Another set of steps, these young and lithe, came running down the passage. Handsome young oaf in overalls. His gun was on its shoulder sling, gripped firmly, and pointing at them.

"Shots in here," he said. He stared at the three immobile figures and the bag of clothes on the floor. "Who're you?" he asked.

"I'm the owner of this house," said Alberthe in quite a social

195

voice, as though explaining to tourist sightseers that sorry, these
were private quarters.

"Castang, PJ," said Castang automatically. "This is my wife."
Light dawned.

"Ah. Hostages. We were looking for you," superfluously.
"Who's this?"

"That is the chief of the band," in a stilted tone that must sound
laughable. "You were looking for him, too."

"Is?" said the soldier, poking with his foot. "Was, you mean.
Somebody a pretty good shot," looking enquiringly at Castang; ol'
John Wayne there had a spare gun up his trouser leg.

"I shot him," said Alberthe.

"Oh," sounding inadequate. "Well. Uh – good riddance, no?
Pretty good shot," again; admiringly. He jerked his thumb back up
the passage. "Uh – they'll be expecting to see you, upstairs."
Finding himself in excess of requirement he scratched, turned, and
went.

Was indeed a pretty good shot. Fatality, no? An experienced
person always shoots at the body. It's a bigger target, and anything
above a popgun jumps as it fires. Holding a gun as Alberthe had held
it, stiff and rigid, and aim at a man's head, you'll make a hole in the
ceiling. She'd hit him square in the teeth first crack. Fatality.

Processionally, they moved upstairs, the lady of the house
leading the way, as was right.

The hall was like that of the Gare Saint-Lazare. The French have
a beautiful and descriptive name for this sort of space where
humanity eddies aimlessly about. *Salle des Pas Perdus* they call it.
There seemed to be no damage, except that a flower vase, a pretty
one and valuable, in blue Vincennes porcelain, that had held pink
carnations on an occasional table, had been knocked over and, alas,
broken. A skilful restorer would fix it so that the damage would be
unnoticed save by an expert. Alberthe advanced to the centre of the
hall where a little group stood. Regally she introduced herself to the
paratroop commandant, in overalls since he had jumped with his
men, the section-leader, a couple of footmen, runner or ordonnance,
whatever they're called in paratroop jargon.

"Baroness de Rubempré. I wish to welcome you to my house, and
to thank you for freeing us." She still had blood upon her chin, and
her handbag clutched in one hand. "I know that you have been as
careful as you possibly could. But there were dreadfully loud bangs,

outside. I do hope you haven't had to cause too much damage." The commandant, without any clue at all how to cope with this amazing vision, fingered his chin and endeavoured to gain a countenance. Castang thought of the negro bystander in the Chester Himes book, who said with the greatest simplicity 'Lady, your ass is out'.

The officer was saved from further embarrassment by the door opening to admit the reception committee, headed by the Chief Stationmaster in full regalia: stars on his hat, flags, lanterns and whistles.

"Ah," said the Prefect, in a voice so fruity that the cottonwool beard wagged, and 'Are you all being good boys and girls?' was surfacing behind it.

The Prefect stopped dead. Everybody froze without knowing why. There was a strange horrible silence.

Richard, looking English, deliberately insignificant in a grey tweed jacket and flannel trousers, a thoroughly commonplace maroon tie, had come in just behind the Prefect. Alberthe saw him and all her fur rose stiff, as the mongoose that sees the snake.

"Torturer," she said in a small, stiff voice, reaching for her handbag.

If she were quicker this time so at last was Castang. He took four steps in a patter and put his arms round her shoulders as the shiny, nickelled gun came up. He held her wrists as gently as he could, his face in her hair.

"No, dearest girl, no."

She held herself stiffly, throwing her strength against his, a tall, strong woman, but she did not have the muscle in her forearms. When she realised it was futile she did not struggle, and let him hold her hand. Then she turned calmly to look at him. Then she spat straight in his face.

The commandant's military training came to the rescue.

"Outside! The lot, there." An absurd echo of Kranitz, ringing sarcastically in Castang's ears. He hugged her gently, saying 'Hush dearest, hush.'

"Monsieur le Préfet," in a parade tone, "I have prisoners to turn over to justice."

"Excellent, excellent," face-saving like mad, hurrying out to the terrace.

The young gendarmerie captain, tallish, thinnish, a pale, well-cut face unexpectedly sensitive above the bulky bulletproof jacket, was

197

collecting evidence in a corner; impressive pile of large, unpleasant, ugly ironmongery with which he could go off to Paris and say smoothly, 'Glad you didn't expect me to conduct an assault against that little lot: next time I'll take tanks'. He came up to Alberthe, gave her a gentle smile, said, "Take it from you shall I?" and cupped his other hand under the crook of her elbow, as lightly as a boy lifting a bird's egg.

"I want you to meet our doctor." She followed him; docile; dignified. Richard turned and said something to the rugby-fan from Pau: the Section Paloise, as the violence-squad had inevitably come to be named, was standing about expectantly dangling handcuffs. He walked up to Castang, who said formally, "In among that crowd will be found whoever killed Viviane. And Orthez."

"Orthez isn't dead," said Richard. "His head is harder than yours or mine." He turned aside to Vera. "Are you safe and sound, my dear girl?"

"Perfectly." She took Castang by the arm. He was standing there with his eyes shut, because salt water was stinging them. Richard touched his elbow.

"I owe you a debt, boy. And I'll see that it's paid. You bloody idiot," he added in his usual voice.

Normal republican institutions were restored by the Prefect, who came back from offering republican felicitations to the army, a pleasant task over which he was rubbing his hands and smiling.

"Richard, you represent justice here, since you hold a mandate from the Examining Magistrate." Who will be much relieved, that all the Tactful Line of Conduct lectures from the Proc might prove after all unneeded. "And, of course," with a dreadful false facetiousness "I don't know the criminal code in quite the detail you do, but that's surely a Section Sixty-Four if ever I saw one." It is that valuable paragraph which says that persons deemed unfit to plead, hm, shall not be held responsible for criminal performances.

"She killed Kranitz, poor woman," said Castang, sweating all down his back.

"I know, I know," answered the Prefect reassuringly. "We'll have the medic look at you too; you've had a rough time." The fruitiness was swelling afresh. "I need hardly say that as the representative of the civilian – and military – authority I instruct that none of you shall speak any word whatsoever to the press. I'll handle them. As regards, uh, various occasions upon which strict obedience to the regulations may have been at times overstepped, I think I may say that devotion beyond the call of duty may be deemed to obliterate . . . meuh, longanimity might avert official displeasure. Since the matter is being held to depend, uh, upon the conclusions I shall be drawing in my official report, I can possibly find means to condense . . ."

The use of 'condense' for 'condone' (Richard was to remark later) is good, and so is longanimity, which I had to look up in the dictionary.

"A sixty-four for Alberthe," said Castang in the car, "that's a bit too crude, isn't it?"

"Yes, boy, and one for you and me too. She's had a bit of a nervous depression," explained Richard with longanimity, "and so did you. A few tame shrinks will juggle the dates a bit."

"You mean I haven't been given the sack?"

"Well at first things looked a bit sticky. Minister frothing somewhat at the lip, and Ottavioli with his public-execution face. And then it turned out you had friends at court."

"Uh?" Nonplussed.

"Monsieur Marc Vibert was very pleased with the way you handled things – meaning largely Madame Vibert. And while of course they're politically in separate camps, do recall that he and the Minister were all blood-brothers together at the National School of Administration.

"It was held furthermore," went on Richard at his blandest, "that the Companions of the Liberation, not quite so powerful a lobby perhaps as Inspectors of Finance but one can't have everything, would be vexed if I were to leave the service prematurely under a cloud. Can't think why it's called a cloud: seems like an uncomfortably glaring light from where I stand. Let's say that a veil was interposed, and since it's the same veil that Alberthe benefits by – the Whip of Calamity was stayed. Even though I was told in private, in a very nasty way indeed, to stick to planting cabbages for my remaining days."

Maryvonne had gone home and Judith, unpretty and beautiful Spanish woman, was babysitting. Lydia, thumbsucking, with enormous round eyes, was lying very happily listening to a song. Judith, extremely self-conscious, broke off and blushed. Nobody paid any attention. Vera went and got a drink for the men. Judith, so

199

shy that she was scarcely ever known to utter at all, decided that she was being ridiculous and went back to singing the cradle song from the Caribbean. '*Duerme, duerme, negrito.*' Sleep, little one; your mother is in the fields.

Then there is a highly-unsuitable bit. And if the little black one does not sleep, the white devil will come, and Crunch, will bite off its little leg – Chacapumba.

They clinked glasses softly, and together with Vera's glass. First time she'd had a drink since becoming pregnant, but deserved now, don't you think? Yes.

"I'd like some cocoa if there is any," said Judith.

They sat still and quiet together, the men holding a puddle of juice on the knee (good scotch juice from islands) in the small chinking noises of Vera's housekeeping. The little, bitter, gentle, rocking song went on.

'*Trabajando,*
trabajando duramente,
trabajando, si.
Trabajando y no le pagan,
trabajando, si.'
Working,
working,
working so hard.
Working, and nobody pays her.
Working, yes . . .

Vera passed Judith the cup of cocoa, with a little coffee in it, a thimble of whisky, and a little cinnamon.

All four were nodding, ready to go to sleep before the child was.

200

ABOUT THE AUTHOR

Nicolas Freeling was born in London and raised in France and England. After his military service in World War II, he traveled extensively throughout Europe, working as a professional cook in a number of hotels and restaurants. His first book, *Love in Amsterdam,* was published in 1961. Since then, he has written numerous novels and nonfiction works. His most recent books have been *Castang's City,* the fifth Henri Castang novel, and *Arlette,* the second in a series about the widow Van der Valk. Mr. Freeling was awarded a Golden Dagger by the Crime Writers Association in 1963, the Grand Prix de Roman Policier in 1965, and the Edgar Allan Poe Award of the Mystery Writers of America, Inc., 1966.

Mr. Freeling lives in France with his wife and their two children.